Dedicated to Kathryn and Elsa

Acknowledgements

My thanks go to Ellie, Jenny, Joann and Pauline for their critical consideration of the early draft of this story; to Shirley for her patience and advice; to Elsa, Frances, Ellie and Shirley for checking the content and text – and to Gill for skilfully assembling the whole.

The co-operation of GASPS' members (Gay Authors Self Publishing Services) has made this publication possible.

MY LIFE OUTSIDE
CHAPTER 1

'Are you coming, Helen?' That's Corinne shouting from the corridor.

'No, I'm not ready yet.'

There's no point in me going across to the main hall until it's nearly time for the Neston Horticultural College diploma presentation cum graduation ceremony to start.

It's fine for the other students. They've got parents coming and boyfriends. They look with surprise when I say my parents can't come but they don't ask me why. I don't tell them it's more a matter of, 'my parents won't come'. I never discuss 'why' with them and they know by now that it's not a good idea to question me – they know I can't be coerced into talking, for example trying to get information out of me with, 'What a shame! Why can't they come?'

I never allow myself to talk freely because I must never let slip what happened before I started this college course. Once you start talking it's easy to get caught out. I've had to be very careful not to accept more than one drink at a time, a sherry, one glass of wine, one beer, so there's never been any danger of me talking carelessly. It's made me lose some of my spontaneity. Once upon a long time ago I was considered to be a lively addition to any group, though the more serious person I am now seems to be acceptable.

The students don't know for example that I used to be called by my first name, Mary. I dropped the Mary as soon as I left prison and use my middle name Helen. The name Mary Burns might have been recognised. Some of the prisoners in Stonebridge Women's Prison used to call me 'Contrary' because I wouldn't sit and listen to their rubbish or invective without challenging it. I was labelled because of the nursery rhyme, *Mary, Mary, Quite Contrary how does your garden grow?* I suppose that, as my interest in horticulture started when I was inside, the reference was apt on two accounts.

The prisoners weren't comfortable with me. They resented the fact that I'd finished my first year at University before I was sent down. Most of the prisoners I mixed with had played truant from school and skipped much of their secondary education. But they were not short on native wit. They kept me on my toes. I was continually mocked but they never gave me grief.

Not like a woman in the same prison wing who was called Dee Livesey. They wouldn't leave her alone and finally beat her up and put her in hospital. It was a pity because I liked talking to her and hoped we'd be friends on the outside. I'm not sure what happened to her when she left hospital, maybe she went to another prison. There were rumours that she was sprung, escaped. Rumours are rife in prison; you never know what to believe.

I would have liked my parents and sister to come today. I sent them an invitation, just so they know I haven't gone from bad to worse. Their disapproval started when I was sentenced to five years for manslaughter, at the start of my second year at University. The following is a summary account of the painful story; I don't let my emotions go there.

My friend Enid Thompson and I arranged to room together. Second year students had to move out of residential hall and into lodgings. We'd no sooner moved in than there was an accident. Enid died as a result of the push I gave her. She wanted a sexual embrace and I was trying to get her to back off.

Mr and Mrs Thompson were kind and didn't blame me. Their first reaction was that they wanted to keep in touch with me, for Enid's sake, but once I was in prison the situation was too awkward. They met my parents and spoke openly about Enid being gay, explaining to my father that Enid was in love with me. I was tainted by association.

My father picked up on everything I said and made it sound incriminating.

'You agreed to the arrangement,' he stormed 'you wouldn't have done that unless you had feelings for the girl.'

I was beaten by the enormity of what had happened. I couldn't bring myself to tell him that I didn't know Enid was gay – I doubt he would have listened to any protestations from me in the heat of that moment. Enid hadn't said, 'I love you Mary and I want you to room with me.' I liked her, we'd weathered the first year together and I thought we got on well enough to share lodgings. She told me she was gay two minutes before she died.

'We'll never condone lesbianism,' my father said. 'The accident with Enid and this prison sentence we could forgive. We know that you wouldn't deliberately assault another person, but we can't acknowledge a daughter who's a lesbian.'

My mother wrote me a letter in the same vein, in which she explained as nicely as she could that the whole situation, was more than my family could countenance. She and my father wouldn't tolerate perversion. I wrote back, saying that I was still the same person whatever my sexuality. I added that lesbianism isn't perversion, that a pervert is someone who inflicts harm; they only had to look the words up in a dictionary. But I suspect that their minds were shut to any information of that kind. Communication between us ceased.

I come from a home that is large and imposing, an expression of my father's success in banking. He's strong on outward appearance, on conformity and the literal interpretation of the bible. I say he's got stuck with the judgemental God of the Old Testament. He might get a shock one day if he reads and takes to heart that this same God says in Leviticus, '*You shall not seek revenge, or cherish anger towards your kinsfolk; you shall love your neighbour as yourself.*'

My invitation to the graduation ceremony will have let my parents know that I've successfully completed a college course. They'll be able to say that I've gone in for horticulture and I'm working away from home – if anyone asks. My mother ... I don't like to think about my mother. We were close. I hope she misses me.

My sister hasn't made any effort to contact me. She was seventeen when I was put away and had already begun to mix with stuffed shirt friends – who weren't exactly the social types to condone lesbianism. She must have found it more comfortable to forget her sister, once she'd decided it was necessary to reject her.

My parents remember birthdays and we exchange Christmas cards. I include notes to let them know I'm fine and that I have plans for the future. I can't accuse my parents of financial neglect. I knew they'd taken out a five thousand pound bond when I was born, to mature when I was twenty-one. I was in prison at twenty-one. My father sent a correct note in the summer of 1972, toward the end of my first year outside.

Dear Mary

Now seems a good time to send you the money we promised for your twenty-first birthday. You will need money to finance the college course at Neston. We have added a little to the interest to make a round figure. We wish you well. Yours sincerely, Mum and Dad.

Inside the letter was a cheque for ten thousand pounds. I shed a lot of tears. If only they could be as generous with their affections. I'm my father's daughter in money matters. I banked the sum and use it sparingly.

It helped that Stonebridge Women's Prison was miles further north than my home, my middle class home. The distance made the rejection easier to bear. I was reeling with the horror of my situation when I arrived at the prison late one evening. I was shown to my cell and introduced to the inmate as 425 Burns. A black woman was lying on the top bunk reading a comic. She peered round the side of the comic to look at me. I saw large eyes in a strikingly good-looking face. She didn't speak. I started to make up the bottom bunk but I was all fingers and thumbs. Twice I got the sheet the wrong way round and I dropped the pillow. I tried to hide a sob of exasperation and panic and held up the blanket to see which way it went. The woman dropped down from her bed and removed it from my grasp.

'Shift out the way,' she said and finished making up my bed.

The rough kindness moved me. I wanted to thank her but she obviously didn't want to communicate. She hoisted herself up on to her bunk and returned to her comic. I sat on the edge of the bed feeling totally lost. A bell rang.

'Lock in. Twenty minutes before lights out,' the woman said.

I got ready for bed and loosened my hair from its long pigtail. My hair is thick and wavy. At that time I wore it fastened up in the daytime and brushed it every night.

'Give it me,' the woman said and took the brush out of my hand. 'Sit on the chair.'

The woman sort of took charge of me after that, never offering more than a few necessary words of information. She was a silent protective presence for which I was immensely grateful. She was older than me and strong. She had a shapely figure with firm breasts and a big bottom. Her hair would have been a mass of tight curls if the prison hairdresser, Marylyn, hadn't kept it to within half an inch of her head. Perhaps that was why she liked to play with my long hair. Her name was Noreen. She'd attacked her father when he was ill treating her mother but she didn't know when to stop ...

I looked forward to the quiet time in our cell when Noreen would brush my hair. I noticed the first time she touched me. She lifted the neck of my nightshirt into place on my shoulder and left her hand there. The next night she adjusted both sides of my nightshirt and ran her hands down my upper arms. I enjoyed the sensation and realised my body was lonely for physical contact – but this silent stroking was not like any of the touch I'd experienced with my family and friends.

The lesbian talk in the recreation room, refectory, shower room, exercise yard, was full of sexual allusions and jokes. I'm quick on the uptake and learn fast. When Noreen finally cupped my breasts in her large hands, I'd anticipated the likely sequel to her previous contact. I was expectant and intrigued. I leant back and let her know that I welcomed her touch on my skin and her lips on my forehead and hair. The thrills did surprise me. I encouraged Noreen to keep on with her exploration. The hair brushing rather went by the board on ensuing nights. Noreen liked to bury her face in my tresses when we'd made love.

It was a shock to realise that, each time the door shut Noreen and me into our cell, the very enjoyable time that followed must mean I was a lesbian – or was I a 'gaol turn out'? I'd assumed that I would meet someone, marry and have kids. I'd have liked a family life with kids. I think at that stage I believed that could still be my future.

The young men at university hadn't impressed me, though I was pleased to be asked out. The first kiss was a disappointment; it was a wet open-mouthed affair which I found revolting. The second young man barely took time to kiss me before I had to prevent his hand from getting inside my briefs and the third was nice and correct but boring – whereas the sex with Noreen made me feel loved and great. Unless I was to meet Mr Right in the future, it was likely that my parents did have a lesbian daughter.

There's one tutor here at Neston that I've had to watch, Miss Horsfall, the floral arts tutor. We've studied with her since the spring term. She invites tutorial groups up to her room, lovely room. She's very gracious really but with rather a gaunt face and angular figure. Her dress sense is tastefully classic and she always looks good; has beautifully coiffured brown hair. She gives the students nibbles and a glass of wine but from the start of the year she showed too much interest in me. She asked probing questions and seemed to want to know more about me. She took every opportunity to touch me.

Not that I object to the actual touch. Apart from the occasional non-sexual hug, I've had no loving contact in the two years I've been at college. If there's any homosexuality here I've seen no signs of it.

Miss Horsfall would walk behind my chair and smooth her hand over my shoulder. I was aware, and I'm sure she was, that her fingers were only inches from my breast. It was when I saw her run her hand over her figurine of *Venus de Milo* that I knew where she was coming from.

'Would you like to stay and discuss the project further, Helen?' she said more than once after tutorials.

I said 'no' every time she suggested a solo session because I don't fancy her. I wasn't going to discuss personal matters with her and an affair would hardly have been wise. Here I am today with an unblemished record. Any misdemeanour would have led to instant dismissal. I know that my background was discussed between the college principal and the prison governor, Miss Pennyfields, before I was admitted to Neston. The outcome was an agreement that no record of my prison sentence would be kept on the college premises.

Concealing my sexual inclinations has been a difficult aspect of these two years at college. It's my fault that I'm alone. I've been so scared of my lesbianism being discovered that I haven't dared to make a friend of a woman since I got out of prison. Some of the young women have wanted to be close friends.

'My room is my cell. My cell is my sanctuary. I am the nun that must labour therein,' I joked. But my point was taken seriously. Goodnights were said outside the door of my room – invitations to be alone with any of the women in their rooms were declined.

The shrink is partly to blame. He instilled into me that, 'Attachments hurt rather than help relationships,' so I've just behaved casually with everyone and kept the women in my year at a distance. The shrink wanted me to give myself time to get to grips with life outside. Here I am today with a clean slate for two years but I can't stop wishing that someone cared about me. I'd rather have the pain associated with attachment, Mr Prison Shrink, than this knowledge that there will be no friends watching and applauding this afternoon.

I'm not sure how I'm going to cope with the ceremony. I don't feel part of the prevailing excitement.

I'm sitting here in my college room, on this old tubular steel bed, swinging my legs as though it has nothing to do with me. The bed's just the right height for swinging legs but I know I'm only sitting here because I need the rhythm. It's my equivalent of comfort rocking. I indulge whenever I'm putting off the next move, can't make up my mind and feel unsure of myself – like now.

'Helen, sorry to bother you, can I come in?' That's Amy.

'Yes, come in.'

'Are you going to fasten your hair up with your bead hair band?'

'No. I'm wearing my hair loose.'

'Can I borrow it please?'

'It's there on the window sill, you're welcome.'

'Are you okay Helen, you're not dressed yet?'

'I'm fine, I'll be there in time, don't worry.'

Before I left prison, I asked Marylyn (who plied her hairdressing trade in one continuous effort whether inside or outside prison) to cut my hair to shoulder length. I wanted it long enough tie back when I'm working. I felt there was less chance of me being recognised, just in case anyone was hanging on to an old press photograph of me taken at the time I was sent down – the photograph with the caption STUDENT DIES: ROOMMATE ACCUSED OF ASSAULT.

The end of term is oppressively near. It was simplistic of the prison shrink to say, 'Aloneness is when you're enjoying yourself.' The pretence, that keeping me to myself has been enjoyable, has got me through this college course. Now that I have to leave the security of the college, the will to pretend that I'm okay has taken flight. My stock of energy and determination is depleted. I'm actually frightened of feeling this cut off and alone. There doesn't seem to be enough air to breathe in here, even though I've opened the window.

I can hear voices along the corridor. I've only to open the door if I want to speak to one of the other students but it's not that sort of contact I want. The loneliness and keeping quiet are added penalties. Suffering doesn't end when the prison doors clang shut behind you; the tougher than ever before, nitty gritty life, starts all over again and this time without friends.

I'm strict with myself when I feel emotional. I say, 'You were given this opportunity to start a new life and you took it, now stop belly-aching. You chose this way because someone encouraged you, had faith in you, opened the way to a career that's interesting. You've worked hard to succeed and to prove that their support was justified.'

Two super women supported me. One was the dishy prison governor Miss Pennyfields. A lot of the prisoners fancied her. We called her The Penny behind her back. The other was Miss

Priestley, the vice principal of the further education college near the prison, Deanswood.

Miss Pennyfields is great. She arranged for the prisoner I mentioned, Dee Livesey, to have a privileged job in the prison forecourt garden. I told Dee that I'd like to take over from her, when her three month remand sentence was up. As it happened, the prison bullies did me a favour by getting rid of Dee. She disappeared from the prison scene after a fight, the gardening job became vacant, and yours truly filled the place earlier than expected. I'd asked for an interview with The Penny, hoping she'd tell me how Dee was. It was at that interview that my transfer of labour to the garden was arranged. She told me to sit down and proceeded to check my file.

'Mary Helen Burns,' The Penny read out from my file. 'Eight O levels, three A levels and a first year credit in your science foundation course at University.' She raised her eyebrows at me. That was her way. She waited for you to say something.

I didn't like to be reminded. My eyes filled up. My life was going swimmingly up to that point.

'Would you like to take responsibility for the garden down there,' she said, taking me over to the window. 'Unfortunately, Prisoner Livesey's injuries will prevent her from doing any gardening for some time to come.'

She seemed to take it for granted that I would be interested in gardening because I'd been studying for a science degree. I didn't know anything about gardens at that point. I wanted the job because I could work on my own, outside and away from the other prisoners. My father grew prize dahlias and chrysanthemums but his interest in gardening was all very serious and competitive. He never let me near his plants. I accepted the offer of the gardening job of course and that was the last I heard of Dee.

It wasn't long before my scientific interest kicked in. I wanted to know the names of the plants already in the garden; learn their Latin names and read about Linnaeus who designed the classification system. I tried the prison library and complained because they hadn't got the books I wanted. That's when The Penny brought in Miss Priestley.

I think the woman was nervous the first time we met, she must have thought prisoners had a habit of attacking on sight whereas she was perfectly safe because there was a prison officer present in the room.

'Mary Burns?'

She knew damned well that I was Mary Burns! The frustration, that I was probably well on the way to being this woman's academic equal, choked me. I didn't speak – had a wild desire to behave like a crazy woman and scare her. Not fair of me really. The Penny must have let her know that I wasn't dangerous, even that I was pretty high on the *compos mentis* scale.

'Miss Pennyfields says that you need some help with reference books.'

'I'd like books on horticulture and horticultural sciences please, particularly illustrated books of flowers and roses.'

'I'm very fond of roses,' she said, 'I'm gradually adding favourites to my garden. I've recently moved house and it'll take me some time before I get the garden as I want it. People tell me to be patient. They say it takes seven years for a garden to become established.'

'I wouldn't know,' I said. 'I'm starting from scratch.'

It was churlish on my part because she had a pleasant voice and was doing her best in an awkward situation. I liked the way she ran her fingers through the wisps of blonde hair that fell forward over her eyes, in a sort of shy gesture. I could have suggested that she caught her hair back neatly with a comb, and tie the rest up in a pony tail, but I suppose that style contributed to her pretty, feminine image. She was into making the best of her attributes; the summer dress was a perfect fit with an alluring neckline. I observed from my greater height that the latter was not revealing enough to flout the rules of decency but offered a tantalising view of beautiful breasts. Oh yes, Miss Priestley was aware of her charms and it made me angry. She appealed to me and I couldn't relate to her as woman to woman. I suddenly wanted the meeting to end and motioned to the officer that I was ready to leave.

I didn't see her again. The books arrived and were on long term loan. The crafty woman sent a novel, *Silas Marner* by George Eliot, with the first batch and I read the story hungrily. I'd neglected English after the compulsory O level English Language examination. I returned that book with a request for more books by the same author. Fiction was a good way to forget my situation. I could empathise with the characters that suffered misfortune.

That's how my association with Miss Priestley began. She slipped in other women authors that she thought might interest me, Elizabeth Gaskell, Jane Austen and Virginia Woolf. I wasn't sure whether the basic French grammar was sent deliberately. Perhaps it was scooped up with my pile by mistake. I enjoyed revising the French that I'd learnt in the first years at High School, did a few exercises each day, and hung on to the book. Occasionally by way of communication, I inserted a query, an appreciative comment or a thank you note, when the books were returned to her.

In the year following prison I attended night school classes at Deanswood Further Education College – all part of the plan to make a life for myself outside. I needed to get back into the habit of studying and in the autumn of 1973 I hoped to gain entrance to Neston Horticultural College. It was extraordinary that the prison gardening experience had paved the way for a possible career.

I used to think of excuses to waylay and talk to Miss Priestley if she stayed late. She didn't seem to mind. It helped that she knew about my prison sentence, and probably my lesbianism, so I didn't have to be guarded. Once after class, I asked her about a novel I was reading.

'Helen, would you go with me to the cafe over the road please,' she said and took hold of my arm. She was sort of clinging to me heavily and her hand was shaking. I sat her down in a chair. 'Ask for a fresh orange, if they've got one or a glass of milk quickly.'

I headed to the front of the queue.

'You'll have to wait your turn Miss,' the man behind the counter said.

'I think it's a medical emergency,' I whispered urgently and pointed at Miss Priestley who was sitting with her head in her hands, as though it was too heavy to hold up unsupported.

'What'll it be?'

'Have you fresh orange?'

He had. I added a packet of plain *Marie* biscuits in case she needed something to eat. She had trouble holding the glass so I cupped her hand round it and held it to her mouth until she'd drunk it all. I sat opposite her. There was a hush in the cafe as everyone watched to see if she was going to recover without sending for help. A number of the clientele were college students who knew her. It was minutes before the colour came back into her face. She looked dreadfully tired.

'I'm sorry Helen,' she said eventually. 'I'm diabetic. I had some work to finish. I thought I'd be okay until I got home.'

I hadn't met anyone with diabetes and didn't understand what was involved.

'With a diabetic, the pancreas doesn't function properly, make enough insulin,' she explained. 'I have to inject myself with insulin and balance it with my intake of food. I was in a meeting at four o'clock when I usually have a snack. This evening there's been one student after another with a problem and I forgot to eat. If I don't get the balance right, this is what happens, or worse. I can go out completely, into a diabetic coma. I felt it coming on and you were there at the right time. It doesn't happen often. Do you mind walking with me to my car please? We'll talk about the novel some other time.'

'Are you okay to drive?'

'Yes, I'll be fine, Helen, thanks. It's only a mile to my house.'

I was shaken by the experience. When I got back to my digs, my landlord Mr Hurst poured me a drop of whisky and Mrs Hurst made me a hot drink. I wondered if anyone was looking after Miss Priestley.

I hugged the episode to myself. 'Deputy Principal needs ex-con,' and I'd done the right thing. I wouldn't be surprised if she and The Penny are in an affair. They suit each other, both handsome women and authoritative in different ways. I suppose I'll always be the ex-prisoner to them.

Miss Priestley and I did have a few more coffees after class that term. I was preparing for the O level English Literature exam. Her time-table, apart from her administration duties allowed her to teach a few classes of English and French. Her mother's French and lives in Paris. She wasn't my tutor. That suited me because she prefers more modern novels and at the time I was into the classics. Life felt too tough for me to want to read about present day dramas. The past was comfortably distant, however hard the life portrayed in the story. Mr Dawson, who took my class, was a Charles Dickens fan which suited me fine. I'd also pinned a few romantic notions on to Miss Priestley by then and might not have been able to concentrate if she'd been at the front of the classroom.

I did get a shock in December.

'Would you like to come to a small end-of-term party at my house, Helen?' she said.

I only managed to say 'Erm ... ' because so many thoughts were going through my head like – why was I being invited? Who was going to be there? What should I wear? Would I have to take a present?

'It's a women only party, I'll be providing a buffet, no need to bring presents or booze and we'll be dancing to records.'

'Sounds too good to miss,' I said as we walked across to the car park. I held her bag and jumble of books while she opened the car door. We had to move close together so that she didn't drop any of her bits and pieces and I looked at her face. For a split second we were within kissing distance.

'I'd better get going, curfew and all. Goodnight,' I said gruffly and walked away.

'You'd better call me Annabel,' she called after me.

Mrs Hurst knew I was nervous about going to the party. I got out my red waistcoat and trouser suit from three years ago. Was it a bit loud? Mrs Hurst suggested a white jumper and we agreed that it would be Christmassy. I bought a fine lambs' wool, long-sleeved jumper. I would have preferred the white blouse with puffed sleeves that I saw in the shop but it was winter and practicality ruled the day. Mrs Hurst lent me a little twist of spotted, red silk scarf.

Annabel Priestley lives in a detached house, Leahurst, with a drive and considerable area of private garden all round it. I peered at the garden but her progress wasn't evident on the dark winter night. I walked there in my work shoes and changed into my patent pumps when I arrived. Everywhere was brightly lit and festive. I felt as though I fitted in with the Christmas theme, but my outfit was dated and colourful compared with the clothes worn by the rest of the guests. They were standing around holding wine glasses and the voices were upmarket. I couldn't imagine why I'd been invited and what I was doing there. Was I an object of Christmas charity? Was it an attempt to rub the prison image off me and re-introduce me to refinement? It was my first all women party.

I went to genteel 'straight' parties in my teens. I didn't 'come out' until I was in prison – if I did 'come out'. As I said, the prevailing sexual climate was lesbian and I was thrust into it. The terrible truth is that if I hadn't been ignorant and afraid of lesbian sexuality, I could have responded to my roommate Enid's offer of a clinch instead of being unnerved by it. I would not have said, 'No Enid, don't!' and pushed her away from me when she put her arms round me and wanted to kiss. She would not have tripped backward over a stool and hit her head against the corner of the mantelpiece. She would not have died. I would not have been sentenced to five years for manslaughter. By now I would have a Bachelor of Science degree, have completed my post-grad teacher-training, and be well established as a teacher in a school. Sometimes the horrible reality is overwhelming. I have to brace myself to carry on.

Annabel set me up with a glass of wine and seemed pleased with the cellophane-wrapped Cyclamen I'd brought. She introduced me as a student to Claudia, a chemist. The main topic of conversation was Claudia's work and I wasn't sorry when we were joined by a teacher who asked her to dance. Being a one-sided audience relieved me from having to tell her that my post-prison job was that of an assistant in a fruit and veg shop.

    I stood weighing up the talent. I got used to doing this in prison every time we had new admissions. This was the first time I'd been among only women since prison. They all looked frightfully nice and correct, straight or straight lesbian, if there is such a term – not like the obvious dykes in prison. There was one good-looking, confident butch woman with a porcupine hairstyle and very tight-fitting pants. I only fancied Annabel and was quite happy to dance by myself.

I was surprised and pleased to see the prison governor, The Penny, walk in late. She and Annabel hugged and moved together into a dance.

'School Nativity play,' I heard her say. 'You know she's sorry to miss this.'

The Penny held Annabel loosely with one arm and the two of them looked very familiar and comfortable. The Penny's hip movements were sexily intriguing. I'd fancy having her for a dance partner. Who couldn't come to the party with The Penny? She was in a noticeably good mood. Something must be very right with her!

The music was okay, pop with good rhythms for dancing. I got moving with *Freedom come, freedom go* and as I was singing the words I thought, 'I bet a lot of this crowd does have doctors for daddies and debutante mummies like the *Freedom* in the song.' I was quite happy by myself but the spiked hairstyle woman moved in on me and we started dancing together. She said her name was Deirdre. I don't know what was wrong but a ripple seemed to go through the room and the next thing I knew The Penny had excused Deirdre and was dancing with me.

'Your song, Helen?' she said as though nothing was the matter.

'Very much my song, apart from the living in a mansion bit.' I said.

'That's my prerogative,' she said and when I looked puzzled she explained, 'I live in a mansion.'

It was nice. She stayed to chat after the dance, seemed to be interested in how I was getting on – one of her protégées I suppose.

No one was allowed to walk home from the party. My curfew had been lifted for the occasion. I was safely deposited outside the Hursts' front door. They'd stayed up to hear how I got on and I had them laughing at my imitations of the posh voices at the party. But I made sure they understood that I'd enjoyed myself, that everyone had been very kind and that my clothes had felt okay.

I had to work hard in the spring term; exams were coming up. Apart from an occasional meeting on the college corridor, when Annabel was perfectly friendly, I didn't see her again by herself. Without understanding how, I felt vaguely as though I'd in some way blotted my copy-book at her party.

I've done my best to fit in everywhere. I didn't give enough thought to life beyond a prison sentence; how it would restrict the way I talk to people or the constant fear of being exposed as an ex-con. How naïve was that? Perhaps it was better not to know. Would I have set out on this course if I had?

The sad thing is that I can't really enjoy my success today because I can't share it with anyone special. There'll be a new set of people to get to know when I move into digs in July and start work at Kerryhall Nursery. I like the boss who interviewed me. I keep hoping that one day I'll have a friend, a friend with whom I can be open about myself, perhaps a woman like me, whose life is less than hunky-dory.

This afternoon I'll have to go up on the platform, collect my certificate and be thankful that working my guts out has paid off. The students and some of the tutors make a fuss and say I must celebrate. I'm Student of the Year you see, whether anyone is there to clap me or not.

It's afterwards. I'd like there to have been someone who would accompany me into the conservatory where they'll be serving cream teas. Later we could stroll round together. I could show off the college grounds and my den, this room that's been my haven for the last two years.

I have enjoyed this room. Like now, sitting here looking at the results of my two year occupation – the little red check remnant curtains that I tacked up to hide the books in my orange-box cupboards, the beech nuts that are hanging as a fringe from the lampshade, the British Museum poster of Meadow Wild Flowers, the 1974 Calendar of Redoute Roses and my work table which I keep beautifully neat and tidy.

Among the books that Miss Priestley sent to the prison was Virginia Woolf's *A Room of One's Own*. At home I felt I never had any privacy. My younger sister would walk into my room without knocking. If I objected to her making free with my clothes, she bewailed the fact to my father. He would then lecture me kindly on my good fortune and how blessed it was to share one's possessions. He didn't see my sister smirk and remove the item she wanted to borrow from my wardrobe. This college room has been my refuge, nurturing my privacy and independence. It's helped me to feel that despite everything, my achievements matter.

I sent invitations to Miss Pennyfields and Miss Priestley for this afternoon. I wanted to let them both know that their encouragement had paid off, as well as hoping that they would be impressed by my success. They haven't replied, not that I expected them to.

I suppose I ought to think about getting ready, half an hour before I need to go across to the main hall.

I'm wearing a dress, which is unusual for me. It's ready on a hanger and I've had a bath. My hair's nearly dry. The girls said I had to get out of my trousers for the occasion. They helped me to make the dress in the sewing room – well, they did most of the sewing. I'm not very adept because I haven't been interested in sewing, much to my mother's disappointment. My mother ...

'God Helen, give it here!' Corinne was fed up last week. 'How many rows of your crooked stitching have I had to unpick? Where've you been all these years that you don't know the first thing about sewing?'

It was pretend exasperation. The exchange of labour between Corinne and me is fair. I've often done her a favour by explaining the theory she couldn't understand.

I'd better get dressed ... in a minute.

The girls were full of admiration when I tried the dress on this morning. They don't realise that in a dress my image worries me. I feel safe in trousers. In a dress I send out the wrong messages. It showed straight away this morning.

'You've no excuse that a boyfriend'll take you away from your studies now,' Fay said, with the usual assumption that studying is the only reason why I've discouraged attention from the male students. The girls can't understand why I'm not interested in having a boyfriend. They think I'm an attractive woman.

I said at the beginning, 'I'm older than you lot and have more sense.'

I'm twenty-seven. They stopped teasing me about boyfriends when they saw from my determined attitude to work that there was no room in my plans for romance.

'I'm sure Nigel Atkins has always fancied you. Wait till he sees you in your dress,' Fay said. She and Corinne went off laughing.

Neither of the girls notices my tightly compressed lips whenever Nigel Atkins is around, or mentioned.

When I arrived at college I kept my confident attitude to my shapely figure and sex appeal. I didn't go all Puritan with my limited wardrobe. I left neck buttons unfastened because I've got a winning cleavage. I tied my shirts so that my midriff was bare, turned up my jeans to show my slim ankles and fastened my mane of chestnut hair in colourful bands.

In those first weeks I listened to the lectures earnestly, did the homework assiduously and threw myself into the practical lessons in the greenhouses and gardens. I wanted to prove that I was as capable as the younger students. They were mostly eighteen to twenty years old. I thought nothing of working late, for example, if a last tray of plants needed potting on. I have a tidy mind and I like jobs to be completed.

October was strangely warm in that first term. My group had been assigned to work in the long greenhouse, tidying up the still fruiting tomato plants. My shirt was knotted as usual and I was wearing shorts because of the heat.

'We'll leave you to finish the last section of that bed, Helen, okay? There's not room for more than one ... well that's our excuse,' one of my co-workers said at the end of the afternoon session.

I nodded without looking up from the cane and stem I was circling with raffia. They knew by then that I rarely socialised before or after the evening meal. When the job was finished I collected up the tools and took them to the potting shed. I love the smell of wood and the quiet, the order of rows and rows of neatly arranged gardening implements

It wasn't until I reached up to slot a pair of scissors into place that I felt the hands on my waist and heard the triumphant laugh. I dropped the scissors onto the bench and tried to prise the hands off my body, twisting myself round to see who it was that had stolen quietly into the shed.

'Work's over for today Helen,' Nigel Atkins whispered, 'time for play.'

He tightened his hold so that his hips pinned mine to the bench.

'It's been torture working alongside you this afternoon, you fascinating creature. I've never gripped a spade so hard to stop myself from wanting to touch you.'

'Let me go Nigel, you're hurting me,' I pleaded.

'This doesn't hurt you, silly woman! You're just not used to a strong man's arms round you. Let me feel ... ohhh! I love the way you wear your shirt.'

'Nigel, stop it! Take your hands off me!'

Up to that point I wasn't panicking. Having my breasts felt up wasn't a new experience ... the situation could surely be brought under control.

It was when Nigel's hands grabbed my thighs, high up so that his fingers reached inside the legs of my shorts and into my briefs that my alarm bells rang. He was smothering my neck in kisses and fiddling with the zip on his jeans. I became unsure as to whether I could escape from the vice like pressure of his body against mine. He was aroused and determined.

Months of patient counsel vanished. The prison shrink would have wrung his hands. My suppressed anger rushed to the surface, emotions hurtled into rage. I hadn't come this far to get raped! I didn't want to get pregnant! This man was endangering my body and jeopardizing my future.

My hand closed on the scissors ... I could stab his hand, his leg. But in a flash it all flooded back ... the ambulance ... the police ... prison ... the end result of being blamed for assault.

The predicament triggered despair. I screamed. It came out as a piercing protracted wail, anguish that travelled out of the door and into the dusk. I suppose it was a terrifying sound to anyone that heard it. It was me letting out the pain of rejection and imprisonment and the dread of rape.

Nigel immediately jumped backward and zipped up his jeans.

'What the hell are you doing? Someone will think something's wrong!' he said furiously.

I didn't turn round – I untied my shirt so that it hung loose. I haven't tied it like that since.

'Someone does think there's something wrong,' a man's voice said and we both recognised Liam Spencer. He was a first year student but older than most of us. He had explained to me that he had degrees in Business Studies and Management but needed the practical experience of running a nursery. His father had promised to take him on as a partner in his firm.

'I was just having a bit of fun with Helen,' Nigel said, with a man to man and I'm sure you understand attitude.

'I didn't get the impression that the scream I heard was one of enjoyment,' Liam said dryly. 'Are you all right, Helen?'

I barely nodded, couldn't speak. I was trembling from head to foot. The scream had shocked me and at the same time it had felt tremendous, liberating and it had saved me from striking out. I just wanted to get to my room and have a hot bath, wash the experience away.

Liam hadn't finished with Nigel. He'd arrived at the door in time to witness the hastily straightened clothes and my distress.

'You wouldn't spoil Helen's promising career by chancing that she got pregnant, would you?'

'Christ Liam!' Nigel burst out. 'Get off your soap box and ... and mind your own bloody business! All right, all right! I'm sorry Helen. I shouldn't have tried it on. You looked so tantalising all afternoon with the way you do your shirt and everything and I got carried away. My God! You needn't worry about it ever happening again.'

Liam stood to one side as he hurried out of the door.

'Let's lock up and I'll walk you back to your block,' Liam said gently. He slipped out of his windjammer. 'Put this on, it will stop you shivering.'

'Oh it's lovely and w ... w ... warm,' I said and snuggled inside the woollen garment.

'You can have it,' Liam said with a laugh, 'you'd be doing me a favour. Mother gets these ideas about what I should wear but I don't fancy myself in lovat green tweed so you're welcome. It's a bit long for you but it's got lots of pockets and winter's coming.

There'll be early morning starts and outdoor work. I'll tell Mum I've left it to wear at college.'

I looked at him gratefully. He's a tall, fair man and wears glasses; always has a spare pen in his inside pocket, carries a notebook and makes lots of memos.

Before I went into my block, he suggested that he give me an hour to recover and then call by to accompany me to the dining hall. I accepted. I was grateful. The soak in the bath helped to wash away the sensation of predatory hands on my body.

Liam and I went around together a lot after that first incident. We're both swots and often studied in the library where we compared notes etc. Our conversation usually related to the course subjects. There was pleasant rivalry between the two of us and it became obvious that we would vie for top honours.

I gathered that he was from a well-off family. He drives a Volvo Estate which his dad lets him use. He always insisted on paying if we went out anywhere. I got a bit worried about his attentions. I didn't want to lead him on, nor did I want to alienate the only student who was good company by telling him my sexual inclinations were not in his direction – nor toward men in general.

I had no intentions of sharing the prison experience with him or anybody else, so I was never totally open with him. He seemed to accept me as I was, but I hoped for an opportunity to clear the air re relationships and keep his friendship.

Occasionally we went into town to see a film. We enjoyed *Oklahoma* on a cold Saturday afternoon in late November. Afterward, we ran into a café and sat eating slabs of Flapjack, with hands cupped round our coffee mugs. Liam paid. He waived aside my protest as usual.

'I have a very generous allowance,' he said again.

I wanted to clear my conscience and had decided to broach the matter of 'him and me' at the earliest opportunity, even if it spoilt things between us. I dreaded losing the closeness with him because he was fun and he was caring.

'You're very serious, madam,' Liam said and suddenly the opportunity was there.

'It's better to ask and ascertain,' the shrink said. Momentarily I was brave enough to agree with him.

'I hope that what I'm going to say won't spoil our friendship, Liam.' His eyes become wary. 'You are my best friend.' I paused. 'The only sexual relationships I've had, which finished before I came to college, were not with men.' Saying it that way avoided direct sentences like 'I'm a lesbian' or 'there's no point in fancying me.' Surely he couldn't mistake my meaning.

He didn't say anything. He sat back in his chair looking intently at the ceiling. He was such a fine man, what a shock for him to learn the truth about me. I felt that my worst fears were about to be confirmed. I blinked away the tears that threatened. When he leant forward he spoke quietly. I realised that I was holding my breath.

'Thank you for the compliment, Helen. I'm glad you've enjoyed our friendship as much as I have.' Enjoyed – the past tense. I waited fearfully.

'I've always had girl and women friends ever since I was little. I think you're special and I hope our friendship will continue, for a long time, unless we fall out over the exam results.' He was smiling. The twinkle of fun in his eye disappeared before he went on.

'My sexual relationships, and there have been a few, were not with women.'

It took a split second for the penny to drop and then we were laughing our socks off. It was a marvellous realisation that there were no sexual complications to be faced.

I'm smiling now. We could be absolutely free with each other and were quite happy to let everyone assume we were a couple.

He's been good to me. The first Christmas Ball was an event I planned to miss but Liam had other ideas. I had nothing suitable to wear and didn't feel the occasion justified splashing out on a party dress. After one of his weekends at home Liam returned with a dress for me.

'My sister's your size,' he said, 'and she didn't want this dark green velvet dress. Mum added the red beads and earrings because she thought the dress needed to be more Christmassy. You'll look like a holly bush. Oh ... and Mum wants to know what you're doing for Christmas. I told her you weren't going home. My sister's engaged to be married just in case any flirtatious ideas cross your mind.'

We used to giggle at jokes like that.

It would not have been appropriate to appear at the Spencer home in Liam's cast off jacket! The trains were convenient for Manchester and Kendal Milne's was a favourite shop. I bought gifts for the Spencers and cards for the few people who would welcome a greeting from me. When it came to trying on coats, I felt suffocated with grief because I was there without my mother. I wondered whether she would approve my choice – an Aquascutum hip-length jacket in camel, camel suits my colouring, smart tweed trousers and a set of knitted gloves, scarf and cap. When I got back to my room I posed in front of the wardrobe mirror and could hear Mum saying, 'Yes, very nice Mary.' The tears ran down my cheeks until I grinned sadly and mopped them up – I mustn't mark the collar of my new coat.

My knees knocked when I saw the size of the Spencer house with its huge conservatory that Christmas. There were welcoming lights in the windows. When Liam rang the doorbell and put his key in the lock, we heard a wild barking.

'You won't get attacked,' Liam assured me. 'That's the Rufus I told you about. He assumes that the doorbell is rung on behalf of a bitch that needs his services; seems to know he's a prize-winning poodle and a desirable mate.'

Then the door opened and I began the first of my college holidays in comfortable surroundings with gracious people. No wonder Liam was good natured with such a loving family. In the Spencer family no one needed an excuse to wrap their arms round each other, me included. I felt welcomed and happy.

I didn't do any work that holiday, apart from when Mrs Spencer let me help in the kitchen. Liam walked me round the acres of grounds, the different growing areas, and introduced me to the ins and outs of the Spencer Nursery. In the Easter vacation and following holidays Liam and I worked, either in the shop or in the greenhouses, 'for our keep', as Mr Spencer put it.

If the Spencers were curious about my family background I was not aware of it. They seemed pleased that their son had a girlfriend. It felt a little as though I was there under false pretences but Liam told me not to worry my head about that, his parents had always made his friends welcome. Liam commiserated with me because my parents wouldn't tolerate lesbianism. He wasn't 'out' to his parents and admired me. I couldn't explain that there had been no brave declaration on my part – that it was circumstances connected with my prison sentence that brought me 'out'. I didn't like having a secret from him.

The Spencers will be there this afternoon, mainly to see Liam go up for his certificate but they'll clap me. I ought to be ashamed of myself for sitting here moping. I'm not though. It doesn't harm to own to a specific loneliness as long as I appreciate the friends I do have.

I was only allowed two invitations to today's event otherwise I would have asked the Hursts if they would like to come.

In June 1971 on the afternoon I left prison, my social worker, Miss Martindale, escorted me to lodgings with a Mr and Mrs Hurst, a safe house. Most prisoners had members of their family waiting outside the gates on the day of their release. I was grateful for Miss Martindale.

The awkwardness of first meetings, and getting to know the run of the house, soon dissolved. I was determined that my behaviour would give no cause for concern. I enjoyed my meals, kept my room clean and tidy and spent the evenings, either at night school classes or reading.

I hadn't been there long, when Mrs Hurst saw me one evening sitting quietly on the top stair listening to her husband's records.

'Hello!' she said, 'what are you doing there?'

'I've missed listening to beautiful music. Rachmaninov's second piano concerto is my mother's favourite.'

She didn't quite close the door and I heard what she said to her husband.

'She's not the normal type we get, Arnold, as far as I can make out. They're usually starved of good experiences but this girl's had a good upbringing. She's getting through library books at a cracking rate and she appreciates classical music. I'll see if she would like to go to the ballet with me at the end of the month. It's Prokofiev's *Romeo and Juliet*.'

I liked being called a girl.

'I got her to give me a hand with lifting the heavy pots into the greenhouse this afternoon,' Mr Hurst said 'after she got back from wherever she goes on Wednesday afternoons. She was very distant with me. I wonder what her father's like?"

We did go to the ballet. I paid for my own ticket. It was almost too beautiful to bear – the sadness of the story and remembering the times my mother took me to the theatre. The music for the love duet made me cry. Mrs Hurst held my hand. I was glad she'd ordered a glass of wine for the interval. I borrowed a complete Shakespeare from the library in the following week and tried reading *Romeo and Juliet.*

'It doesn't jump off the page at me,' I said to Mrs Hurst.

'Have you seen Shakespeare acted on the stage or telly?'

'No, we read *Twelfth Night* in my first year. I missed a chunk of it because I had tonsillitis.'

'Would you like to come down and watch *Hamlet* on telly next Sunday? It's the production with *Laurence Olivier* playing the part of *Hamlet*. If you see one of the plays acted, it might help with understanding the text. I'll light a fire in the front room because Arnold won't want to watch *Shakespeare*. He's a *Conan Doyle, Sherlock Holmes* fan.'

I was amazed at how acting made the words come alive. What a miserable story! Death, death and more death ...

Night school classes started and the tutor handed us a copy of the syllabus for the O level English Literature exam. We had to study *A Midsummer Night's Dream*. Fortunately a local school put on a performance before Christmas and my class went to watch it. It was well done and a good laugh. Weird fairies! My idea of fairies is that they're pretty beings with diaphanous wings. These fairies were strange unearthly creatures but I understood the story much better after seeing the love plots untangle.

The work that had been arranged for me was in a fruit, veg and flower shop within walking distance of my digs. My hours were nine to five Monday to Saturday with Wednesday afternoons and Sundays free. I had to keep up with the counselling sessions from two o'clock to three on Wednesday afternoons. At night my curfew was ten o'clock unless I had permission to stay out later ... as with Annabel Priestley's party.

Mrs Watkiss appeared to be the sole proprietor of the shop. Mr Watkiss was an electrician and they had no children. I only saw Mr Watkiss twice, once when a strip light needed replacing in the shop, and the second when the fairy lights wouldn't work for the Christmas tree.

My employer was forthright and a sharp business woman. Her hair was bleach blonde and permed. I never saw her without an overall and trousers. She liked to tease me and if I was embarrassed, she threw her head back and laughed loudly. It was good really. She got me out of my over-sensitive state and into the way of finding things funny, as though she was determined to make me put prison behind me – introduce me to normal workaday life. I began to feel happy.

I seemed to bring out a maternal instinct in her, though she wasn't old enough to be my mother. I wasn't allowed to slip the green overall over my head and fasten the ties myself in the mornings, which was unnecessary attention. Mrs Watkiss would smooth out the wrinkles over my hips as though I had to look the part to serve fruit and vegetables. After I'd put the overall over my head she would free my hair and fasten it up in a pony tail. I remembered what else I heard Mr Hurst say.

'Helen doesn't seem interested in getting a young man.'

'Millie Watkiss won't be backward at asking questions about her love life.'

'Yes, but didn't you say that Millie was ... you know?'

'We never knew for certain about Millie. She got married didn't she? If Helen can survive prison, she can cope with Millie Watkiss.'

The last person to play with my hair was Noreen. Noreen ... the picture is vivid in my mind of my woebegone cellmate on the day of my release. I couldn't bear to return to the prison to visit her. I sent the occasional letter or card and then she was transferred to another prison. I decided to let the association drop.

I worked hard.

'She's a cracking worker,' I heard Mrs Watkiss report to Miss Martindale. 'The sections of fruit and veg have never been kept so well stocked and she has a way with flowers, displays them attractively. She's spot on with serving the customers.'

At the end of the first week I hung up my overall at ten past five on Saturday afternoon.

'There's a bag I've put up for you,' Mrs Watkiss said. 'The apples'll give you a bite while you're doing this reading you tell me about, though what a young woman like you is doing reading instead of going out dancing on a Saturday night, I wouldn't know – not that you've had time to get acquainted with anyone round here. The anemones'll look nice in your room and the freesias are for Madge Hurst. I ought to know by now what she likes, we were at school together.'

By the end of the third week the bag of goodies was a certainty along with my wages.

'I'd have thought you were a Libran,' Mrs Watkiss said on my birthday, the twenty-ninth of October, 'you seem to me more of an air spirit than water. On the other hand you showed your Scorpio tendencies with that pushy young man this afternoon, poor sod,' and she laughed.

I was weighing out 5lb bags of potatoes when she made that remark. I wasn't into astrology and just smiled to myself at the inaccurate reason for my reaction to this afternoon's customer. It wasn't the first indication I'd had that my employer was more than a little interested in me.

There were two sherry glasses set out in the back of the shop at closing time and a cream cake each before I went off home. When I unpacked the bag of goodies I found a pair of green woolly gloves and a pair of warm, striped tights.

The approach of Christmas was great fun. It was cold in the shop in the mornings. I had to move quickly to keep warm; my breath rose in clouds while I set up the array of fir trees, holly branches and wreaths on the pavement outside the shop window. Mrs Watkiss gave me the job of decorating a fir tree with baubles and lights and held on to my legs when I was up the step ladder, fastening a star to the top of the tree.

'These are nice firm limbs I'm holding on to,' she said and ran her hands from the sensuous spot behind my knees to my ankles.

When no one touches you day in day out, you notice things like that.

Underneath the tree I arranged pots of red poinsettias and tubs of white lilies. We were both very cheerful and weary by the time we put up the shutters on Christmas Eve.

Mrs Watkiss sank down onto the bench near the coat hooks.

'Pour us both a drop of brandy, love, that'll perk us up. The mince pies are in that bag on the radiator. They'll be nice and warm now.'

I sat on the edge of the table, in my mini-skirt, swinging my striped legs. The unfamiliar alcohol made me glow. I was feeling great. The Hursts were fine about me staying at the digs over Christmas. It was considerate of them not to pry into my family situation. I suppose Miss Martindale had given them the bare outlines.

'It'll be nice to have you here over Christmas,' Mrs Hurst said, 'a bit of young life about the place. Arnold'll have you playing cards. I have to say it though, Helen, it grieves me for you that you won't be spending Christmas with your own family.'

My parents would have received my Christmas card and the note I enclosed with brief news about my work and studies.

I took off my overall and reached up to hang it on the hook above Mrs Watkiss' head. As I did so, I felt a warm hand place itself firmly on the inside of my thigh.

I didn't know what to do!

If I made a fuss, it could ruin our working relationship, I might lose my job. I hadn't the presence of mind to laughingly make a comment and remove her hand. The last time I objected to a sexual approach I got five years in prison ... this was serious stuff for me. Fingers near my genitals set off the usual thrill. Indecision made me groan. I leant my head against the overalls and coats and wondered what the hell to do. I wasn't expecting sex to be included in the spirit of Christmas. It hadn't been mothering attention after all.

But I liked and trusted her. There'd been no instance of her abusing or belittling me because I was an ex-prisoner. We had fun and were comfortable with each other, a sexual dabble couldn't do either of us any harm. There was something cosily secret and intimate about our cluttered little space at the back of the shop, so near to the main street and no one knowing we were there. Mrs Watkiss interpreted my groan and silence as acceptance.

I stood burying my face in the coats as my tights were pulled down and my thighs encircled surely by her hands. She brushed kisses everywhere, causing shivers of excitement. Mrs Watkiss had done this before! She touched and smoothed between my thighs, lightly brushing my pubic hair, feeling her way to stimulate the spot that made me draw in a quick breath. By then I was ready to open and welcome her probing fingers, sensations so powerful that my knees threatened to give way. I let myself go to her and let out a post climax sigh.

'A little Christmas present for us both love,' Mrs Watkiss whispered and pulled up my tights. I sat down heavily opposite her. 'I was right about you, wasn't I love?' she said.

That was the beginning of the strange friendship that kept me loved and petted by an employer who seemed to revel in the extra-marital involvement. The morning apron routine in the back room often included appreciation of my breasts and if we were both early for work and in the right mood we had an amorous start to the day. 'I know, I'm a sexy bitch,' Mrs Watkiss laughed, 'I like doing this with you even though I've a man at home. Don't worry; I see to it that he doesn't go short.' She laughed again. 'Just as long as you enjoy it.'

I did enjoy it and the drops of brandy at closing time on Saturdays, as well as the varied sexual intimacies my employer devised for those occasions ... when we weren't too tired. It was a joy that Mrs Watkiss valued my work – and me. I was happy at college, in my digs and at work. Perhaps life outside was going to be okay.

The end of August 1972 brought about a sad leave taking.

'You go and get on, love,' Mrs Watkiss said, 'you'll do well at that college, a clever girl like you. We both knew this little job was only to tide you over until you found your feet and got a bit of money behind you. I'll miss you like anything. Call in and see me when you're round these parts.'

We exchanged birthday and Christmas cards but it wasn't until after Easter the following year that I visited the shop. The name had changed. The window displayed small items of furniture and lamps of all sizes. I went round to my former lodgings.

'She had no need to work, Helen,' Mrs Hurst said. 'After you left she decided to sell the shop. They've bought a place abroad, in Spain.'

It was a disappointment, but meeting up again might have been awkward after we'd been so intimate.

I've been sitting here feeling sorry for myself. For a whole year I enjoyed the friendship of the Hursts, Annabel Priestley and Mrs Watkiss. Here at college, I've had Liam's companionship and friendly contact with staff and students – just no close women friends – or sex.

It's time to get ready.

CHAPTER 2

I stay seated after we've sung *Jerusalem*. The principal closes the proceedings formally by issuing an invitation to the refreshments in the conservatory.

Once the front rows empty, I can appreciate the flower display along the front of the stage. Miss Horsfall is remarkably talented. She knows just which flowers and greenery to choose for each event and she makes quite sure that we follow her instructions. She's the most elegant tutor in the hall this afternoon, in her smart white suit. Our floral arts module is finished. Miss Horsfall informed us that she's going off to attend a course on Monday and then it will be her summer vacation. I shan't have to worry about Miss Horsfall in future.

'Helen!'

I turn round and there are the Spencers. Hugs all round.

'We couldn't leave without congratulating you, Helen,' Mr Spencer says, 'though of course I shall never forgive you for wresting Student of the Year from my son.'

'Aren't you staying for a cream tea?'

'We've got to get back for the hounds as usual.'

'As soon as you're settled you must come over for a weekend,' Liam's mother says. 'You and Liam will have a lot to talk about, not least being waged individuals.'

'I'll go back home with Mum and Dad now, Helen,' Liam says, 'take advantage of no classes tomorrow. I'll see you on Monday.'

The loneliness is back as soon as they walk away. I face the stage again, though I can't see the flowers properly because my eyes are full of tears.

'You're looking very attractive this afternoon, Helen.' Miss Horsfall appears from nowhere. 'Are you all right?'

'Fine thanks,' I say hurriedly and brush the tears away with the back of my hand. I don't trust being with her when no one else is around. 'I'm heading for the refreshments.'

I turn quickly and collide with a person who catches hold of me. It's The Penny! She's come after all! I'm so surprised to see her, and so overwhelmed that she's responded to my invitation, that tears spill down my cheeks. I stand there feeling very foolish. There isn't a pocket in my dress. I've no hanky. An older woman is at my side immediately and a hanky's thrust into my hand before anyone can speak.

'We got here late, Helen,' The Penny says, 'but we saw you go up for your award and clapped like mad.'

'Yes, well done, Helen.' Miss Priestley adds. She's come too!

'Meet my mum.' The Penny says and I'm introduced to this older version of the handsome prison governor. She was the one so quick to see that I needed a hanky. 'Mum's the gardener and we couldn't keep her away from the chance to see the grounds at Neston. You're just an excuse, Helen.'

And there's Dee! Dee Livesey! What a surprise!

'Gosh, how lovely to see you,' I say and we hug and laugh. 'What're you doing here?'

'Are you going to introduce me to your friends, Helen?' Miss Horsfall sidles up to our group.

Panic! These people are all connected with my prison sentence – surnames, traceable surnames. Miss Horsfall is the last person I want to know. I try to control my scared expression but I needn't have worried. It appears that my visitors are prepared for this contingency.

'We're friends from the past,' Miss Pennyfields explains easily. 'I'm Jane, this is my mother Margaret, Dee is another keen gardener and Annabel was the tutor that encouraged Helen to take this course at Neston. We're delighted with her progress.'

'This is Miss Horsfall.' I introduce her as, 'our Floral Arts tutor.'

'Do you mean to say that you are responsible for these amazing creations in the hall today?' Margaret asks. I love the way this woman comes to the rescue. She must have been primed by The Penny.

'I design the display, the students do the arranging.'

'Well, I think they're beautiful and the students are fortunate to have you as a tutor.' She addresses her daughter. 'Now Jane, can we head towards the refreshments please? Excuse us Miss Horsfall, but I'm dying for a cup of tea.' The awkward moment has passed. I could hug Margaret for relieving the dangerous situation. The Penny must have seen my fear. I wonder if she clued in to Miss Horsfall's sexuality. She's had enough experience of lesbians at the prison.

I'm not sure the admirable tutor is satisfied. She follows us, engaged in conversation by Miss Priestley who is equal to any social occasion. Fortunately, the Principal comes across to Miss Horsfall and steers her by the elbow to meet one of the dignitaries.

I feel proud! They include me in the conversation as if I'm a celebrity that belongs to their family. We take our tea outside and sit away from the crowds. It isn't long before Margaret Pennyfields wants to fulfil her purpose in coming to Neston and I'm asked to lead the tour. I want to get Dee away from the rest of them and ask questions.

Margaret lingers longer over some plants than others. The roses intrigue Miss Priestley and soon we're not all together. I fall behind with Dee and suggest that we sit on one of the benches under my favourite cedar tree, while the others walk along the herbaceous border.

'Miss Priestley seems quiet,' I say before I dare tackle the real reason I want her on her own. 'She usually has a sort of enthusiasm about her.'

'She hoped her partner Deirdre would come with her today,' Dee says. 'Deirdre backed out this morning and Annabel is disappointed.'

Deirdre! The porcupine head and Annabel Priestley! Now I know why there was an all change of partners at Annabel's Christmas party – and probably why she wasn't interested in spending as much time chatting with me the following term. I don't say anything. I'm wondering what married Deanna Livesey is doing with the prison governor, her mother and friend? I now know that Annabel Priestley relates to women and she's not partnered with The Penny. I can't wait any longer to ask her.

'What are you doing here? How is it that an ex-jailbird like you is in the company of the powers that be?'

'I did tell you I was innocent, Helen, but neither you nor anyone else knew what to believe in prison. You know the first interview that prisoners have with The Penny? Well ... when she heard my account of what had happened, she believed that I was innocent, that I hadn't pushed my mother-in-law to her death, but she couldn't let me know or shorten the remand sentence. It was lucky for me that evidence of a footprint was found at my house which proved my mother-in-law had stepped up to the open window and taken her own life – otherwise I might still have been inside.'

'Yes, but what's happened since then and how come you're here with The Penny and her mother?'

She opens her mouth to launch into the story but just then The Penny calls, 'Dee, come and look.'

I noticed Miss Priestley have a quick word with The Penny and the way they both turned to look in our direction. I couldn't hear what was said, but now I see The Penny put her arm round Dee, pull her playfully toward her and kiss her hair. That explains it – Dee is with The Penny! The unfaithful husband must have been ditched. The Penny could have left us a few minutes to catch up on our association. Is she unsure about Dee's renewed contact with me, an ex-con? Daft if she is. Dee's very attractive. She's tough too. I knew the prisoners that gave her a rough time. She's well equipped to stand up to The Penny yet she didn't stay and talk to me this time did she? She went at The Penny's bidding. I'm evidently not to be allowed an opportunity to be alone with her and I would have liked us to be friends.

'Helen, this Cineraria, the colour would look well in my garden. Does the college have plants for sale?' Margaret addresses me when I rejoin the group.

'Yes, there are some ready for sale and as I was in charge of the potting I know where they are. Would you like me to go and get them?'

'I'll come with you if I may.'

Margaret is very easy company and I'm glad to spend some time with her. She comments on the colours of flowers as we walk along and asks to visit the hothouse, where she's in raptures at the sight of the blooms, but it becomes clear that the diversion is intentional. She wants information from me. She chooses five plants and then suggests that we sit down together for a few minutes.

'Helen, Dee has often spoken about you. She says you were the only light in the tunnel at 'that place'. She smiles. 'Did you not want to keep in touch with her?'

'I did. I really did! I was sure we'd be good friends. But I'd no idea where she was living. I looked up the name Livesey in the phone book, when I got out of 'that place.' We both smile. 'I tried a number in the village where she lived and the line had been disconnected. She hasn't written to me, yet my address has been no secret. It's just that she and I had the experience of 'that place' in common and there would have been one person in whom I could confide. I didn't know that Dee was in contact with Miss Pennyfields and Miss Priestley. They must both have had access to my address. I was on file at Deanswood College for a year and Miss Priestley knew I'd come to Neston. Perhaps Dee didn't think to ask them.'

Margaret looks thoughtful. She changes the subject.

'Your parents were not at the ceremony this afternoon?'

'My parents don't want to know me.'

'And that is because?'

'I'm an embarrassment to them. In their eyes I'm a homosexual criminal, an out and out sinner.' I smile but my chin quivers. Margaret's gentleness makes it difficult to keep my sadness in. If I start to cry it will be hours before I can stop. She puts her hand over mine and the firm touch steadies me. She cares.

'I must pay you for the plants,' she says, fishing in her shoulder bag.

'I'd like you to have them as a present from me,' I say.

'Oh Helen, that makes them very special! I shall point them out to my friends as plants grown by the ace student of Neston Horticultural College.'

We meet up with the others and I conduct them to my room. Dee asks a lot of questions about the course. She seems hungry for information, as though she envies my position at the start of a new career. They all want to know about my job.

'I shall expect to see you at the Kerryhall Nursery stall when I pop into town on market Saturdays,' Miss Priestley says. 'I often buy plants for my garden at the market.'

That feels nice, the continuation of this association. But it's time for them to go. I help them to find their car in the packed car park and wave to the party in the maroon M registered Jaguar as it cruises out of the college gates.

'Keep in touch,' I say to Dee, as she waves through the open window, but I realise that none of my visitors has the address of my digs. She could contact me at Kerryhall Nursery.

What an interesting afternoon! Margaret Pennyfields is fun and such a supportive person – fancy having a mother like her. She accepts her daughter's sexuality and partner.

Poor Annabel Priestley – and she is a lesbian. That Deirdre must be a fool if she doesn't make an effort to appreciate such a nice woman. Annabel looked lovely in her silky top and flowing skirt. It showed her slender ankles and pretty sandals. I'd like to see her wear tight fitting pants and tie up her blouse, bare her midriff and emphasise her bosom, that would suit me. But then, she's still out of my reach. Must go – it's my evening to do the watering in the greenhouses.

CHAPTER 3

At seven thirty on the first Monday morning in July, the bus drops me off at the bottom of Eaton Lane. I walk the mile up the hill to Kerryhall Nursery. The first part of the walk is past houses but the road narrows into a lane with dry stone walls and open moorland on the right hand side. On the left, the wooded slope drops down to the village below. The boss, Mr Harrison, is in his office. He makes me a coffee but says pointedly, 'This is the first and last mug of coffee I make for you, your job in future.'

The office is untidy, unchanged since my interview. While I listen to Mr Harrison explaining the market day schedules and rota for the greenhouses for the next few days, I pick up a pencil and pen and slot them in a holder, group paper clips and rubber bands and shuffle scattered cards into a neat pile. I'm longing to restore order to this messy workplace.

'Well, I think you'd better carry on as you've started, young woman. It's the first time there's been a clear patch on my desk in a while. Read all the invoices and letters and file them. That'll give you the best idea of the business we do.'

At ten thirty Mrs Harrison comes across from the house with a mug of milky coffee and a warm fruit scone.

'I thought this would be a good excuse to meet you,' she says unashamedly curious. 'I wasn't sure whether you'd brought any snappin' with you – that's what we call packed lunch.'

'I've got a Cornish pasty for my lunch.'

'If you give it to me I'll heat it up in time for your break. You've made a good start here,' she says, looking round with admiration. 'I don't know how Roger has managed to work in this mess. He wouldn't let me near it. He hasn't had a woman assistant for years and then it wasn't one he would trust to let loose among his papers. He must have high hopes of you.'

She goes off up the yard in search of her husband. He's employed me because of my academic record and college success. I pray that he never finds out what happened in the gap years for which I haven't provided a reference.

It takes two days to get the office ship-shape. I meet the rest of the workforce when they come in and out for information. They seem a nice crowd. I'm included in the Wednesday market run. The plants for sale are grouped the day before. The work is heavy, a matter of loading the lorry, unloading it in town and setting up the stalls. Then we stand and wait for customers.

There's one nice young Asian customer, with a toddler in a pushchair. She looks harassed.

'Cheer up, it might never happen,' I say and smile.

'It's been one of those mornings,' she moans, and pays me for three primulas.

'See you,' I say hopefully.

Miss Priestley appears at my first Saturday market, to buy a variegated holly. 'I wanted to make sure you'd got started,' she says.

'Is your garden looking good two years' later?' I ask.

She pulls a face. 'So, so, it's going to take the next five years I think. I'm trying to find a gardener who'll come and do an end of summer prune and tidy.'

'Would you like me to give you a hand? My Sundays are free.'

I see that the idea appeals to her but she hesitates and takes out her diary. 'We're off on Monday to spend the rest of the summer with my mother. I won't be around until term begins. Would you be willing to come in September?'

'Yes, book a day when you get back. Lucky you going to France; have a good time.'

I notice the 'we'. A day out at Neston College didn't suit Deirdre but a holiday in France does.

That's the pattern for the rest of the summer, office work, outdoor work, lots of potting-on in the greenhouses and market days.

I'm happy! The young woman shops regularly in town and stops by for a chat when we're not busy. She's called Myra and her toddler is Nathan. She has no partner.

I spend the last weekend in August with the Spencer family and Liam and I compare notes. He's rather excited about a good looking, fair young man that his father has employed.

'No such luck in my department,' I grumble. 'The lads at the nursery are good fun but I haven't had time to find a social niche.'

'They'll be starting back at Neston in a fortnight,' he says. 'Wish you were still at college?'

'No, this job suits me fine. I miss my college room though. There's not much privacy at my digs and the furniture in my bedroom is big and ugly.'

He commiserates.

I return to my new life and leave him with best wishes for his romance.

Miss Priestley appears on the second Saturday in September. 'Can I take you up on your offer of help in my garden, Helen?'

'You can. Is tomorrow okay?'

'Not tomorrow,' she says quickly, 'next Sunday would be more convenient, at ten o'clock?'

'Yes, fine. What about gardening tools?'

'I have the tools you'll need.'

The weather is fine the following Sunday. The shed door is open when I arrive. I change into my wellies and gloves and get cracking. I'm in my element with plants that need pruning. Annabel comes out in gardening gear and rakes up the trail of dead heads and twigs in my wake. She brings out coffee and cake and we sit companionably on a bench and talk about her ideas for the future of the garden. At half past twelve, she seems anxious and I assume it's time for me to go. She shows me to the downstairs toilet and I wash my face and hands. I note the coats, macs and pairs of shoes that belong to more than one person.

'Are you there, Annabel, I'll be off now?' I call and open the kitchen door. She looks up from laying the table and I register the two settings. Deirdre must be in residence and expected soon. No wonder she's getting anxious.

'Here you are, Helen, and thank you so much.' She holds out an envelope.

'What's this?' I say warily.

'It's a little something for your time.'

'I don't need payment,' I say stiffly, 'I offered to help because I wanted to make you feel happier about your garden.'

'You've certainly done that.'

'Then I'm satisfied. Cheerio.'

I decide to take a field path back to my house, just in case Madam Deirdre should drive along the road and recognise me. I chuckle to myself. How will Annabel explain the improvement in the garden? Has she said that she's booked a gardener for the morning? I doubt if Madam Deirdre will even notice.

I mention the digs' problem to Mr Harrison one day and his response surprises me.

'Ever thought about buying a little place?'

'No! Could I?'

'I reckon that you could apply for a mortgage now you've got a steady income. Have you any savings for a deposit?'

'I have seven thousand pounds.'

'Have you by Jiminy! Five will go a long way toward buying a small property, which will leave you with a minimal mortgage.'

'My father's in banking and my parents took out a bond to mature when I was twenty-one.'

'Well, that was sensible of them and the money's going to be handy. One of the estate houses is up for sale in Hylton. They've got a grant on them and go cheaply. It probably won't be in very good shape; there's usually a reason why those houses are sold, but they were well built and you're not afraid of hard work. It would take a few years to get it how you wanted. Madge wants rid of a few pieces of furniture and we'll ask around. Shall I ring the estate agent and ask if you can view the property?'

'Will you go with me?' I ask breathlessly.

'Aye, I like looking round houses and we'll see what's what – if it would suit you I mean.'

I'm on top of the world! The house is rough, needs a thorough clean and decorating. I'm longing to apply scrubbing brush and steel wool to the Marley tiles on the floors in the downstairs rooms; a former resident has been careless with paint. The floors will look nice and light with a mat by the sink and perhaps a carpet square in the living room with a warm red hearth-rug in front of the gas fire. I'll shop for readymade curtains. The back garden's overgrown but getting that in order will be my pleasure. The essential services function. I can't wait to get started. According to the estate agent, it'll take about six weeks for the transaction to go through. I'd never have been allowed a mortgage if Mr Harrison hadn't backed me – I'm of no fixed address. He says he'll stand security for me. I suppose he would have the house if I defaulted. 'Please God, let nothing go wrong.'

But it does go wrong. Not the house, my happiness. It vanishes into insecurity at five o'clock home-time on the following Saturday.

I come out of the office to see a smart black car parked in the yard. Standing by it, is tall stylishly dressed Miss Horsfall. Her clothes always reflect the occasion. Today she's wearing tweed slacks, a Viyella check shirt and Barbour waistcoat. It's her outfit for visiting students that are out on work experience. Her hair is immaculate. My hair hasn't been cut since prison. I trim the ends because I can't stand rats' tails and I keep it tied up in a pony tail for work. I'm very conscious of my sweaty shirt and dirty jeans. I don't want to be rude and try not to show my dismay.

'Good afternoon Helen,' she says. 'Term is well under way and I thought I'd come over and see how you're getting on.'

'I'm fine,' I say (about everything but her I could add). I'm certain there's a reason why she's here.

'I won't ask you to show me your work this late in the day. There'll be another time for that but if you haven't anything particular to do this evening I thought you might like to join me for a meal.'

'I'm not in a fit state to go out,' I can genuinely say. 'I need a bath and I haven't really any going-out clothes.'

'That's not a problem. You can clean up at my place while I put the finishing touches to the meal I've prepared.'

I groan inwardly. I can see her perfumed bathroom, everything soft and dainty. For two years I've avoided what lay behind the closed door further along the hall. How can I get out of the invitation?

She moves a little closer.

'I spent some of my summer vacation in London, Helen. While I was there, I met someone at The Star gay nightclub who knows you,' she says confidingly. Her name is, 'Elvira Morgan, formerly an officer at Stonebridge Women's Prison? She was quite forthcoming on the subject of one of the former inmates of Stonebridge, Mary Helen Burns.'

I'm stricken. She waits to see if I'll say anything. Speech is out of the question. My gut couldn't hurt more if I'd been kicked.

'Don't look so upset,' she murmurs. 'I'm not going to tell Mr Harrison. I see he's standing over there watching us. Perhaps we should go over.'

How my legs carry me across the yard I don't know. They're on automatic pilot.

'Good afternoon, Miss Horsfall,' he greets her. 'Have you come to check up on your ex-student? I'm very satisfied with her.'

'I'm pleased to hear it. I thought you would make good use of her talents. We had great hopes of her at Neston. I came over to see if she would like to come over to my place for a meal, as a Saturday night treat.'

'Now that'll be nice for you, Helen. It's been very much work and more work up to now and not likely to get any easier with Christmas round the corner.'

I attempt a smile but it's a hasty, worried response. My past has caught up with me and Miss Horsfall knows it. How long before Mr Harrison learns the truth about me?

'I think you owe me a little of your time if I'm to keep your secret, don't you?' Miss Horsfall says as I sit in the passenger seat in her car feeling helpless. She reaches across me to fasten my seat belt. 'I hope you can make up your mind to enjoy some aspects of our liaison, Helen. There's nothing to prevent our association now that you're not my student.'

She switches on the engine. I move with her into the faultlessly prepared trap.

'It won't all be bad,' she murmurs, 'perhaps just not your choice.'

I would be some sort of churl if I couldn't enjoy the luxury of that bathroom – hot perfumed water, soft sage green towels, creams and talcum powder and a peach satin bathrobe. I begin to relax when I realise that I'm to be left alone to enjoy it.

I emerge from the bathroom very conscious of the smooth satin gown clinging to my naked curves. My clothes have disappeared into a washing machine; unless Miss Horsfall has a dryer that means an all night stay.

'There you are. Feel better? That colour suits you. I thought it would. Let's eat now.'

She draws a chair out for me and stands behind until I'm seated. My early suspicions are confirmed. This is to be a sexual relationship. The 'hands on my shoulders' routine is for starters, she doesn't stop there. For a moment I suspect that the meal will be put on hold. She fondles my breasts but then stops and buries her face in my damp hair. She utters brokenly, 'Oh my bright, beautiful girl. I've waited so long to do this,' and seems to pull herself together. We raise our wine glasses and she makes a toast.

'To Helen, the subject of my affection, may we eat, drink and be merry for many days to come and Helen, please call me Edith.'

I'm not sure about the 'merry' bit but eating and drinking is fine for now. Calling her Edith is okay, better than Miss Horsfall every time I want to address her and I suppose that, in return for her silence, I'll have to put up with whatever follows dessert.

Follow it does. Edith's flat is on the fifth floor of a modern building. As soon as I enter her bedroom, later that evening, I'm drawn to the wide window that overlooks the fields beyond the college. What a view! Edith comes up behind me.

'Can you see why I wanted this room?' she says softly. 'I knew that I could stand here with a lover, slip off her robe and caress her as though she and I are alone in the world. At last it can happen, my Venus.' Actions accompany her words. The peach satin robe is on the carpet. The she-cat has caught her mouse. I won't be going home tonight.

The contrast between my jeans and wellingtons day and the fragrant, silken world of my night is astonishing. I've no choice but to abandon myself to this lover. My sensuous body is quick to respond to her touch. She must know from my response how lonely my lips and body have felt. I guide her fingers where they most excite and demand greedily that her rhythm matches mine until she feels the tremor of my orgasm. After that, it's up to me to satisfy her desire ... not once ... Edith Horsfall's desire, like mine, has built up over a long period. She rides to her pleasure with the help of lubrication and vibrator, a thigh, fingers and endless kissing. Her body is lean and hungry. We drink wine and fall asleep only to rouse to her passion as soon as we wake.

I stretch out on Sunday morning and experience pleasure in the licentiousness of the night. In a way it's similar to being in prison but with better quarters. I can't escape so what does anything matter? Why not just enjoy the lust and luxury? I can't admire the woman for forcing me into her bed. Perhaps I admire her audacity? On her head the responsibility.

She serves coffee, warm croissants and apricot jam. We laughingly brush flakes of pastry out of the bed.

The necessity of returning to our everyday lives makes us withdraw from each other as the day progresses. We shower separately, dress soberly and prepare for the drive back to my world. I tell my landlady that, unexpectedly, I was invited to a talk at the college and stayed overnight in a room there. Edith Horsfall drives away and the glow of sex fades.

I'm no longer my own master. I can be controlled, manipulated by this discovered knowledge of my past. What a small world! In the great expanse of the city of London, how was it that Miss Horsfall bumped into Elvira Morgan? I suppose that both being gay and professional women they were likely to go to the same places. How unfortunate for me.

However much I remind myself that it isn't all bad ... delicious food and drink, comfortable elegance, being cosseted and sex ... I can't dismiss the realisation that the situation is very far from good ... and how long will it go on? Can there be an end? Edith Horsfall has given her orders; they are that I won't be needed next weekend, but the one after that she'll come for me. She says we'll celebrate my twenty-eighth birthday.

I've asked her to wait for me down the road. I don't want Mr Harrison to ask questions. She advises that we continue to meet at her flat. When I move into my house I'll have a telephone, so that she can make contact and arrange to pick me up. There's no escape.

CHAPTER 4

In the weeks that follow I work just as hard but fear of discovery, and being beholden to another person, has driven the joy out my life.

The purchase of Number 12 Willoughby Street is almost an anti-climax. The excitement gets lost in the knowledge that I'm not a free agent. I have dark thoughts … can understand victims planning murderous ways out of a trap. I don't sleep well.

I'm back in pretence mode. Pretending to Mr and Mrs Harrison that I'm delighted with my new home, pretending that I'm happy, pretending to Edith Horsfall that I can cope with our relationship – always keeping the different factions of my life apart and hoping that no one will notice.

It occurs to me more than once that I should confess to Mr Harrison and take the consequences but I hope vaguely that something will happen to change my circumstances.

I can't celebrate Christmas in my own home. It's arranged for me that I'll be whisked away on Christmas Eve to all the delights that Edith Horsfall can offer.

Early in December, I send a Christmas card to my parents with my new address.

We have a little party in the Harrisons' home after Christmas Eve market day. I've prepared packages for each of my workmates and they've looked for items that I will need in my kitchen, wooden spoons, a ladle, tea pot stand. The Harrisons give me a set of pans. I've bought them a Flower Calendar and Bendicks chocolate – the latter is what I would have bought for my mother …

It's the first time I've drunk mulled wine. We need the spicy warmth after standing out in the cold market square. I sit in one of the comfy armchairs, relishing the cheerfulness of the coal fire but miserable because I must leave this honest gathering and sneak off for a deceitful Christmas holiday.

'You okay, Helen?' Mrs Harrison perches on a stool beside me. 'Roger says you seem to be less cheery than when you started to work here. Is anything bothering you?'

'It's been an eventful autumn.'

'I hear you're not spending Christmas in your own house.'

'No, I've been invited to stay with a friend from college. In the New Year I'll invite you and Mr Harrison down to my house one evening and make you suffer my cooking. Next year I'll be more organised. I might manage a party at my house.'

'We'll look forward to that. Meanwhile you just see if you can get a bit more rest over the next few days. The circles under your eyes are too dark for a young woman.'

I have a job not to cry. The simple kindness is difficult to bear.

So too is Edith's kindness and affection – love? She must have spent days shopping to make sure that I'll be pleased with my gifts; pretty underwear, toiletries, a jumper, slippers and a leisure suit. I had to tell her about my parents. I think she's hoping I won't miss them too much. Perhaps she's trying to make up for the loss. I'm overwhelmed, grateful for the gifts and I feel awful because I resent the whole situation.

I looked for a present that Edith would like and had bought her the latest book on floral decoration. She's thrilled. I knew she'd seen it advertised in The Guardian and was planning to buy it. I filled one of my socks with choc bars, an orange and an apple, a lipstick and a sixpence at the toe. She didn't hear me put it on the bed last night and was delighted this morning. I can't begin to repay her for her generosity. It makes me uncomfortable to be so much in her debt. I hide my emotions, expert at pretence, and convince my lover that I'm enjoying my Christmas.

Bed's not now as exhausting. As the months progress, desperation gives way to playful and innovative sex. Edith and I have much in common, correct upbringing, good school record, university – and disapproval from our families because of our sexual orientation. We chat companionably all the time we're getting on with meal preparation and the chores. She's planning to buy a bungalow in the country. We lie in bed talking, reading and listening to music. My feelings toward her are a complicated mess of gratitude, friendship, admiration and pity. If I was in love with her the situation would be wonderful but I can't get away from the fact that she's stooped to sad lengths to snare a lover.

In the second week of May I brave an invitation to Myra, my young woman friend in town.

'How would you like to bring Nathan round for tea on Saturday,' I say. 'It's my day off. (Edith's away at a conference). I need to practise my cooking on someone. I promised to make a meal for my boss and his wife and I never got round to it. I want to try the dish out on someone first in case I get the sack, that's if you and Nathan don't mind taking pot luck.'

'What about me getting home?'

'There's a good bus service or you could stay over if you haven't to be back for any reason. I've a spare room and am the proud owner of cast-off bunk beds. We'll play it by ear.'

The meal is a success. It's only a lamb hot-pot but the potatoes crisp up nicely and I don't overcook the veg. I make extra mash for Nathan and he enjoys my apple crumble and custard. Myra and I drink red wine.

'I don't think you'll get the sack if your meal for your boss is as good as this,' Myra compliments me.

She dries the dishes and then we both kneel on my red hearth-rug in front of the gas fire and build towers for Nathan to knock down, until it's his bedtime.

'Shall we see if he'll settle upstairs Myra?'

'Okay. I'm enjoying myself and I don't really want to go home yet.'

We both watch him splash about in the bath and he falls asleep before Myra has finished reading a second picture-book story.

Myra and I finish the bottle of red wine and lounge on the ex-Harrison settee. I'm not into making a pass at Myra, not that it hasn't crossed my mind. It's nice to have a friend of my own age and she needn't know about my time in prison. I've bought a portable record player and some pop music forty-fives. Myra checks to see that Nathan's sound asleep and then we play the records and laugh and dance.

Suddenly there's a mighty thud against the window. We both stop dead and stare at each other. It's followed by two more thuds and shouting voices. Myra's face blanches. I switch the record player off and we listen. I don't want to open the curtains and let anyone see me peering through. Is it a matter for the police?

'Bloody lesbians!' I hear quite clearly. 'We don't want lesbians in our neighbourhood.'

'Oh! I can't cope with this,' Myra says, terrified. 'I must go.' She runs upstairs and starts gathering her's and Nathan's belongings together.

There's nothing I can say to convince her that she should stay. I open the door and see the ugly crowd of teenage girls. They're inside my gate, standing on the drive. The thuds have been made by clods of earth, now lying on the path underneath the window.

Myra, with her head down so that she needn't face the girls and Nathan complaining loudly at having been so rudely snatched out of bed, rush out of the gate and along the street to get to a bus stop as far away as possible.

That's right, you piss off,' the gang shouts after her. 'The sooner we're rid of types like you the better. We've still got this one livin' 'ere to sort out.'

The voices get fainter. I watch from behind the net curtains in my bedroom window as the crowd straggles along to the shops. Perhaps it was a one-off assault and I needn't call the police. I drag the quilt off my bed and take it downstairs where I crouch on the rug, hugging myself, shaking and weeping with shock and rage and hopelessness. Other people are bent on ruining the life I'm making for myself. Has someone been watching Edith collect me on a Saturday night and drop me off on Sundays – occasionally bring me back on a Monday morning? Myra is my first woman visitor and now she won't want to be my friend. My own home isn't sacrosanct. I lie in a wretched heap, curled up in front of the fire. I don't think I sleep. I'm in a semi-conscious state until dawn.

On Sunday I work in my back garden, where I can't be seen from the street. When I hear voices and footsteps in the drive, I investigate. A teenage lad is posing against my railings, with his hands in his pockets. A gang of three or four lads hang over my privet hedge.

'Sorry to bother you,' the poser leers, 'is my girlfriend here?'

'She's not,' I say and the onlookers snigger.

'Bloody Les!'

I'm trembling. Does this mean that a lesbian is not going to be permitted to live undisturbed in this village? Will I have to move away? Will I be forced to accept Edith's suggestion that we could live together in her bungalow?

I see Mr Harrison look closely at my face on Monday morning. I smile as best I can and open the mail.

The girls are there at the same time that night. More thuds on the window and shouted jeers. On Tuesday morning when I leave for work, I'm dismayed to see that the soil I turned over has been trampled down and the newly planted annuals are flattened. Branches have been torn off my beautiful flame-coloured azalea.

Tuesday night is the same. I hear shrieks of laughter followed by the clatter of my letter box. A pile of dog dirt drops on to my door mat. I throw the mat in the dustbin and have only just finished cleaning and disinfecting the door and hall tiles when the phone rings.

'Helen, its Edith, see you at the usual time on Saturday?'

'Yes, okay.' I must sound less than enthusiastic.

'You all right dear?'

'Rather more frustrations than usual, I've just about got my head above water.'

'I hope you get rid of your frustrations by Saturday. I've booked us into a hotel at Windermere for the night. My conference was stuffy last weekend. We could both do with a change of scenery. Pack your mac and walking shoes.'

It will be a relief to get away but will my house be damaged in my absence? What a choice – fleeing to a hotel, staying at someone else's home under duress or being besieged in my own home! Where in the world can I be at peace?

On Wednesday morning, Mr Harrison calls me into the office.

'Make us both a coffee, Helen.' He draws a half bottle of rum out of his jacket pocket and pours a liberal splash into each mug. He motions me to sit in his chair and occupies the one used by visitors, positioning his body between me and the door.

'Now, young lady, you've a story to tell and we're not leaving here until it's told.'

I collapse in tears. I couldn't speak if I tried. This time I have my own man-sized hanky. Mr Harrison sips his coffee and says, 'I thought as much.'

Where to begin? Is there a key point that will explain the mess I'm in?

'I'm a lesbian.'

'Yes, I thought as much,' he says again. 'I told our John not to bother you with his attentions when I saw he was a bit keen. You very tactfully put him off.'

I stare at him in amazement.

'Nay lass, I've a cousin that's queer and an old girl-friend that lives with a woman. We never pry into what sort of set up they've got. It isn't such a big deal for some of us older ones, now what else?'

'There's a group of teenage girls. They started on Saturday night throwing clods of earth at my front window and yelling lesbian abuse. I had a young friend and her toddler over for tea – you know, Myra, the woman I talk to at the market. We were having a quiet drink and listening to music. She was going to stay over but she fled, terrified. There's been abuse every night since. They've damaged the plants in my front garden and they posted dog poo through my letter box.' I break down.

'Well, we'll soon put a stop to that! What time did you say the nuisance starts?'

'About eight o'clock.'

He picks up the phone.

'Sergeant Graham, its Roger Harrison, Kerryhall Nursery. Can you get two officers in plain clothes to my house at seven thirty? ...

It's a nasty outbreak of homophobia. ...

A group of teenagers is targeting the house of one of my employees. ...

We need to approach the village unobserved. ...

Right, I'll see you then.' He puts the phone down.

'That's that settled,' he says. 'I want to see who's responsible, I may know their parents. You stay up here with Madge tonight. She knows there's something wrong and she's got the bed made up ready.'

There's a pause.

'Now, let's hear the rest of it. That trouble only started on Saturday night, so you tell me, but I saw your spirits plummet at the appearance of a certain smart lady from Neston College.' He waits.

'Did you notice there were gaps in my references when I applied for this job?'

'I did. There could have been any number of reasons, illness, divorce, I didn't ask because I was prepared to employ you on your college achievements.'

'I was in prison.'

'Ah … now that does surprise me. Which prison?'

'It was Stonebridge Women's Prison.'

'I know the governor Miss Pennyfields, or rather her mother. We go back a long way. I can check your story.'

'Miss Pennyfields and her mother came to graduation day at Neston.'

'Did they indeed! But I'm not surprised. Margaret Pennyfields wouldn't miss a chance to see the grounds at Neston. I hope you get to see her gardens at Hattersley House. Now, what were you in prison for?'

'My roommate at University was a lesbian. I wasn't into homosexuality at that time and when she wanted a sexual cuddle I pushed her away.'

'And … '

'She staggered backward, hit her head and died. I got five years for manslaughter. The judge said it was assault.' I grip my coffee mug and am grateful for the kick of the rum.

'That was a stiff penalty. Sounds more like accidental death to me. I suppose someone had to be seen to be punished. And what's the connection with Miss Horsfall?'

'She was my floral arts tutor at college. She fancied me and I avoided a relationship with her. The deputy governor in prison was a spiteful lesbian called Elvira Morgan. She was dismissed after a breach of conduct.'

'I think I get the drift of this story. I suppose Miss Horsfall has had the good fortune to meet this woman, discover your history and hold you over a barrel ever since.'

'Yes,' I whisper.

'And do you want to put a stop to that?'

'Yes.'

'When do you see her next?'

'She's picking me up from my house after work on Saturday.'

He sits thinking for a moment.

'I'll drive you down and meet her on Saturday. She can know that your secret is out and that I don't think any the worse of you because of what happened in the past. After that you can decide what to do about her.'

'I'll discuss the affair with her when we're in the Lakes this weekend.'

'Are there any more skeletons in your cupboard?'

I smile ruefully, 'No, not that I know of.'

'Right, go across to the house and spend the day with Madge. She's making cakes for a Spring Fair at Chapel.'

'Thank you, Mr Harrison.'

'Nay, I don't need thanks. I just want to see you restored to the bright lass you were when you first came here.'

Mrs Harrison is expecting me.

'Have you got things straight now? We've both been worried about you for some time. Roger said, 'If you meet a young woman with so much about her she's likely to have some tangles to cope with.' He's just phoned across with a message that you're to stay here tonight.'

I sleep soundly.

CHAPTER 5

We arrive in Windermere in time for Edith to spend half an hour with her ninety-five year old aunt before she retires for the night.

I notice her aunt's hearing-aids whistle fitfully; her bag of curlers and a hairbrush are on the chair beside her, ready for bedtime. The well read *Daily Mail* is neatly folded and there's a postcard from Switzerland propped behind the clock on the mantel piece. I sit on a chair while Edith is grilled by her inquisitive relative.

'How long are you here for, Edith? Have you done anything about buying yourself a place?'

It's obvious from the insistent flow of words that the briefest of replies are expected from Edith and few of those.

'Still no man on the horizon? No wonder if you will wear trousers all the time. Never mind, Edith, I don't regret not marrying. As long as you don't get involved with any of those homosexuals – there was a case in the paper today. It's ridiculous. You can't have sex between women! You get yourself nicely settled before you retire. Now, off you go and have your late meal with your young friend. I'm doing all right. Mr Simpson gets my shopping and I can walk to the corner shop on a good day. It's time I was getting ready for bed.'

We are dismissed, the aunt having shown no real interest in her niece's life.

On Sunday morning, Edith and I stand in the bay window of our hotel room looking out over Lake Windermere. The mist is rising from the trees on the far hill-side.

'Let's not drive anywhere today,' Edith says. 'It's going to be a fine day. We can go down the wood, have lunch in Bowness and just enjoy the few hours we have to spend here.'

'That suits me fine.'

She's not very sure of herself after the encounter with Mr Harrison at my house. She didn't talk much on the drive up and was shy about sex when we got into bed last night. I managed to tease her out of it. I don't know what I'm going to say to end our affair. She's become a friend of sorts, one with whom I need have no secrets. It's just that for months I've had no choice but to be in the relationship. Edith has planned this trip as a treat and I feel it would be mean to say, 'Right, I don't want to see you again.'

We walk a little way down the main road and see the sign post for Sheriff's Walk. The path is narrow and we stroll in single file until we clang through the metal swing gate into the hush of the wood. Here the path's wide and Edith takes my hand.

'This is my favourite place in the whole world,' she says. 'My aunties brought me here when I was little and we had to hunt for sticks for kindling. The house they lived in then had a big old range. The sticks were put to dry in one of the ovens. The ground here used to be covered with wild raspberry bushes, yellow and red fruit, but it's the policy to clear the undergrowth these days. Breathe the smell, Helen. It's peculiar to the Lake District. I recognise it when I step off the train or get out of my car. I feel I'm back where I belong.' She laughs self deprecatingly but not before I notice that enthusiasm softens the taut muscles in her face.

Tall trees are sprinkled with the light green of opening leaf-buds and underfoot, the path is soft with aeons of crushed beech nuts. The sensation is that of being in a living cathedral. A chattering beck runs parallel to the path. When it reaches a deep cleft in the rock, it cascades to the pool below with a roar. We move back from the sound simultaneously and sit on the seat with a view of the waterfall.

'I want to be buried here, well ... I want my ashes to be scattered into the water down there,' Edith says.

I look at her startled. I don't know whether to laugh or be serious. Is she doing a 'poor-me' act, feeling sorry for herself now she's been rumbled by Mr Harrison? Does she hope I'll carry on with her out of pity? She's avoiding eye contact.

'The trouble is – I don't have any relatives who would oblige.' Her voice is unsteady.

God, she is serious!

'I'll just have to leave instructions in my will and hope that some considerate lawyer will see to it that my wishes are carried out.'

I'm so flabbergasted that I can't think of anything to say. I sit watching the force of the water as it pounds into the depths of that dark pool and shiver. Fancy wanting to have your earthly remains churned about down there. Is that all she thinks about herself, chuck what's left of her into darkness and depths? Jeez! This woman's a pill! Now she's got me feeling sorry for her.

'I'm not sure that would be a loving enough gesture toward yourself,' I venture. We're still not looking at each other. The topic's a new one for me. How would my bible-bashing father go about it? He'd probably be unsure as to whether the Lord would welcome a lesbian into life everlasting so the method of her disposal would be of no consequence. I'm not my father. I'm much more into the message of a loving God. I choose my words carefully. 'Your ashes are the last remains of your being. Your life is honourable, you are hard working and kind and you create beauty with flowers. I think you need a gentler burial place.'

Why do I feel I have to be firm with her and jolt her into a greater regard for herself? I start off by loathing the woman, hating her for the hold she's got over me, then I learn to respect her because of her artistry and her care of me. Now I'm beginning to like and attempt to comfort her!

'I can understand you wanting your remains to be in this peaceful wood,' I say, 'but down there it's too violent, too sudden. What about having your ashes scattered in the beck at the top of the wood?' Is this me talking respectfully about scattering ashes? I'm twenty-eight. I haven't got round to thinking about death and its attendant responsibilities. 'Your ashes can lie among the stones then eventually trickle down toward the waterfall and out into the lake.'

She turns to face me and nods with a tight smile. I take hold of her hand and then she cries. It's my turn for hanky duty. I can't bear the weight of her loneliness yet I don't in any way feel forced to ease her mind, I'm genuinely concerned.

'Put my name in your will as an ashes scatterer,' I say irreverently and then more seriously. 'Wherever I am, the lawyers will find me. I'll bring you here to say goodbye.' I kiss her hand, give her a hug and stand up. 'Come on misery guts. That's your end dealt with. Now, let's get on with today.'

We walk along the bottom road, past the rugby field where her dad used to play, and arrive at the Bowness shops.

'Never mind belonging,' I say mischievously, 'I'll turn you into a tourist.' We each choose a flavour for an ice cream cornet. She objects to me paying but I insist. Dammit, the woman has to learn to take! I'm snowed under with her consideration.

We window-shop on our way down to a pub where I order two coffees and two measures of rum (Mr Harrison's given me a taste for the combination) served with a crunchy peppermint choc. Our seats are by the window, facing each other.

'Why did you come away with me?' she asks in a voice that other customers can't hear. 'I've got no hold over you now. You've known that since Wednesday. You could have cancelled the trip.' Her bottom lip quivers. 'You must despise me for using your past experience to get you into my company.'

'I didn't think too kindly of you to start with I can tell you!' I whisper fiercely. 'And wasn't your plan to get me into your bed?'

'Yes, I hoped ... I'm not proud of my behaviour, Helen. I had to do it that way because I don't attract anyone. Look how you avoided me. I'm not ... I haven't ... I mean, no one wants an intimate relationship with me. I was desperate.'

'Do you mean desperate for sex?'

'No, I wanted you.'

That gives me a boost! Good for my ego to be wanted! Noreen, Mrs Watkiss and Edith, they each wanted me as a lover and made the moves. They know how to 'want' and are not afraid to act out their desires. I wouldn't know how to initiate a sexual relationship. I haven't fancied anyone enough, even Annabel Priestley, to contemplate how I would go about asking for a date.

But with Edith there's a lack of self regard that's sorrowful. I'd be unkind if I said anything to hurt her.

I grin.

'You said, as you strapped me into your car and carried me off to your lair, that it wouldn't be all bad and it hasn't.' She looks as though she can scarcely believe her ears. 'You're a bit of a goof Horsfall woman, do you know that? Don't you realise that you really understand what makes a woman feel wanted? Lovely meals, comfortable surroundings, transport everywhere and this trip. Okay, you're a demanding bitch in the bedroom but you're lucky because that suits me.' I let her take this in but it doesn't alter her serious mood.

'But you would never love a person like me?'

Oh boy, am I having to rack my brains today! Honest answers need careful thought. I must tackle this truthfully.

'Hm ... I came away with you, knowing quite well that I didn't have to, because you had arranged the trip and you wanted my company. I haven't been to the Lake District before and I knew you would have organised the details as beautifully as ever. You care about me and you've been very good to me, Edith. I appreciate your kindness and I've grown fond of you. I learnt more about you yesterday evening, when I saw you with your aunty.'

'What, as a subservient, frightened relation?'

'No, as a patient, caring woman who puts up with narrow mindedness rather than upset an old aunt. Yes – I despised you in the beginning. How could I not? I used to dread Saturday night and seeing you waiting for me in the car; that got us off to a very bad start. But on Wednesday, when the compulsion to be with you was removed, I was free to decide if I wanted stay friends with you.'

'And do you?'

'If neither of us throws a spanner in the works I don't see why we can't be friends.'

'Just friends?'

'We could never be 'just friends' Edith. Isn't ours a loving friendship; one in which we can relax because we've no secrets from each other? Liam is my only other friend and he doesn't know everything about me like you do. Don't you think that, in a way, friendship is a more secure relationship than lover? I watched lesbian couples during those years in prison. They were jealous and scared in case the relationship failed, in case someone seduced their partner. There's a freedom with friendship. We can be sure of each other and go our own way knowing that there's someone we can rely on. The sex would have to go if either of us falls in love. Neither of us would two-time a partner.

'Meanwhile woman, my tummy is growling and you promised me lunch – lunch and an afternoon by the lake. I'm enjoying being with you, Edith, and I'm glad we're staying for another night even if it does mean an early start tomorrow. Now if you would like to fasten that button on your shirt I would be obliged. You're revealing more enticement than I can cope with if I'm to eat a good lunch.'

She suppresses a delighted response. I think this woman will find herself a mate. Our eyes meet as we collect our belongings, hers blue and wistful, mine hazel and commanding. Yes, this woman and I have a lot on each other, we'll be good friends.

CHAPTER 6

Life has become pleasant! I can't believe that there's nothing to worry about. Myra talks to me but I issue no more invitations. There's a surprising phone call one Monday evening, later in the month.

'Mary Helen Burns?' a voice enquires.

Who knows me as Mary Helen? I think I recognise the voice.

'Would it by any chance be ex-con Deanna Livesey asking the question?' I hear her laugh. 'What are you doing ringing me?'

'Is there a reason why I shouldn't? I've been hearing so much about you lately that I thought I'd get the news straight from the horse's mouth. It doesn't sound as though your life has been very straightforward with that college tutor stitching you up.'

'Someone's been telling tales. How do you know about that?'

'Your boss was here with a delivery and he and Margaret got chatting. Margaret took me on one side after he'd gone and told me about your conversation at Neston. She's very good at making things come right. I don't suppose you know that it was Margaret that organised my kidnap from hospital.'

I didn't even know you were kidnapped from hospital! Dee, how can I possibly know about that? I thought you'd been transferred to another prison. There were rumours that you'd been sprung but we didn't know what to believe. I haven't talked to you since 1970, that day we had a chat in the potting shed at Stonebridge.'

'Ah yes, the famous tete-a-tete in the shed that rattled Jane.'

'What do you mean?'

'Even seemingly confident prison governors can be jealous. Jane saw you and me go into the shed for our little exchange of confidences and she was afraid we were having sex. She was absolutely beastly! At that stage I had no idea that she liked me. I just thought she was hammering home the rules of the place.

'After your boss had gone today, Margaret told me that you and she had talked at Neston, when you went off with her to get the cinerarias. She thinks it may be Jane who hasn't wanted you and me to correspond. I confirmed that Jane had been jealous of our friendship when I was in prison. Jane owned up to the reason for being horrible, after we got to know each other, but there's no need for her to be suspicious of the friendship between us now.

'Margaret asked Mr Harrison for your phone number. She's canny. If she gets an idea into her head beware. It's not the first time she's overridden her prison governor daughter; the kidnap was the prime example. I'll tell you that story at a future date. What's with the college tutor at the moment?'

'Her name's Edith Horsfall and it's turned out okay in the end. We've agreed to be friends. I can do with friends who know all about me. I've had to hide the prison and lesbian information from everybody. Edith was desperately lonely, with no good opinion of herself. I say was, because she's in a much better frame of mind now. She knew she wanted me for a lover when I was at Neston and guess who she met up with who gave her the opportunity – or did Margaret tell you?'

'She did; Elvira Morgan, you unlucky ex-con.'

'I resented the situation terribly, but as time went by I realised that my attitude wasn't helping either of us. Edith's good company and she treated me like a princess. Even so, it feels great to be in charge of my life again.'

'That's good news. I'm glad Elvira Morgan's nastiness didn't harm you in the long run. Would you like to meet up with me? I'll extend the princess treatment to you, Mary Helen Burns, in return for the *Helen Burns/Jane Eyre* biscuit sneaked to me in prison.'

I laugh at that.

'Join me for dinner at The Manor in town? I could do with someone to talk to. Is Thursday any good, at seven o'clock?'

The velvet dress isn't suitable for a warm evening. I wear a cotton shirt, pants and sandals with a denim jacket. I'm puzzled as to what Dee wants to talk to me about. We choose to sit on a leather settee in a quiet corner of the hotel lounge and order sherry.

'Is it okay with The Penny that you're out to dinner with me?'

'She doesn't know.'

I can see that she's trying to get to grips with wobbly emotions. I wait.

'We're not on good terms. She's living at her flat and I'm at Hattersley House, the family home.'

'God Dee, you and The Penny mustn't pass up on each other! You looked happy together at Neston, as though you were made for each other. Have you gone off her?'

'I adore her.'

'Then what's the matter?'

She fumbles in her handbag, takes out a packet of tissues and fights to bring her emotions under control.

'Adoration isn't enough, Helen. It's the everyday living that has to work.' She sighs wearily.

'In the early days, Jane used to insist that we thrash out our problems. Lately, she swans along with her own life thinking that everything's great. I'm afraid to mention the things that upset me.' She pauses to deal with more tears.

I'm dismayed to see her so upset.

'The trouble between us erupted after that day at Neston, when we came to see you strut your stuff. You were so full of enthusiasm. You had a whole new career in front of you. I felt dejected and realised I was making comparisons with my life, questioning my lot. You see, on the surface everything's wonderful; Jane, the girls, Hattersley House and Margaret and her partner Frances. Maddy and Thea are seven and eleven and really happy at the village school. I've no reason to be dissatisfied.'

'But you are.'

She nodded.

'For a couple of days I was very quiet and Jane noticed. She took offence when I tried to explain my feelings, took it as criticism. She said that we'd better have some time apart so that I could sort myself out, decide what I wanted, and removed herself to her flat in town. I'm not sure she understood where I was coming from. She may have thought I was disturbed because I'd met you again.'

'So what is wrong?'

'I don't feel fulfilled as a person. Thea and Maddy don't need me except for basic care; which means, food, clean P.E. kit, endless ferrying to the swimming baths, piano lessons and ballet classes etc. I help to keep the Hattersley House gardens looking good. None of it is mine, Helen. You know I used to paint and write as often as I could but now I feel guilty if I shut myself in for any length of time. I miss the creativity. There's always something that needs doing, and Jane likes me around when she's at home.

'Jane's got her job. She's often invited to evening functions. That's a sore point with me. If I was her husband I'd be included in the invitation. I think she should say that she has a partner and brave the fact that her partner's a woman. We have great holidays abroad. She doesn't mind us being seen together when we're on foreign soil. But for social events connected with prison business she doesn't come home. I never see her in her glad-rags and you know how handsome she can look. She could have another love in her life for all I know. She wouldn't be the first woman to have two relationships on the go.'

'Oh Dee, I hope not. But she's a closet dyke ... that's not good news. She could put lesbian relationships on the local map if she came out in public. Have you discussed it with her?'

'No, I'm hurt and resentful. It's part of the barrier that's grown up between us. I envy you. You've established your own identity, I feel as though I've lost mine. I want to be more than a mother and part time gardener. I'm restless and lonely for something.'

'I'm not surprised. The life you describe doesn't sound personally fulfilling.'

She shrugs her shoulders hopelessly.

'Did you start to feel unsettled that day at Neston?'

'No, we've been uncomfortable with each other all winter. She moved out in April.'

'That's a month ago! Have you seen her since?'

'I went round unannounced last Wednesday to see if we could sort something out. Wednesday evenings used to be our nights on the town; we'd dine out and go to the theatre or a film. Jane had the phone in her hand when she opened the door and she seemed agitated, even more so when she caught sight of me. I could see through to the lounge and it all looked very cosy.

Annabel Priestley was fast asleep on the settee and there were wine glasses and candles burning.'

Annabel was asleep? That's odd if Annabel had been asked round to Jane's for the evening. My mind whips back to that evening after night school.

'Annabel was asleep. Are you sure? You know she's diabetic? She could have been in a hypo and Jane was phoning for help.'

Dee is aghast, her face a picture of misery.

'I never thought of that. I haven't seen anyone in a diabetic hypo.'

'I think they're sort of asleep until they get some sugar to the brain. The ambulance is usually sent for and an injection brings the person round. I made enquiries after the experience I had with Annabel, when she was weak one night after college, because of lack of sugar. What did you do?'

'I fled.'

'Oh Dee, you are an ass!'

She's too upset to speak.

'Don't you and Jane fancy each other now?'

'I can't answer for Jane but I've only to see her to want her. I'd say our sex life is second to none.'

We both manage to smile at that confession.

'My unrest is really nothing to do with our love for each other. It's more an emptiness in who I am ... and the whole situation is so awkward with me living at Hattersley House. Its Jane's home not mine, well I suppose it's my home now, but Margaret and Frances miss her and I feel I'm to blame. They've been so kind to me. Do you know what my Christmas present was in 1971?'

'I'm listening.'

'The Pennyfields had a daughter my age called Julia. She died of drug related causes in 1967. Julia's inheritance was my Christmas present, divided between me and my daughters. I'm well off, Helen! The girls have to wait till they're twenty-five to draw on their money. You know, how can I be dissatisfied when my life is so comfortable?'

'It's probably too comfortable, boring, no challenge.'

'What I'm really worried about is that I'm ready to pack it all in, for the girls and me to leave Hattersley. I'll give the money back. I've travelled this way before you see. I was ready for single parent-hood and a return to teaching when I prepared to divorce my husband. The challenge appealed to me but Jane happened along, we fell in love and I went to live with her instead.'

'Yes, but you'd gone off your husband, whereas you still love Jane. You'd be hurting yourself and life would be tough. What about the girls?'

'I know. It would be drastic. The girls would have to make another huge adjustment. Part of me feels wild, doesn't care, because it would be a way of escaping from the pain of another broken relationship. It's the only plan I can come up with that would give me the freedom to be me. Wouldn't I be branded as a selfish bitch? But an unhappy mother isn't much use to girls as they're growing up; they saw enough of me in that state before my remand sentence. I thought Jane and I discussed the issues relating to co-habitation satisfactorily, but obviously we didn't. I trusted to the initial falling in love – as I did with my husband Jon.'

'We can all be wise after the event.'

'Yes, but I should have known better, having made the mistake once. Jon's divorce wasn't through when he and I fell in love and I ended up living with him, which was not the 'done thing' in 1958. I had to keep it secret in case we lost our jobs. Here I am in the same position, having to keep quiet about being gay, largely because of Jane's high ranking position. The only people I meet regularly are the mothers at the school functions. I'm friendly with one or two of them but I've only disclosed that the girls and I live in rooms at Hattersley. I doubt Thea will say much to her friends; she knows it's unusual to have two mummies. But Maddy will probably have let everyone know that Jane and I sleep together.

'Oh Helen, I've had it with going against my own will in order to suit other people! I can't credit that I went to Somerset House to collect Jon's divorce papers because he said he couldn't spare the time from his studies at the British Museum! Or that I agreed to arrange our runaway marriage with the registrar at Guildford, for the same reason. I hated what I was doing and yet I said nothing. I even lied to please him.'

'That doesn't sound like you.'

'It's not me now, but it was me. I was always afraid of displeasing him. When my best friend invited us to her wedding I let Jon persuade me to ring up on her wedding day and say we'd missed the train. That was the end of that friendship ... and she was a very special friend. Regrets like that never go away. What a price to pay for keeping in with your partner!'

Dee is into self-laceration in a big way tonight, ploughing up these old regrets and my tummy's rumbling. I'll have to wait until she's got the woe out of her system before I mention eating.

'I would like to try living on my own. Jon was an academic and he excluded me to the point where I was nothing more than the little wife at home. Now, I've become Jane's little lesbian partner at home. I'm trying to summon up enough nerve to insist on what I want to do. God, Helen, I'm sorry ... bringing up all this stuff.'

I decide this is a good point to take a break.

'Let's eat and think what to do.'

'You'd have to go back to teaching if you leave Jane?' I say when we've eaten our starter and sit with a glass of wine, waiting for our main course. She nods miserably.

'Do a refresher course, yes.'

Over dinner I ask her if there's any branch of the arts or sciences that she's interested in. Could she stay where she is and go to college? Do a degree? Join a choir? Join the Townswomen's Guild? Learn how to play a musical instrument; get involved in any activity that will introduce her to fresh company and stimulate her mind. I notice that the latter suggestion initiates a response but she says that she's too old to learn to play a musical instrument. I say I'm sure that it's practice that matters, with learning to play a musical instrument, rather than age. She's not aiming to be a solo artiste! I mention a violin, a flute, a piano accordion. I'm not very up on musical instruments. It seems to me that she needs to succeed with some new venture.

(I think I'll start an advice column, *HELEN CAN HELP: problems relating to life and death thoughtfully considered.*)

'I can play the piano, 'Dee says. 'I wonder if I could try a piano accordion.'

'I've only seen them played by folk groups,' I say. 'Mr and Mrs Harrison went to hear an accordion band that played in our village hall recently. You could join a band. I'll ask Mrs Harrison, my boss' wife, if she knows where to begin and I'll let you know. You've had quite a lot to drink, Dee, are you okay to drive home?'

'I've booked a room. It's a double, do you fancy staying the night?'

I don't answer. I can tell that we're both considering the implications of a night together. I speak first.

'I could very happily spend a night with you but guilty consciences, even if we didn't have sex, would rule out friendship. I need your friendship, Dee.

'You're right of course, that was foolish of me – alcohol and loneliness talking. It would be jiggering up our friendship just when we've met up again.'

The Harrisons are helpful about the local accordion group. They put me in touch with a member of the band who waxes enthusiastic about the instrument over the phone. I have a job to get a word in edgeways, to say that it's not me that wants to try an accordion. The next evening I relay the information to Dee, as to where she can buy an accordion and how to go about joining the beginners' group.

How to get her back with Jane is another matter. Can learning a musical instrument work relationship magic? It seems to me that her need to assert her individuality is pressing. Jane's neglect of Dee with regard to social events is a bummer. Am I the right person to be involved if Jane is afraid of my friendship with Dee?

I'm still pondering this question on Saturday, during a slack period at the market, when who should come along but Annabel Priestley. She stops for a chat.

'Annabel, have you got time to join me for a coffee?' She looks rather taken aback. I call across to Mr Harrison. 'I'm okay to go for half an hour Mr H?' He gives me the nod.

'I hear you've been having a tough time,' she says. So she knows as well.

'Hasn't scarred me for life and its all practice for when I meet the one and only,' I say with a laugh. She's politely amused.

'Annabel, do you believe that learning how to play a musical instrument could change one's life?'

'I'm sure it could. Why? Are you thinking of yourself?'

'Me? No. I'd like to be a rose growing specialist, that's learning enough for me. I'm talking about Dee.'

She reacts as though I've no right to be talking about Dee.

'Look, Annabel, Dee rang me up last week and we went out to dinner because she was desperate to share her problems with someone. She and I got on well in the prison.'

Her shocked disapproval is evident. 'Are you ... do you think you are the right person in view of ... well, your reputation?'

I can't believe I've heard her say that! Is this the woman I looked up to?

'My reputation has nothing to do with this. What do you know about my reputation anyway – gossip behind my back? I'm not a two-timer, Annabel Priestley. You needn't worry about me attempting to seduce Dee. Dee's my friend and I know that she adores Jane. I don't move in on other folks' relationships. By the way, did you have a diabetic hypo when you were at Jane's flat last week?'

She nods.

'Did Jane tell you that Dee called round at the flat while you were unconscious and thought you were asleep?'

She has the grace to look horrified.

'I told Dee it wasn't likely that you would be asleep. She thought you and Jane were into a cosy twosome. I've only asked you for coffee because I'm concerned about Dee. She needs a new interest in her life. She's feeling stale, as though she's done it all before.'

'Isn't living at Hattersley and having the children enough?'

'Come on! Would she and Jane be in a fix if that was the case? I didn't realise that Jane's a closet dyke. She's gone down in my opinion. I feel sorry for Dee being left at home while Jane fandangos at dances and civic functions. Anyway, why do you consider that being a wife and mother should satisfy Dee? Her creative self is stifled. Didn't you tell me that you go to Italian and pottery classes? Aren't you always keeping fresh interests in your life? You often travel abroad. Good God woman! Why should Dee be satisfied with domesticity and some gardening? Jane's got her career, the prison staff and lots of social contacts.'

I wait to see if she'll acknowledge any truth in what I'm saying. She doesn't speak.

'Dee and I discussed some possibilities that might get her out of her rut. The only idea that lit her up was learning how to play a musical instrument. She can play the piano but you can't carry a piano around, play in a group and meet people, and she needs to do that. She likes the idea of a piano accordion. My boss and his wife have been making enquiries. We know about two shops that sell accordions, one in Manchester and one in Blackpool. The local club holds a beginners' class on Tuesdays and has a band to join, if she makes good progress. I've passed the information on to Dee.' I stand up. 'Huh! I wonder what made me think that you might put in a word in the right direction. Sorry to take up your time, Miss Priestley! I must get back to the market.'

Now I've been rude! I've let her make me mad. Good job I didn't say what went through my head, words like 'prim unimaginative cow.' God, why have I allowed her to hurt me? Suddenly, I'm late of Stonebridge Women's prison, reported to have been involved in an unsavoury affair and not a fit companion for Dee? I wonder how the woman overcame her fears about helping a prisoner in the first instance. She must have felt it a real imposition.

'And what was she thinking of when she invited me to her home for the party and then let me help in her garden? She offered payment didn't she? That's probably how she thinks of me, as belonging to an inferior class, not someone to relate to as an equal. Oh damn! She mattered to me. I was thinking that we had reached an amicable friendship. I hoped her pleasantries were not feigned though I did suspect her motive in inviting me to her Christmas party.

So ... I discover that the attractive woman is inflexible. Has she the imagination or know-how to help Jane and Dee? I don't feel diminished by her attitude. I'm too fond of her to persuade myself that I've outgrown Miss Schoolmarm Priestley. I just won't make any effort to pursue the acquaintance, won't give her other opportunities to snub me. I was right in one thing. I'll always be an ex-con to her.

The phone rings on Monday night. A very different sounding Dee is on the other end of the line.

'Helen, I don't know what you said to Annabel but it's changed a few things. Jane came for lunch yesterday.'

'How was that?'

'It was pretty tough going.'

'Did you get it together?'

'Lots of things are under consideration.'

'Did you tell her about the wanting to leave bit?'

'Yes and she was genuinely concerned. She recognised that I wasn't making an idle threat.'

'Did she stay over?'

'No. I think we're too awkward with each other. She gave me one kiss that nearly set us off but Maddy came into the room and it was time for Jane to go. I felt that we were both longing for each other but sex isn't the answer to the problems.'

'When's she coming again?'

'Wait for it – I'm invited to accompany her to the opening of an art exhibition at the City Gallery. I'm to stay the night at her flat.'

'That's great. Next thing you'll be dancing with her at the Civic Christmas Ball.'

'I would love that. We dance together wonderfully at home. I thought you'd like to know that I've put thoughts of quitting the relationship on the back burner. Helen, thank you so much.'

'That's okay. I'm relieved to hear your news. I didn't say much to Annabel you know, I was disappointed in the woman. She's a limited stuck up schoolmarm. She had to remind me that I've an unsavoury past.'

'Oh Helen, she didn't!'

'Yes she did. I'm so much libidinous jail fodder to her and someone that filled up the quota of desks at her establishment for a year.'

'I'm sure you've got her all wrong.'

'No I haven't and what's more, I'm not surprised that Deirdre woman doesn't want to go about with her. You'd better introduce me to her. We might have a lot in common'

'For your information Deirdre hasn't been around since the week after your graduation.'

'I can well understand that!'

'Oh Helen, Annabel's lovely!'

'She might be in your experience. You didn't hear the way she spoke to me. At Neston I felt I was one of you and it made up for my awful loneliness. But on Saturday I was definitely made to feel that I belong to an inferior species. Let's not talk any more about her. What about the piano accordion situation?'

'We're going to Manchester on Jane's day off.'

'It sounds as though you and Jane will work things out.'

'You've certainly helped in the process, Helen, thanks again.'

'Do I get to have dinner with you a second time or have I served my purpose? You could always sample the cuisine at my humble abode.'

'You get to have dinner with me again and yes, I'd like to see your place and eat one of your meals. You must visit us at Hattersley as well. We'll keep in touch. I'm claiming myself within our relationship and that self wants to see you again.'

'Great! I'll expect a phone call.'

Half an hour later an excited Edith is on the phone.

'I wanted to thank you, Helen.'

(This is my night for being thanked.)

'What have I done this time?'

'The way you talked to me at Windermere. It made me feel better about myself.'

'And ... ?'

'Yes, well, it's too early to say but ... '

'You've met someone!'

'Yes.'

'Great! Tell me.'

'She was there at that disappointing conference and I said she was welcome to visit us at Neston. She came on Saturday and we got on rather well. She loves my room and my work.'

'Taken her to bed yet?'

'Oh Helen!'

(That's the third, 'Oh Helen' this evening.)

'Okay. That's super news. Don't rush it.'

I feel empty after the phone calls and on my own again. I'm still adjusting to living without anxiety. I make a mug of tea and pick up this week's *Amateur Gardening* magazine.

CHAPTER 7

Mr Harrison encourages my interest in rose growing. He suggests that I get up early and travel to other nurseries on alternate Saturdays in June and July, the months for rose blooms. It's nice of him, because we're busy at the market, the season for selling bedding plants. I think he hopes I'll develop a rose section at Kerryhall. Twice I stay overnight in bed and breakfast accommodation and come back with extensive notes and brochures.

'The more you know the better,' Mr Harrison says. 'You can choose a name for the rose you'll grow eventually but you'll have to be patient. It takes years to cultivate a new flower.'

Edith meets me at the station one Friday night and we travel down to London. She's booked the hotel and I pay for dinner on the Saturday night. She's learning to accept. We spend a fascinating afternoon in the Queen Mary's Rose Garden at Regent's Park. I couldn't have a more interested companion. I have to listen to a lot of stuff about her new friend, Grace. Fortunately for me she hasn't introduced Grace to her silken sheets so I have two nights of blissful relief from my sexless existence.

Dee keeps her promise after the summer holidays, when the kids have gone back to school. We go to the cinema to see *One Flew over the Cuckoo's Nest* and then have a late meal at the pub by the canal. Dee has joined the beginners' class and is well into her music. We catch up on everything that has happened since we were in prison together. She admits that being scooped up into the Pennyfields family, and living in a mansion, has made her transition to a lesbian lifestyle easy. She says that my life, with no parental support must be tough. I tell her about the nice happenings, about Mrs Watkiss, Liam and his family and now the Harrisons. She's interested in my travels in connection with roses.

'That explains why you haven't been at the market on Saturdays.'

'Were you looking for me?'

'No, it was Annabel who mentioned that she hadn't seen you there during June or July. She wondered if you'd moved to another nursery. Annabel likes roses.'

'I remember.'

I still feel upset about Annabel. How am I supposed to prove to her that, despite my unfortunate past, I am now an upright, hardworking citizen who cares about her friends? It's no good. I've let myself be affected by her attitude and want her out of the conversation. Dee and I have plenty of other topics to cover. I wonder if there's a rose called Dee.

Annabel appears again after the summer holiday. Each time she comes to the market in September I make quite sure that I'm busy with a customer. I know its petty behaviour. I can't make myself truly dislike her. I watch her when she isn't looking in my direction, intrigued again by the blonde hair and the way she fiddles about in her colourful woven shoulder bag, trying to find her purse. She dresses so attractively. I would have difficulty hiding my pleasure if she made the first move and came over to me, but she doesn't. Mr Harrison enjoys chatting with her.

'Miss Priestley was saying that the rose gardens in Paris are worth a visit,' he says when she's gone. 'She's a nice woman.' So he's been telling her I've been visiting nurseries and rose gardens, or Dee has. 'You save up and get yourself over there next June.'

'I might do that.'

My own garden is clear of rubbish and weeds. I've designed an initial layout. Mr Harrison lets me have trees at cost and these I plant at strategic points. When they grow, my back garden will be more private. I plant spring bulbs and wallflowers in containers until I know where to site the flower beds.

I keep my promise about a party but I hold it for my twenty-ninth birthday in October. I invite the Harrisons, Dee and my workmates and their partners to come to my house on Saturday 25th October. Edith has a prior college engagement and Jane is working a late shift.

I prepare a buffet meal and the visitors bring what they want to drink. My staple offering is the lamb hotpot and I add a savoury bean stew and baked potatoes. I cheat with packet lemon meringue pies and make a successful sherry trifle. Mrs Harrison contributes my birthday cake with eleven candles.

'Two candles for two tens and nine for nine units to be precise,' she says. 'It'll be easier next year when you'll only need three candles for thirty.'

The men are in good voice after a few beers, and sing the easy songs that Dee has mastered on her accordion, *Bobby Shafto, Blaydon Races* and *Loch Lomond*. The Harrisons and my workmates have clubbed together to buy me a radio cassette player with a cassette of pop music. We jig around to *That's the way I like it* and *Bye Bye baby, baby goodbye*. The neighbours must hear our rendering of *Rhinestone Cowboy*.

I wash up and clear away after they've gone and play my tape quietly in the kitchen. Work doesn't seem like work when music's playing. Twenty-nine, celebrating with friends in my own house – I'm making a life.

CHAPTER 8

November is a dreary, routine month, until the shops brighten up at the latter end with Christmas displays and Christmas lights. I haven't mentioned that I've been invited to stay for Christmas at Hattersley House or that Kerryhall Nursery has provided them with a ten foot Christmas tree. I'm curious about a house that can accommodate a tree of that size.

Dee is keen for me to go. She wants me to meet Thea and Maddy and show off her home. She says Jane is now convinced that I'm no threat to their relationship but I'm not sure whether to accept the invitation. Would I fit in at Hattersley, particularly as I know that Annabel Priestley's going to be there? It would be nice to see Dee's girls and Margaret but I might spoil the atmosphere for the family if I'm uncomfortable with one of their guests.

Edith is otherwise occupied. Grace will be keeping her company this year. Thoughtful as ever, I'm told to open my present before I go downstairs on Christmas Day so that I can wear it. The memories of my last luxurious Christmas make me envy Grace. Every now and then I suffer from 'sorry for myself' feelings.

Jane phones. 'What about our invitation to Hattersley, Helen? We would very much like you to join us.'

'It's nice of you to ask me Jane. I'm sorry I haven't given you a straight answer. I'm nervous because I don't know any of you well. On the other hand, I admit I don't fancy being on my own.'

'Make up your mind then,' she says with prison governor decisiveness.

'It's Annabel Priestley that has made me hesitate to accept your invitation. I'm not sure I can spend two days in her disapproving company.'

'You're not still worrying about last September, Helen? Didn't Dee tell you that Annabel had to do a rethink about a few things? She says you're a pill that provided a dose of enlightenment. She won't give you any trouble.'

'I wish she'd tell me that. She hasn't spoken to me since.'

'From what I hear you've given her the cold shoulder every time she's seen you.'

(That's true.)

'If anything untoward happens will you bring me home?'

'I will.'

'Okay. Thank you for the invitation, I do appreciate it, Jane.'

'I'll pick you up at six o'clock on Christmas Eve.'

I'm prepared. My market day lunch breaks are spent buying presents. These are parcelled, beribboned and labelled.

I post a Christmas card to my parents as usual. This year I glue a postcard of my village, photographed after snow, on to a piece of white card. My house is in the background and I mark it with a little cross. They've had my address since last year but, apart from my birthday card, I've received no mail from them. I wonder what my sister is up to and whether my card gets thrown in the waste paper basket. Christmas, baby Jesus, love ... I'm still their daughter.

Jane arrives promptly on Christmas Eve and I have my first ride in a Jaguar. The leather seats are comfortable and there's plenty of leg room.

'Are you warm enough?' Jane asks 'I can turn the heating up.

'I'm fine thanks.'

I could ride for hours like this, it's a luxurious experience compared with the couple of rides I've had in Dee's practical Land Rover.

We arrive at Hattersley House. What a house, it's huge! And the hospitality ... Dee chatters excitedly as she takes me upstairs and along corridors to my room. (I hope I'll find my way down.)

There's a double bed covered with a patchwork quilt in pink and white fabrics, Margaret's work Dee tells me. The deep pile carpet is rose pink. The wardrobe is fitted and there's an en suite bathroom. She leaves me to unpack. I spread my toiletries in the bathroom, drape my nighty over the radiator and hang up my green velvet dress for tomorrow.

A glass of sherry is in my hand the minute I enter the drawing room. Here the carpet is a pretty pale green and the background of the settees and chairs is cream, patterned with large camellia type pink flowers and green leaves. The effect is light and pleasant contrasting with the mahogany furniture and floor-to-ceiling bookcases. I intend to examine the contents of the latter as soon as politeness permits. The long velvet curtains are drawn and I feel enclosed in warmth and welcome. Elegant tables with attractive porcelain coasters are placed so that there's somewhere near to place one's drink without worrying about any damage to a polished surface.

I assume that Margaret is responsible for the colour schemes.

'Helen, meet my partner Frances,' Margaret says. With her arm round Frances she explains. 'Frances came here as the housekeeper when my husband was an invalid and she stayed on as my lover.'

'Don't you believe it, Helen, 'Frances says, 'I still do most of the work round here, the lover position is just tagged on.'

It's tactful for neither of them to mention that Frances was my prison visitor and that I met her in that capacity. I liked Frances when she came to see me at the prison, every week for the first month. She listened, sat quietly while I wept, and helped me to adjust to the dreadful shock of imprisonment. She knew about Noreen and about my parents. I missed her when I was no longer on her visiting schedule. I'm glad to renew her acquaintance. She withdraws to supervise the kitchen – whence delicious smells waft – but not before I see the two of them embrace and kiss. Oh boy! I hope I'm in a relationship like that some day.

Margaret introduces me to her son Barry, who has his own hairdressing salon, and to his partner Jim, an ambulance driver. They're a dissimilar pair, Barry tall blond and willowy and Jim tall, dark and broad. It strikes me that it's unusual to have so many same sex relationships in one family but that suits me fine.

'I hear that you're interested in rose culture,' Barry says.

'I am, but I haven't got much further than a few visits to nurseries and reading at the moment.'

'Harrison won't be able to teach you enough. You may have to widen your sights to working for a specialist rose growing firm.'

'You may be right, all in good time.'

'Have a rummage through Mum's books or, tell you what, I'll root some out for you later.' He goes off to attend to replenishing sherry glasses and hands me a dish of nibbles. I don't want to spoil my appetite but I'll be tipsy if I don't eat something. I sample the nuts and savoury biscuits.

I realise that I needn't worry overmuch about contact with Annabel. I can easily avoid one person amongst so many. When she arrives I shake hands with her courteously, not with my usual warmth. I notice how fetching her bosom looks in her soft pink jumper with a scooped neckline. She smiles and I hope it's not because my eyes betray my admiration.

Thea and Maddy, Dee's children, have been allowed to stay up to meet us. They're obviously very fond of Annabel and carry her off upstairs to read the bedtime story. Barry takes me over to the bookcase containing Margaret's library of horticultural reference books. I'm in my element until dinner is served.

My place at the table is opposite Barry and Frances and next to Dee. The meal starts with a clear beef consommé and warm rolls, followed by home cooked ham and various salads.

'We thought it best to keep the meal fairly light so that we have plenty of room to indulge tomorrow,' Frances says.

The sweet is a creamy coffee concoction, an Italian recipe that I've never tasted before. It's divine! There are cheeses and biscuits and coffee and chocolates served in the lounge. I'll be interested to compare the difference between this dinner and a heavy meal tomorrow.

I'm not best pleased that Annabel approaches me after dinner.

'Any room on the sofa for a limited stuck-up school marm?' she says sotto voce.

I look at her in alarm but she's smiling and her eyes are laughing. I move up to make room for her, a little discomfited by her pert sense of humour and very much aware of her perfume.

'Do you remember the last time we shared a seat?' she says.

'It was in your garden. I remember making a hasty retreat on that occasion to avoid a certain Madam Deirdre.' She laughs.

'I'm sorry, Helen. I wasn't managing things too well three years ago. Not that I've managed things very well since then, in your opinion.'

'It did seem that there was room for improvement the last time we spoke together,' I allow cautiously.

'Well you've made a good job of avoiding me since, or perhaps you didn't notice me when I came to the market?'

'I noticed you.'

She laughs again. 'So you were being stroppy?'

I can't help smiling, relieved that she's adopted a direct approach. 'You were not nice to me. I wasn't going to encourage a repetition.'

'Helen, will you accept my apology? I got a shock when it was obvious that you were far more aware of things than I was. I had no right to speak to you as I did.'

I assume a mock severity. I'm enjoying this private exchange.

'I shall observe the sincerity of your penitence and see if I'm convinced by it. You have two days in which to redeem yourself.'

Suddenly she slips off the sofa and kneels in front of me. The conversation stops and everyone looks at her good humouredly.

'This Christmas Eve, my friends,' she delivers in good Shakespearean style, 'I Annabel Priestley, of sound mind and limb but obviously with a sad and wicked heart, do here beg forgiveness from Helen Burns for my unkind words last September.' With this kiss,' she takes my hand, 'I promise to mend my ways.' She looks beseechingly into my face.

Everyone is laughing.

'Don't believe a word of it. Helen.' Barry says. 'A bit of play acting from the wench doesn't convince us that her intentions are pure.'

I'm very much in favour of giving her the benefit of the doubt. I would like to believe that she wants to please me. I help her up which means holding her hand and touching her soft jumper, all of which I find pleasant despite my determination to be cool with her.

We're all rather mellow. The conversation is general and good fun. It isn't long before we retire for the night because an early start is inevitable with two children in the house.

'Come down for breakfast in your dressing gowns in the morning,' Margaret says.

I take Dee to one side.

'Traitress! You told Annabel what I said.'

She laughs. 'I'm not good at keeping secrets.'

'What time do you expect us for breakfast? I didn't bring a dressing gown.'

'I think excited voices are likely to wake you early, or the heating system will. It tends to gurgle round the pipes until they warm up. Come down when you're ready and don't forget to open the parcel I've left in your room ... tonight. Sleep well.'

The label on the parcel says, 'Happy Christmas to Helen, love from us all.' It's a soft pinky-beige woollen dressing gown edged with a multi-coloured cord, from Italy. I slip it on and feel cosy and precious.

In the morning I obey Edith's instructions and open her presents before I go downstairs. There's a box of tights. She must have mixed up my present with someone else's. I only wear tights with the little velvet dress and I've brought those with me – a second pair will be useful I suppose. The next package contains a satin petticoat, even more peculiar. Then I unfasten the main parcel. It's a straight through, long sleeved Jaeger woollen jersey dress with a tie belt and collar, in French navy and green stripes. A dress! Now I understand the tights and petticoat. I look at it in dismay. What is Edith trying to do to me? I try the dress on and then I know. It shows my figure beautifully. My hair curls nicely on my shoulders and I look good. Edith intends that I should feel comfortable in these elegant surroundings. I hope she likes the red Amaryllis plant and crystal posy bowl I bought for her. She was complaining that her vases were all too big.

Christmas morning is spent enjoying presents.

Annabel and I play board games with the children. Barry joins in but he's an outrageous cheat and the girls banish him. We eat biscuits and drink milky coffee then go for a walk to encourage appetites for the Christmas meal. I'm shown the grounds. We leave by a side gate in the estate wall and follow the frosty lane, to where the ducks slither on the frozen canal. The girls have remembered scraps for them.

Christmas lunch at two o'clock is delightful, smoked salmon starter then turkey with trimmings; crackers and party hats, silly jokes, and wine with each course. Jim lights the brandy on the Christmas pudding. We each manage to eat a little portion with white sauce and brandy butter. Coffee is served at the table then Margaret and Frances are dismissed from the kitchen. Jane, Dee, Annabel and I set the kitchen to rights. Dee ties me into a big apron. I wash, Annabel wipes and Jane and Dee put away.

No one is hungry for tea but we can't refuse a sliver of Christmas cake. Dee plays carols and we sing round the impressive Christmas tree. She's on top of the world because she's been asked to play in the local accordion band, in a black and white uniform with a green satin bow tie.

Once the children are in bed the adults flop into chairs until Barry says 'Come on, let's dance.'

This is dance with partner dancing, to records. I go over to the bookcase, pull out a couple of Margaret's gardening books and choose an armchair out of the way of the dance floor. If I watch these couples who are in love I shall feel lonely.

'Will you dance with me Helen?' The only single person in the party is asking the question.

'I'm not very good at this sort of dancing.'

'Neither am I but I don't think its ballroom competition standard.'

'Do I do the honours as I'm the taller of the two of us?'

'Please.'

This undoes the policy of no direct contact with Annabel Priestley that I've managed to maintain since Christmas Eve. How can I pursue my 'keep her at a distance' if I take this light, fragrant woman in my arms?

'Lighten up Helen,' she says. 'You're still wary of me because I upset you last September aren't you? Can't you forgive me? I'm trying hard to be nice.'

Her wicked smile doesn't make her look very repentant.

'Don't forget that I've got a reputation,' I mutter ungraciously.

'How could I forget?'

That makes me smile.

'See me tremble.' She lets go with one hand and swings herself away from me with mock horror. Dramatic madam! I spin her under my arm and catch her in a tighter hold.

'So you should tremble. Do I take it that this reputation of mine has been discussed by everyone here?'

'It has, endlessly.'

'Then why have you asked me to dance?'

'Don't feel too flattered, you were the only available partner.'

'Of course, how silly of me!'

The record comes to an end. Barry changes the discs and dims the lights. Jim pours us another glass of champagne. The edges of my resentment blur. I remember how much I admired this woman when she was Miss Deputy Principal Priestley, willing to help me at every turn. I remember lusting after her jokingly at Neston, imagining her in neat pants and a silky blouse. My partner is waiting to dance and she's wearing neat pants and a silky blouse ...

'The real reason for asking you is that I want to be held,' she whispers.

That does take me by surprise.

'Pardon me if I find that difficult to believe, held by someone of my ilk?'

'Who better?'

'Ohhh ... be careful,' I breathe against her hair.

'I didn't ask you to dance with the intention of being careful.'

I put both my arms round her, shaken by a fierce spasm of passion, and hold her tightly.

'Now look what you've done.'

'As long as I'm the one it's being done to,' she murmurs with her face against my hair.

I draw back from her so that I can see her expression, amazed by her unexpected and very obvious advances. Her smile is less certain which is not surprising as I've been severe with her since autumn. The exchange brings us to a standstill.

'You've let me go,' she whispers sadly.

'That can soon be remedied.'

This time I fold her gently in my arms, this woman that I've known for five years. As the dance ends and we move apart, I decide that her upturned face presents every reason why a gentle kiss should contribute to this fabulous Christmas Day.

Hugs and kisses all round end the evening.

I close the door of my room and lean against it. What a wonderful day! What a tantalising woman! My stimulated state can be excused after holding a body like hers. Annabel Priestley is definitely not a prim schoolteacher tonight.

I hang up my finery and soothe myself by splashing my face with warm water. A quick wash is all the rest of me will get tonight. I don't want to wear my nighty. Desire doesn't want to be covered by fabric – it needs the sensation of bare flesh against sheets. How can I calm down and get to sleep?

I can't.

Does she really like me I ask myself? Was she counting on the reputation of my affair with Edith to give her a festive clinch? Has she consumed just enough alcohol during the day to make her daring? Will they laugh behind my back tomorrow for rising to her bait? I squirm. If she's using me for a cheap thrill it would be in line with her earlier opinion of me. There's a seven year gap in our ages and all we have in common is a love of roses and reading – unless there is mutual attraction.

Margaret and Frances want breakfast in bed tomorrow morning, so do Jane and Dee. The girls will have trays and sit watching children's Boxing Day programmes on the television. Barry and Jim will eat in the kitchen with Annabel and me – she and I have been put in charge of the breakfasts. I'll see what she's like to work with, pretend tonight never happened. She leaves tomorrow after lunch to spend New Year with her mother.

Eleven thirty by the glow of the alarm clock.

She doesn't knock. The brief glimpse of light from the corridor shows her the way to my bed and she sits on the edge. She's wearing her dressing gown. I switch on the bedside light and draw the covers up over my breasts.

'I thought I'd better make sure that we both get up at the same time as we're on breakfast duty,' she says. 'Have you set the alarm?'

'Yes.' I determine to find out if there's anything going on between her and me. 'Annabel, tonight, was that you playing with me?'

She's quiet for a moment.

'I was attracted to you the first time we met, Helen. I noticed the way your eyes took in my appearance. You made me feel an attractive woman rather than a teacher. But you were a prisoner and frustrated by the circumstances. In the year you studied at Deanswood you were busy with your job and you seemed utterly preoccupied. Sometimes I deliberately stayed late to have a word with you after class. When I saw you without your pigtail, with your wavy hair loose and your arms full of books, hurrying about, earnest and energetic, I wished I was younger.

'That night you helped me I was thrilled because we actually touched. I wondered how I could legitimately get into your company again and that was when I invited you to my end of term party. But what you didn't know was that Deirdre and I were having an affair. We weren't getting on too well which is why I wanted some attention from you – yes, I was using you at that point – probably trying to make Deirdre jealous. I also quite genuinely wanted you to have a bit of fun. Deirdre picked up on the fact that I liked you; you were the only new girl at the party. Her way of dealing with her suspicion about anyone who threatens to compete for my attention is to attract the person to herself.'

'Why Jane moved in between Deirdre and me?'

'Yes. Then you were off to Neston. There was no chance to see you while you were at college and anyway, Deirdre and I rubbed along until quite recently, as I believe you've been told. Not much joy for either of us, as it turned out.

'Then you see I heard that you were embroiled with the Neston College tutor and you were attracting unpleasant attention where you lived, that all seemed very unsavoury; perhaps association with you meant trouble. I was in that set of mind when you asked me to have coffee that Saturday morning.'

'So, what's changed?'

'That's not how I think about you now. Dee told me that you'd successfully negotiated the affair with the college lecturer and that the two of you are friends. I was mortified when I realised what I'd said! Actually I've been envious too because you brought about a happy ever-after situation with the tutor whereas I felt I'd made a woeful exit from the relationship with Deirdre.'

'You could have dropped me a line, explained, or rung me up.'

'By the time I was seeing sense I felt it was too late.'

'So what's going on tonight? Have you had one too many? Are you sexing up Christmas with the only unattached woman at Hattersley?'

'I flirted with you tonight because I rather hoped you might want me.'

'Annabel ... my antennae have been tuned in your direction since we first met but I haven't known how to take you. You've been friendly one minute and cool the next – and you were Deirdre's partner. When you came to Neston for Graduation I thought again how lovely you were and I dressed you sexily in my imagination.'

The darkness makes it easier to be honest.

'I did let your words get to me that Saturday morning. It's not easy to feel an upright citizen when you've done time, your parents have cut you off, and you have to keep a chunk of your life secret. Even though everyone at Hattersley and my employers are kind, I'm quick to feel that I'll never escape my past.

'I've complied with sexy demands on me, yes. The affairs were forced on me but because there was no emotional attachment I could make the best of the situation. I pleased the women concerned in bed. Perhaps I believe that I don't deserve anything more. I make my work important and don't think about a loving relationship. The first woman who wanted me to love her ended up dead. Wouldn't you be justifiably wary?'

She doesn't answer.

'I responded to you tonight because we were both a bit merry, but I want to avoid feeling foolish tomorrow amongst these super friends. I'm not going to make the mistake of assuming that Annabel Priestley is serious about Helen Burns.'

We sit without speaking.

'Do women satisfy you in bed?' she surprises me by saying.

'I'm lucky that my reaction to stimulation gives me an orgasm.'

'I never experience orgasm with a person,' she confesses. 'Lovers go off me. I make them feel a failure in bed.'

'You would prove a challenge.'

'That's what lovers think, both of them, and they leave with their egos dented.'

'Did you love them?'

'I loved the idea of them I think, and wanted to see what sex with a woman was like. The first time I was disappointed. I felt I was watching the moves and it was all over so quickly. With Deirdre I was just there to satisfy her. The sex never felt as though it was part of loving.'

I keep quiet. It won't have been easy for her to tell me this. I can't think myself into her situation. The sex turns me on whoever I'm with but it's much better when I'm wanted. I wonder if she was never sure if it was her or sex that her lovers were after.

'Do you think an old fashioned type courtship might suit you better than the 'jump into bed because I fancy you' tack? Perhaps you need to grow to love someone instead of acting on attraction and hoping the sex will work out okay. If you made yourself have sex with me, because you thought I wanted it, your mind wouldn't let go. You might wonder how you compare.'

'But could one have a relationship with someone that doesn't include sex?' she asks doubtfully.

'I suppose that as long as there could be cuddles and kisses and lots of holding each other there wouldn't be the need to go the whole way.'

'Do we like each other enough to try?' she says tentatively. 'I like you but I feel I would be asking too much.'

'I would have to prove that you're not asking too much. I've never been in love with a woman. It would be wonderful to love like Jane and Dee or Margaret and Frances. It's you Annabel that I want to get to know. We'll leave it that we tell each other when we want to make love or it just happens, or we decide to pack in the friendship. Forget about it for now. We'll see whether we can work together in the kitchen in the morning.'

'Do you think we could start the cuddles tonight?' she says.

I move across to the other side of the bed and put my arm round her, pulling the sheet up over my breasts and rather wishing that I'd put my nighty on. It's lovely to have her in my arms. After a few minutes she says, 'I must get some sleep, I've a long day tomorrow. Goodnight Helen.'

She initiates the goodnight kiss, not me. I know how kisses fire me up but I'm not refusing this one. I offer tentative lips but her response is passionate. We seem to melt into each other and I'm momentarily lost in wanting her. She shudders and gasps, briefly buries her head in my breasts – then slips off the bed and the door closes after her.

I lie wide-awake, hugely turned on by that kiss. At what point did my careful control over my feelings vanish and leave me lit up like this? All the excuses I've made as to why I couldn't possibly love Annabel Priestley! I've persuaded myself continually that I don't care about her and now I feel helpless. I've let her in, admitted to myself that I'm in love with her. And Annabel, she's far more vulnerable than I would have thought. If she can kiss and let go to that degree, surely the desire must reach her loins. Why don't they let go like mine? Or did they? What was that shudder and gasp about and her head thrust against my breasts? Surely she must feel something for me to have been as intimate as that? Perhaps I'll find out in the morning.

I wake long before the alarm, tingling with anticipation. I'm down in the kitchen before Annabel arrives. I'm longing to see her and ready to chivvy her for her lateness. I'm surprised to see Jane and Dee are there before me. Jane's leaning against the sink and Dee is at the table with a mug of tea.

'Happy Boxing Day,' I say cheerily, 'what are you doing up? Didn't you trust Annabel and me to get your breakfast ready?'

There's something wrong. The atmosphere in the large cream coloured kitchen is chilly in the extreme, despite the smell of toast and the kettle coming to the boil on the *Aga* stove. I look from one to the other but I'm not going to ask.

'Annabel's gone,' Dee announces.

I stare at her, not really seeing her, while the meaning of her words sinks in. I hide the expression on my face by walking over to the window. I hold in the wave of sobs that threatens. My fists are clenched in my jeans' pockets. Jane and Dee mustn't see my shoulders heave or they'll guess.

'Did you do something to upset Annabel last night, Helen?' Dee wants to know.

I'm not going to discuss anything with them. I don't owe them an explanation. From Dee's attitude I can tell that she and Jane have immediately jumped to the conclusion that I'm in the wrong. It's always going to be like this. I'm the outsider. I let Annabel call the shots and offered to fit in with her wishes and now ... no message ... just goodbye Annabel.

I feel a blaze of anger at another dose of rejection. Why is she messing me about with her fears and indecisions? God, she has it in for me! It just seems that I've been invited to stray out of my security and have given permission for her to hurt me again.

'Take me home, Jane, please. I'll wait in the hall.' I run upstairs to pack my suitcase. 'Hi kids,' I call out to Thea and Maddy who are on their way down to breakfast.

'Are you going, Helen? Can't you stay and play with us after breakfast. It was great yesterday, board games are fun with more people,' Thea says.

'It was a lovely day yesterday Thea, best Christmas Day I've ever had, but my holiday is over. I'll be back at work tomorrow.'

'We'll see you again sometime,' Maddy pipes up.

'That would be nice,' I manage to answer, though I'm near to tears.

Dee is standing in the hall. I don't speak, just give her a little thumbs up sign with my free hand and a wave that says, 'cheerio and no, I'm not saying anything.'

Twenty-five minutes later, I'm outside my own front door. I haven't spoken a word during the journey.

'Thank you Jane for inviting me,' I say politely. 'I've had a very enjoyable Christmas. Say goodbye to everybody for me,' and I open my garden gate.

My gas fire has the room warm in no time. I kneel on my red hearth rug and let myself drown in waves of shock and pain – such a beautiful time and then this shattering end. I'll get over it. I'm experienced at getting over knocks.

What state is Annabel in to dash away like that? The more I think about that kiss, the more I feel sure that I've got it right. She did feel something and it frightened her. There would be no need to hang about, getting to the point where we could try sex, if a kiss for Annabel works with Helen. I allow myself a grim smile because what could have come next is commitment. But an ex-con must be prohibitive to Annabel Priestley, just as a lesbian ex-con is prohibitive to my family. I've had to cope with the loss of my parents' approval. I'll have to do the same with Annabel. She may not realise it but I feel she's done her damndest to take me down twice. She won't get a third chance.

I must value the person I am and if possible, without believing that the world is against me, protect myself from disapproving attitudes. It makes sense to keep away from anyone I can't trust to respect me.

CHAPTER 9

Saturday market is in full swing now that Christmas is over. Potted hyacinths left over from Christmas, snowdrop and primrose clumps, some trays of winter veg and the usual shrubs are laid out. We stamp our feet and blow on our fingers and say, 'Hooray!' when trade slackens off in the afternoon. Mr Harrison lets us pack up early.

'Coming in to have a word with Madge?' he says when we get back to Kerryhall and have finished the unloading, the stowing away of unsold plants and garaging the vehicle. 'She wants to know how you got on with your friends.'

I'm very glad to sit in front of the Harrison's coal fire and be served afternoon tea; home-made scones and strawberry jam. Their living room is very different from Hattersley. The windows in the stone walls are small and many paned. The curtains and furniture in the lounge are patterned chintz and the carpet's dark red. It's warm and cosy. There are stools to rest your feet on and rugs for your knees.

'I'm determined not to be one of these people who complain about their arthritic knees,' Mrs Harrison explained last year. 'I'm sure it helps to keep them warm.'

The Harrisons always make me feel at home. Mr Harrison's books are an untidy jumble in the bookcases. Mrs Harrison is the proud owner of a Moorcroft lamp and vase and her precious Doulton figurines are in the glass fronted cabinet.

'I couldn't have been made more welcome at Hattersley House,' I say. 'Have you been to the house?' No point in launching into a description if they're familiar with the place.

'I've been as far as the kitchen for a coffee, after making deliveries,' Mr Harrison says. 'Hattersley's a pretty impressive estate isn't it?'

'I thought it was wonderful. My room was on the second floor and I had my own bathroom. My Christmas present was a warm woollen dressing gown from Italy. We all wore dressing gowns to breakfast on Christmas morning. Miss Horsfall gave me a super dress to wear on Christmas Day. The food was amazing – and the drink.'

'What about the company?' Mrs Harrison asked.

'The company was made up of family members and partners, Dee's two girls and Miss Priestley; ten of us sat down to Christmas dinner.'

'I don't get the impression that you really enjoyed yourself. I've been watching you today,' my observant boss says. 'Your spark's missing.'

'Oh dear ... am I as easy to read as that?' I sit watching the flames for a minute and they wait. 'I had a really lovely Christmas Day.' How much to tell them? 'Twice I've been made to feel that I'm accepted as a friend, by the Pennyfields' family and Miss Priestley. But both times something has happened that makes them turn on me. The kindness, which I hoped was genuine, is I suspect me being patronised. At the drop of a hat, I'm an ex-con. You know I was wary before I went, because Annabel Priestley spoke down to me last September.'

'I thought you'd put that behind you. Sure you haven't got a chip on your shoulder? She's all right, Annabel Priestley.'

'I know I'm a bit sensitive but if I've a chip, it's not without reason. Oh yes ... ' I must watch it, I'm very near to tears, 'Annabel's a lovely woman.'

'But?'

'She's charming, very good at saying come hither when it suits her and then cutting me off. I think it's been a game with her but, as far as I'm concerned, she's played it for the last time. I'm going to steer clear of the lot of them in future.' I stare into the fire and feel miserable. I won't have Dee's friendship or repeat the experience of being welcomed at Hattersley by Margaret and Frances. Mr Harrison breaks into my despondent mood.

'You're still going to the Spencers for New Year?'

'Yes I am. I'm looking forward to it. They're like you – they've never given me a moment's unhappiness.'

'It's just that I've been thinking about your future and now might be a good time to have a change. When you get back from the Spencers I'm going to take you over to Blake's Nursery.'

'The rose-growing firm in Lancashire; or is it in Cheshire now, since the county-boundary changes last year?'

'That's the one, and I'm not sure about the county boundary. I'll check Blake's brochure. It could even be in Greater Manchester. You've learnt as much as a small nursery like mine can teach you and, unless I promote you to manager and give up the reins, there's no advancement for you here. I'm not ready to do that yet.

'I went over to have a chat with Ernest Blake about him taking you on. He wasn't keen. He hasn't got much opinion of women in his line of business but I said you would make him change his mind. He's got two sons, both in the firm, a couple of foremen and a number of assistants. You'd have to live there.'

'What about my house?'

'Yes, well, I've interviewed a young woman that could take over from you. She could rent your place if that suits you.'

'Yes, that would be fine. What accommodation would I have there?'

'Ernest's built a row of chalet-type, single bedroom apartments, for his staff or visitors. He has one vacant.'

'Wow! Quite a start to 1976! The trouble is that I've been happy here and I'll miss you.'

'Which brings me to another matter; I think it's high time you learnt how to drive. You manage the tractor fine. One of the lads there will probably start you off and you could have a few professional lessons to get you ready for a test. You could afford a second-hand car and then you could nip over and let us know how you're getting on. Blake's Nursery is only forty-five miles away.'

'I like the sound of that. I shan't feel cut off from you all. I'd better go now. Thanks for my tea and I'll see you on Monday.' Mrs Harrison always gives me a lovely hug.

My phone has been busy. Four recorded calls. I don't want to hear what anyone has to say. I delete the messages without listening to them; I shut myself in and the world out.

Tomorrow I'm going to lie in, do my washing, prepare for my visit to the Spencers, read and eat. I don't like the idea of leaving my home. It's a grit my teeth and bear it situation for the sake of starting life in a new environment and getting on in my career.

CHAPTER 10

Mr Spencer is not too sure about me working at Blake's Nursery. I see the look that passes between him and Liam when I tell the family my news.

'Blake's a rough sort of chap but he does know his roses. He'll train you up and you'll have to work hard. He's extending his premises and lines of merchandise all the time. His wife's a handsome woman and the two lads work for the business.'

Liam's sister is abroad on a skiing holiday with her husband, so there are just the four of us to bring in the New Year. I'm lucky to have these friends, as well as the Harrisons and Edith, a group of people who like me for who I am. The Hattersley crowd I've cut out of my thoughts. But, it nags at my mind that I've never been honest with the Spencers about my prison past. I'm dying to get Liam on his own to ask about his love life. I half expected his young partner to be here for the New Year celebrations. We spend the evening watching the television and stand ready with our glasses of champagne, to kiss and wish each other well when *Big Ben* chimes in the New Year, 1976.

'Come down after breakfast, Helen,' Liam says when he leaves for his own house. 'I'll see you in the morning, 'Night everybody.'

Liam's house is five hundred yards down the road from the Spencer home. It's a detached modern three-bedroom house and Liam has furnished it comfortably in light colours, with flowering indoor plants on every available surface and a smart streamlined kitchen.

'Doesn't look as though much cooking goes on here,' I tease him. 'I notice you're just near enough for your mum to your make your meals.'

'I cheat and buy in ready-made meals mostly. I cooked when Peter lived with me. Mum's been great. I wrote you that it hit her and Dad hard when I said I was definitely gay and that I wanted to live in my own place with a partner. I think they still hope that some woman will come and sweep me off my feet.

'It didn't work out with Peter. He wasn't really into commitment. He wanted to go clubbing and flirting with other guys so I was kinda prepared when he packed his bag and moved out. Sense of failure and all that, you know ... rejection ... will I ever find anyone? He's gone abroad, to Israel, if he ever got there. He wanted to work in a kibbutz. What about you? The odd postcard hasn't told me much this last year.'

'The up to date news is that I've had a run in with schoolmarm Annabel Priestley. A week ago she was sitting on my bed professing affection and wanting to try a relationship.'

I stop. I realise that I can't give meaning to this story. I can't explain the Edith saga or why Annabel is uncertain about a relationship with me unless Liam knows the secret of my past.

'Liam, I've kept a secret from you ever since we met. It's the reason why I couldn't tell you what was happening this year.'

I pause and sigh. The truth is bound to affect the Spencer opinion of me and I have so enjoyed their confident approval.

'I'll tell you now, Liam, but it may change our relationship. There's no other way to say it – I served three and a half years of a five year prison sentence for manslaughter in Stonebridge Women's Prison.'

I tell him the whole story. He listens without comment.

'The night you heard me scream was the first time I released some of the anger that had built up over the terrible unfairness of the whole situation. I'm grateful in a way to Nigel Atkins for giving me an opportunity to let go of the despair. These days I tend to crumple when I'm upset, hang in with the hurt until it goes away. I've nearly worn a hole in my nice red hearth-rug. I kneel on it and feel sorry for myself. A prison sentence and lesbianism; it's not difficult to see why my parents want nothing to do with me is it?

'You remember Miss Horsfall? She got wind of my story just after we left college. She met an ex-prison officer in London who knew me at Stonebridge and it gave her an excuse to trap me into an affair. The threat was, that she would tell my employer about my past if I refused to get into bed with her. Liam, there are so many more instances of fact being stranger than fiction in my life! As it turned out Mr and Mrs Harrison are okay with the prison information and the lesbian information. I survived the affair with Edith Horsfall – I'd no other option. I can even say bless her! She made up for the dearth of affection in my life. We've ended up being good friends.

'But my past has dogged me, is still dogging me. In fact Liam, I don't think I'm ever going to be allowed to escape it. That's why a move to a different nursery might help. I mentioned the outbreak of teenage homophobia in a letter to you last May, didn't I, when my house was assaulted? Mr Harrison came to the rescue. He and local police officers settled that.'

'My goodness, I felt for you when I heard about that.'

'I thought things were getting better when I caught up with Dee.'

I tell him about my friendship with Dee, about Dee's girls and the Pennyfields, about Annabel and our ups and downs, since the prison book-borrowing days. I end with the details of the passionate kiss that prefaced Annabel's unannounced departure in the dead of night.

'Do you see why I feel that my past rises up and hits me in the face? The friendship can't be sincere – scratch the surface and I'm an ex-con. I feel there's criticism even with Dee. You see, she was wrongfully imprisoned whereas I am guilty, someone did die as a result of my action.

'I was incredibly ignorant as a young woman, Liam! What good was a Grammar School education and being born into an intelligent family when it was all narrow and prejudiced? If only I'd known more about homosexuality! None of this needed to happen. When you think ... Enid was in love with me, Liam! My friend Enid had to die because I didn't know how to cope with a sexual embrace from a woman?'

Tears are welling up – Liam's gentle attention and I'm too near the part of my story that I keep buried.

'Will I ever be able to forgive myself?' I ask him in a despairing whisper.

He puts his hand over mine.

'I'm still the same person you met at college, Liam. Will you still be my friend?'

'Of course I will, silly. I'm glad you've told me though. We've always felt that you were constrained about something or other but we didn't want to pry. I can't see that the information changes anything about the Helen we know and like. Is it okay for me to tell Mum and Dad?'

'Yes, but I'll be sad if they change toward me.'

'I doubt they will. Let's hope that you don't come across any malicious characters in future – anyone who would judge you for your sexuality or for what happened ten years ago. I think you could forgive yourself, Helen. It was accidental death. Anyone who knows you must realise that you wouldn't deliberately harm a person. My God, you've had to suffer for it! Come on, let's walk back, it's nearly time for lunch.'

'I don't think I can stay for lunch, I must go home, Liam,' I say urgently. 'Talking like this has flipped the switch that controls my unfinished emotional stuff. I must deal with it, with the New Year, new start. Can we go now and ask your mum to excuse me please?'

I know I couldn't sit through a happy occasion. My chest feels tight with churning emotion. Liam's gentleness, the bitter disappointment over Annabel ... Enid ... I feel as if there's a sea of sadness that won't be held back any longer. I must get home.

'You pack your bag and I'll run you to the station. Mum will understand.'

'Thanks, Liam,' I say when we're on our way to the station. 'I'm relieved that you know the truth about me and still want to be my friend. Tell me quickly about the Blake Nursery.'

'I didn't care for Mr Blake but I did like his son Gareth.'

'I'll look him up for you.'

'When you do, point him in my direction if you please. Sons of nursery men, we could have a lot in common.' He grins. 'The other son, Nick, he's all right, bit of a womaniser. You should be safe with Gareth.'

'Safe?'

'Men will be men.'

On the way home my mind is a merciful blank. I'm desperate for my quilt, gas fire and red hearth-rug. I make a pot of tea and set the tray down on the tiled hearth but long before my cup is empty, the tea is being salted by tears.

'Enid ... my friend Enid ... I'm so sorry ... years ... with my own predicament uppermost in my mind the whole time ... self-centred clueless bitch! I cause unhappiness for both our families ... a mess of unfinished business for myself and everyone concerned, and then charge ahead with what matters to me. I didn't think about what you felt Enid ... I never stopped to think about your feelings. In prison I just told the story, ha, ha, that's how it happened. It's only now that I love someone and rejection has hit home that I have some idea ... some idea of how magnificent love feels. It's been wiped out of me and I killed it in you.' I kneel, racked with sobs. 'I can't make this better Enid.'

I lie inert, paralysed by misery.

The church clock strikes eight and I stir wearily. At last I've dared to let the sea of sadness, guilt and remorse break through. I was afraid that I wouldn't be able to cope with the onrush of feeling but it hasn't driven me mad. The receding waves leave me drained, washed out. I get up slowly and close the curtains, make more tea, set a lighted candle on my coffee table and sit on the settee wrapped in my quilt. The stillness of the candle flame steadies me.

'You know there is something I can do, Enid. Your parents wanted to keep in touch and I haven't honoured the request. It felt too awkward and you know how sorry I've been feeling for myself.' I smile. I can see Enid smiling. I pick up the phone and hope it's not too late.

I hear, 'Mary Burns! Mary how lovely to hear from you,' but I'm crying too hard to answer. 'We'd love to see you. Are you by any chance free tomorrow?'

I mumble an affirmative.

'John will meet you at Manchester Piccadilly Station. Give us a ring in the morning so we'll know what time to expect you.'

We cry; Enid's dad John, her mum Anne, and her brother Harry, we all cry and then we need a drink of brandy and laugh. They forgive me for letting the years pass. They say they were numb too. We have lunch and talk about Enid. I fill in some of the story from my memories of that first year at Uni. We look at photo albums and I learn more about the Enid that was their daughter and my friend. I stay overnight and sleep in Enid's bed. I let myself own the friendship-love that I felt for Enid.

John and Anne say my visit has opened a door for all of us. I'm ashamed of the years in between but they insist I mustn't worry about them – they say the circumstances were understandable.

It is not easy for me to tell them that it appears I am gay. They're very quiet for a few moments and then John speaks.

'She got that right then?' he says with a sad smile.

Early the next morning, John phones Mr Harrison and explains that I won't be in work until Tuesday and that I'll give him the reasons then. Anne sends me home with a chunk of Christmas cake and sandwiches to eat on the train. We promise to keep in touch.

A NEW START
CHAPTER 11

Mr Harrison transports my luggage and me to Blake's Nursery on Wednesday morning.

'Madge and I were saying we were glad you got in touch with that lass's family. You've had it rough, but you're getting a chance to make something of your life. Madge and I would have liked a daughter. I can't imagine what it must be like to lose one, and I'll never understand your blinkin' parents!' he says angrily. He doesn't talk again until we arrive.

The large signs, car parking space, neat lawns, and tastefully planted shrub beds fronting the Blake's Nursery showroom, are very impressive. This is a huge business concern.

Mr Harrison leaves me with Mr Blake soon after our introduction. There are a few uncomfortable minutes in the presence of my new boss while he looks me up and down and then files the written information about me.

I use the time to assess my first impression of him. He's a big man with a strong handsome face, wearing dark-green corduroy trousers, a Viyella shirt and Barbour waistcoat with many pockets, the garb of horticulturalists it would seem. I'd say he's a grower, a salesman and showman. Success is written all over him but, I don't like the deep creases between his eyes, the result of much frowning and bad temper? His office is reasonably tidy and boasts up-to-date equipment. In a room to the side, a variety of jackets and hats hang on a rail of hooks, wellington boots on the floor.

'Well, you come highly recommended, young lady but that's as may be. I'll find out your worth for myself. Your life's your own out of work hours but I don't want any shenanigans with any members of my staff – not that that's likely if I've understood your former boss rightly. I'll show you round now and then first thing in the morning you start with the tractor and spread manure on the fields. I'll take you to your chalet first. Here's your door key and there's a spare kept in here in case you go out and forget to take yours. My wife will be round this afternoon to see you have no problems with your accommodation. She keeps an eye on the state of the chalets.'

I like my chalet and look forward to putting my stamp on it. The rooms are small but there's a separate bedroom and a shower over the bath which will be great when I come in dirty from work. I unpack my clothes and shoes and put my toiletries in the bathroom. I've brought my towels and bed linen and make up the bed. It means a lot to have my own place.

Mrs Blake arrives at four o'clock. We look at each other with interest. She's a tall woman with a well proportioned figure and beautifully styled auburn hair. I wonder if my chestnut mane could be made to look as attractive. My mother would approve of her straight jersey wool skirt in green and purple weave and her purple jumper with neat little pleats at the front and a collar. She's very much a lady in her green suede, expensive and practical shoes.

'Helen, it's nice to meet you,' she says and shakes my hand. 'I'm afraid my husband's establishment is predominantly male but I'm sure you'll manage. Do you think you'll be comfortable here? Have you everything you want?'

'Yes, thank you and I've discovered the tea bags and milk you provided. Would you like a cup of tea?' She accepts, almost as though it's a relief to sit down where no one can see her. There's unease about her; she looks as if she finds it difficult to concentrate on the present. I can see why Mr Blake would want this woman but I'm surprised that she married him. I can't imagine his heavy body being gentle in love making – why do I always think about that side of a relationship? The fascination of opposites – perhaps he reveres his elegant wife. What does she see in me? A tall healthy young woman with a shapely figure and a mane of hair caught back in a pony tail, open neck shirt, jeans and work shoes.

'I saw on your papers that your name is M H Burns. What does the M stand for?'

I hesitate momentarily before I say, 'Mary.' Mary said on its own will perhaps not evoke any memories whereas Mary Helen Burns said aloud might remind Mrs Blake of newspaper headlines. But she does say it aloud.

'Mary Helen Burns,' thoughtfully spoken. She looks over toward the window before adding, 'Yes.' She turns to look at me with a smile. 'Your mother and I must have shared a liking for *Jane Eyre*.'

I let go of the breath I've been holding.

'I'll warn you in advance when I plan to call on you. It will be in a few weeks, when you've had time to settle in,' she says as she's leaving.

The propagation of roses is work that's unknown to me but, from the hundreds of trays I see in the greenhouses, there will be plenty of pricking out of popular annual and perennial seedlings in the weeks ahead. Meanwhile I'm used for muck spreading.

The men are friendly and straight away, the sexy jokes are told for my benefit. I find these difficult to cope with as I frequently don't understand the punch line or they're not particularly funny. They laugh uproariously at my embarrassment and aren't offended. They let me know that they appreciate my figure, but they've probably been warned about their behaviour as well.

The elder son Gareth is away. I'm told that he's the member of the firm that travels in connection with purchases, sales, shows and development of the nursery.

Nick's cool look takes in the female parts of my body. He's well built like his father, wears his jeans tight and low slung so that I can see his more than adequate bulge in front and the cleavage at the top of his buttocks when he bends over.

I smile to myself. I can't criticise him for the way he looks at me when I'm weighing up his masculinity.

I drop a line to the Harrisons and Spencers, assuring them that I've survived the first two days at Blake's, and I mail my new address to my parents.

I'm homesick. Everything and everybody is new here. I'm tired. I've spread muck since half past eight this morning, apart from the lunch and coffee breaks. I feel desolate as I walk along the pavement to the post office with my letters. The countryside is very flat with wide stretches of fields behind the hawthorn hedge, a brown and uninteresting expanse at this time of year. The village is the other side of a railway bridge. I resist the impulse to 'yoo-hoo' as I go underneath it like we did as kids. I buy a loaf from the baker and mooch round a surprisingly well stocked bric-a-brac shop. I fall for a china mug, made in Staffordshire, and a second hand needlepoint cushion – both decorated with roses wouldn't you know.

A small cafe with plastic topped tables and tubular chairs tempts me. I sit down with a coffee and slice of Eccles' cake. I'm quite pleased when a tall, nice looking young man joins me at my table, though I'm surprised because all the other tables are without customers. I noticed his back when he was standing at the counter ordering his drink. His hair; it's ginger, tight ginger curls. He's got broad shoulders. I do like broad shoulders in a man, probably because I'd like to be held against them protectively. I must be lonely to be thinking like this. He moves with a loose ease of movement inside his grey tailored suit, makes me wonder whether he can dance – and my second thought – is he gay?

'Nice cushion cover, very appropriate in this rose growing area,' he says.

'I happen to like Redoute roses.'

'Me too – it's the bib of your overalls, with the Blake logo, that drew me to you, Madam. I have to add that I would of course have appreciated your bosom had there not been a logo to decorate it,' he smiles cheekily. 'Anyone from these parts recognises the Blake logo. I haven't seen you here before.'

'I'm a new employee.'

'Where are you from?'

'Kerryhall Nursery.'

'Ah! I know it but I haven't seen you there.'

'If you came on a market day I wouldn't be there.'

'Of course, are you going to tell me your name?'

'Helen Burns.'

'I'm Gareth Blake of Blake's Nursery, here for a quiet coffee, out of the way of my demanding father, who will proceed to gobble up the rest of my day as soon as I show my face.'

'Yes Liam,' I say to myself 'I can see why you would like this young man. I like him too and he doesn't take after his father with hair that colour.'

'Dad doesn't usually employ women.'

'I've been told and warned that I mustn't fool around with any of the male staff. That's not a problem as far as I'm concerned. I'm here to learn.'

'Ooh, very noble. Does that mean that you're romantically hooked up?'

'Very much not.'

'In that case I would have thought that one or other of the male specimens here would hold some attraction for you.'

I don't answer him straight away. I'm tempted to say, 'I relate to women.' Instead I take my tiredness and loneliness out on him.

'I would have thought that someone who travels far and wide for the firm would know that there are other things than men that interest a woman. You assume that a woman has nothing better to do than weigh up the male scene wherever she goes. I can't cope with this line of talk at the end of a muck spreading day. I'm going.'

'Hey! Hang on! Okay, I started on the wrong tack. I can try another one. I thought that with you being an attractive woman …'

'Yes, well an attractive woman doesn't always want a man.'

'True and an attractive man doesn't always want a woman,' he flings back at me, which I find interesting. 'So what can we talk about?'

'Where you go to and what you do when you're there, with regard to roses.'

'Ah well … how long have you got?'

'I've finished work for today.'

We drink another cup of coffee and eat toasted teacake while I learn about his input to the family business. It gives me greater insight into the cultivation of roses beyond this nursery. He has a pleasant attitude to his work and to the people with whom he's in contact. I ask him if he knows the Spencer Nursery and he does.

'Good old Liam!' he chortles.

'He is good and he's not old. He happens to be the best friend I have. He gave me this jacket.'

'Oops! I'm not doing very well with you at our first meeting.'

'Perhaps it's time for you to see what your dad wants.'

'You're right. Coming?'

'To let your dad see you and me walk into the forecourt together? No way! I'm the newcomer and I'll stick to the rules. You're the boss' son, the last person he'd want to see with me.'

'Okay cheerio then, until we can arrange a second, perforce clandestine meeting,' he says as though he's every intention of defying his father.

'I'll look forward to the intrigue,' I say with a grin. I walk back in a lighter mood.

I see him again in the morning when he joins us for the coffee break. He's diplomatic. Chats to the other men and then asks his brother to introduce me.

'It's nice to have some female company, Helen,' he says with a wink, 'even if you come with the smell of manure.'

The men laugh.

'From shit grow the sweetest of flowers,' I reply and rinse my coffee mug at the tap.

'Got you there, brother,' Nick says triumphantly. 'She's a match for you this woman. You're off again today aren't you? I thought you'd have gone already.'

'Dad told me about the new member of the work force and I decided I'd better check up on her before I left.'

I hear Nick say to Gareth as I'm walking out of the shed. 'She's not interested in men from what Dad says, pity because she's quite a woman isn't she?'

January is a dreary month. I have to leave the muck spreading when it snows and we work in the greenhouses. I like the way the lads bring in a battery radio and we keep in touch with the charts. I join in the singing and there's a nice atmosphere. Mr Blake gives his orders to the foreman and he relays them to us so I rarely come into contact with my boss.

I see Gareth in and out of the office. He's arriving in his beautiful black car when I knock off from work one afternoon.

'Wow! What a super car,' I say. 'It looks very up to date.'

'It is, latest model, Jaguar XJ6 Mk 2, I cover a lot of miles and like my comfort.'

'You also need a lot of cash to buy a beauty like this.'

'Indeed you do, but I'm lucky. I'm a favoured son of an indulgent mother. Have you met Mum yet?'

'She checked me in.'

'Between you and me,' and he looks at me seriously 'Mum is the money behind this whole operation. Dad's done well with the venture but he doesn't altogether enjoy the fact that Mum holds the purse strings, cause of strife and all that.'

I'm not sure he should be telling me about his family in this way. I peer in through the windows of the car and see beige leather upholstery, a radio and cassette player.

'Do you listen to music when you're driving?' I say to change the subject.

'All the time.'

'Mr Harrison was saying that I should learn to drive.'

'So you should. I could give you a couple of lessons when I'm at home for a spell but not in this beauty, can't have you crashing my gears. We'll have to look out for a practice vehicle for you.'

Mr Blake comes out of the office and we separate.

Our pay-packets are handed out on Friday evenings at the end of the working day. I take mine across to my chalet. On Friday the thirteenth of February there's a stiff little envelope in with my pay-slip and money. 'Open tomorrow,' it says. I'm curious but do as I'm bid. It's a tiny Valentine's card with a pretty pink Redoute rose and it's blank inside. The only person who knows I like Redoute roses is Gareth. I smile every time I see it on the mantelpiece.

There's another new employee, Damian. Bernard the senior gardener instructs both of us in the art of rose pruning then leaves us to get on with the job. We go up and down the rows of bushes, wearing our leather gloves, cutting out the dead wood, measuring the growths to be trimmed, choosing the outward facing bud and every now and then standing up to stretch our aching backs.

On the second Friday in February an extra slip of paper floats out of my pay-packet and falls on to the floor. The writing is in longhand.

'What I've got in mind is a small cafe out of the way.' Billy Joe Spears via GB but not the line about making love to you ... pity. 8 p.m.'

My spirits lift. I switch on my radio and dance round my kitchen singing along with the pop music. Gareth makes me feel good. He's light hearted and fun. Who wouldn't welcome a date with this nice ginger- top guy? I muffle up with a woolly hat, scarf and gloves because it's a freezing night. He's there first drinking a coffee and waiting for me. He drains his cup.

'Come on we'll go to a pub. This was just a convenient meeting place.'

His car is parked out of sight behind the cafe.

'Did you like your Valentine's card?'

'It was absolutely sweet. It'll be one of my treasures.'

He looks pleased and plays a tape of the current songs in the charts. *All by myself, don't wannabe all by myself.*

'That's my theme song for tonight,' he says.

I relax into his care and being entertained. I could get used to this. It's my third ride in a Jag. The pub is a few miles distant in the hope that no one from Blake's will be there to recognise us. We fit into a table near the blazing coal fire and I take off my layers.

'Hmm ... there emerges an attractive looking woman from under the wrapping, pity about the red nose. Beer okay for you tonight, Madam?' Gareth asks and buys the drinks.

We thaw out.

'I've located a cheap car for sale and wanted to ask if you're game to buy it and learn how to drive.'

'How much?'

'One hundred and fifty pounds, Cortina four years old, one owner, clocked up thirty-seven thousand miles, colour green, owned by my friend's mother.'

'I can afford that.'

'It'll fit on the drive in front of your chalet but, if I'm going to teach you how to drive, we'd better keep it elsewhere until you've passed your test. There's a large works' car park near my friend's house. You can have lessons there. You'll have to reckon cash for driving lessons, road tax and insurance.'

'Gosh thanks, Gareth! My own car! As a matter of interest, why are you keen to do this for me?'

He doesn't answer. 'I'll get us another drink, crisps?' I nod.

'Simple answer,' he says when he returns to the table, 'I like being in your company. You make me feel good. I admire your pluck and it pleases me to help you toward something you want. Is that bad?'

'It's very good for me! No strings attached?'

'Not at the moment,' he grins. 'I suspect that our interest lies in other directions but I hope you'll be my pal in the lull between romances.'

'If this evening's an example I'll be glad to. Not that I'll be promised a new car every time we meet.'

'On the night you pass your driving test we'll go somewhere and celebrate. The chap at the local driving school is okay. His dad taught me years ago. The lessons with me will be irregular because of my job. We'll start on Sunday morning, if that's all right with you. Walk along the road and I'll pick you up just beyond the church at ten-forty-five. That will time it so that the church doors have closed on the congregation. I hope I'll be able to arrange the next lesson each time we meet. It shouldn't take you many months to learn because you manage a tractor well – oh yes, I've watched you.'

There's a brief awkward moment when Gareth draws the car to a standstill so that I can get out and make my way home. We've arranged that he should always go in first and then his father will be less likely to see me. I intend to get undressed by the light of the street lamp and the glow from the spotlight on the Blake's Nursery sign. No one will know I've just come in.

'I'm really sorry we have to do it like this,' Gareth says, 'but you're right. Dad would give you the sack you if he knew.'

'I'd rather it was this way, than that I couldn't have you as a friend.'

'Thanks, Helen.' He removes my glove and kisses my hand with old fashioned courtesy. I shiver at the touch of his soft lips. It seems quite natural after that for us to lean toward each other and kiss goodnight.

'What all good friends do,' he whispers.

'Any excuse,' I whisper back, 'on both our parts it would seem. Good night.'

The driving lessons are intermittent. The first is on Sunday and then Gareth and his mother go for a holiday to India for three weeks. I study my copy of the Highway Code while he's away. The first Sunday he's back I'm treated to lunch at a pub, after my driving lesson.

'Stay here for a minute,' he says and brings me a bulky parcel out of the boot. 'From India for you, Madam, sorry you have to carry it home.'

Inside the parcel is an exquisite light-weight Indian rug mostly in warm reds, yellows and burnt orange with a black border and fringe. I'm ecstatic.

'You see I think about you when I'm away. I compose letters to you but I don't want the post to go astray so they're in this packet. Read them when you get home.'

I automatically hug him and when our faces touch, I kiss his cheek. He quickly turns his head so that his lips meet mine and it's not a peck!

'Well, well,' I say embarrassed. 'You're very nice to kiss and I suppose it's an expressive means for me to say thank you.'

He leans back in his seat and laughs. 'I don't expect my gifts to be paid for with kisses if that's what you're thinking. This is a special occasion. I return from foreign parts, my lady accepts my gift. I promise there will be no recurrence of this behaviour ... not today anyway,' and he laughs again.'

Is this what Liam meant – 'men will be men? I'm not convinced that Gareth will wait for another special occasion. Liam ... I said I'd point Gareth in his direction but he'll have to wait. I'm enjoying Gareth's company.

Gareth's letters from abroad are delightful, colourful day to day accounts of what he saw and did. I can smell the hot spices for sale in the market places and see the strings of necklaces and rugs hanging in the narrow streets, illustrated by postcard views. I imagine the evening sea breeze and see him and his mother sitting under palm trees with cocktails. I'm touched that he thinks of me while he's away. Does his mother know we're friendly?

I receive a note from Mrs Blake saying that she will call on me for the customary inspection of my premises on Tuesday evening. The place is tidy but I make a special effort with the cleaning. Gareth's rug looks splendid as a throw over the settee. I would like to range his postcards along the mantel shelf but I never forget the spare key in Mr Blake's office. Mrs Blake is legally correct in informing me of her visit but I'm not sure if Mr Blake would adhere to regulations and what would happen if he saw cards from abroad on view, written in his son's handwriting? I keep them flat, hide them underneath magazines in my bedside locker. The rug could have been mine before I came to work here. I take a chance with the rug as it makes my room more attractive.

I bake ginger snaps and when it gets near the time for Mrs Blake to arrive, I boil the kettle and prepare two mugs in case she would like coffee.

Mrs Blake would like coffee and sits on the settee while I prepare it.

'Do you like Gareth's present?' she asks. I look rather nervously at her and she laughs. 'He bought me one the same, slightly different pattern. I haven't displayed it quite as boldly as you. It's all right. I'm in Gareth's confidence. He's enjoying his friendship with you. How's the driving coming on?'

'I scared him a bit on Sunday. He needed a whisky when we got to the pub.'

'He says you're doing fine. Have you booked some lessons with the driving school?'

'I'm saving up for that, end of April.'

'Delicious ginger snaps. Where did you learn to cook?'

'My last employer's wife, Mrs Harrison, she got me interested.'

'Well, you've made a nice pad for yourself here. Are you happy with your work?'

'It's what I want to do, though my back aches after a day's pruning. Mr Blake is going to demonstrate 'budding' to me in the summer; that will be interesting. The greenhouse work is straightforward but endless muck spreading doesn't charm me. Someone has to do it.'

She gets up to go. 'Thank you for making me welcome, Helen.

Gareth will enclose mail for you with my letters, when he's abroad in future. I'll pop them through you letter box. Until next time ... '

I watch her walk away. Gareth is his mother's son.

My phone rings on Wednesday evening.

'Miss Burns? My name's Mr Ford, Reg Ford, from the A1 driving school. I've instructions to give you eight driving lessons and prepare you for your test.'

'I don't understand! What about ... ' I stammer with surprise but he interrupts me.

'The payment's taken care of, would Friday evening at six suit you for your first lesson?'

Graham, the foreman, asks me to mow the front lawns at the nursery, their first cut of the year. They're kept weed free and smooth as velvet. I see Mrs Blake on her way to her car as I'm shunting the mower up and down. She drives a smart red BMW.

We stand still for a moment. I give a little wave and mouth, 'thank you.' She smiles and opens her car door. She's quite a woman and I like women!

CHAPTER 12

I have a professional driving lesson each week with Mr Ford and am increasingly confident. When Gareth next arranges a Sunday lesson he sees a big difference in my control of the car.

'You'll be ready for your test after Easter, get it booked,' he says. 'It'll make a world of difference to you when you can drive yourself around.

I find a Lindt Easter egg nestling in my pot of tulips on Easter Sunday morning. He is so sweet! I book myself an extra lesson for the following week, to make sure I'm ready, and take my test in the last week of April. I pass!

In Friday's pay-packet there's a ticket.

SATURDAY 1ST MAY, MAY DAY DANCE, 8 PM UNTIL MIDNIGHT – GINO'S NIGHTCLUB, BURTON and in longhand, *Meet as usual, celebration due ... Honey, honey!*

The weather is warm, my favourite month for blossom. I'm aware of the lilac and cherry when I nip into the shops. The flared blue mini skirt I choose and the white sleeveless blouse are both cotton. I go for tied ends and a bare midriff look and don't forget my denim jacket. I hear my mum saying, 'Take a jacket in case it's cold when you come home.' I'm surprised by the hot tears that fill my eyes. She used to sit on my bed and share the excitement when I dressed up to go out. I blink my tears away, walk out to my car, switch the engine on and deliberately switch off the memories of Mum. Tonight I'm driving to the meeting place where Gareth picks me up.

Gino's has a crowded dance floor. We down a whisky and a beer to get us going. I was right about Gareth and dancing. He's a real mover but so am I. We find a corner and make quite a couple, sometimes holding each other, sometimes free dancing. When the music is Country and Western, Gareth spreads his wellbeing amongst the women until they all want to dance with him.

'There's a reason for the sunshine skies
There's a reason why I'm feeling so high'
Just let your love flow and you'll know what I mean'

We have another drink later in the evening. Gareth likes to dance with his arms loosely round me in the slow romantic numbers. I don't mind. I was right to admire the broad shoulders and here I am leaning against them. *Tempus fugit* when you're having a good time. I've never felt so easy in anyone's company.

The last waltz is the old favourite, *Who's taking you home tonight?'* and Gareth tightens his hold. I'm not sure that I should be feeling what I can only believe must be an erection, while our hips are close together. I'm not into male anatomy and look up at his face questioningly.

'Sorry, he whispers into my hair. 'Got a bit out of control for a minute ... a man can't be blamed with a woman like you in his arms. Have you enjoyed your celebration?'

'It's been great! I've never danced like this with a man before and I like it, well, I like it because it's you. I wasn't alarmed by your out of control minute, another new experience for me.'

He hugs me and we hold hands as we walk to the car. 'Do you mind if we stop on the way home?' he says. 'I'd like to talk. I don't really want the night to end.'

'Okay, tuck the car in somewhere, if you can find a space to tuck in a vehicle this size.'

He turns up a country road and we park under some trees. I wonder whether I know what I'm doing. I'm twenty-nine years old and this is the first time I've been alone with a man whom I like and who seems to like me.

'I need to talk about us, because I don't quite understand what's happening,' he says. 'I've only had flings, or brief affairs I suppose you'd call them, with men. The idea that I would be happy with a woman is new to me but it feels good. There's a freedom attached to a man being out with a woman, do you feel it? We don't attract attention or have to hide. Tonight was wonderful.'

I'm not sure how to cope with this information.

'Since the first day we met I've made every opportunity to get a glimpse of you. I think about you all the time. The day brightens when I see you and now I find that I'm sexually aroused when I'm with you. Don't you feel anything?'

'I suppose I haven't thought we'd get into sex. Apart from a date or two with men I've only had affairs with women. I didn't expect to be discussing this. I feel happy and carefree when I'm with you and yes we have great times together. But your father's disapproval and fear of losing my job prevents me from feeling the freedom that you mention.'

'Dad is a pain but he hasn't found out yet. I want to kiss you. Shall we sit in the back of the car?'

I do know that I'm letting myself in for petting if I join him in the back of the car. It seems more serious than if it was a woman asking me. I'm tempted to see whether a man can stimulate me, and how he goes about it. I have no problem responding to the ardour of his kisses. He takes my hand and directs it to his erection.

'What do you want me to do?'

'Get to know this part of my body.'

'This is what we should have been doing when we were kids. We're late developers,' I say shyly.

'Is it okay for me to unfasten your blouse? I've never felt a woman's breasts.'

I feel worldly wise in that connection and willingly give permission. Then I find that yes, a man can and does excite me and what follows takes us to a dangerous stage of sexual exploration.

'Gareth, if we go further we make a baby.'

'I've got a condom so we could go further.'

'You planned this?'

'Helen, a man like me takes a condom everywhere he goes, but I can assure you that I haven't used one in the time I've known you and I have a clean bill of health. Anyway, would it be such a bad thing if we had a baby?' he says plaintively.

'As irresponsibly as this, yes it would! I've never given a thought to being a mother and probably you haven't thought of being a father.'

'Oh yes I have. The one thing I regret about being gay is that I won't be a father.'

'What interests me,' I say to change the subject, 'is that sex is sex is sex. It doesn't matter who gets you excited. Whatever our sexual preference, we have the equipment.'

'But you won't let us use it.'

'Without a condom, no I won't.'

'Here's the condom. You put it on.'

This is where I should put a stop to the inevitable but I don't. I press out the condom and unroll the flimsy rubber over his penis while his hands run up my thighs and draw my hips toward him. I want him to make love to me and meet him half way.

'We could've talked forever, Helen. This is what we need to do.'

I don't answer. With him inside me, I feel as though I'm full of him, up to my eyes, and anyway, I agree.

I don't keep too worried a watch on the days that follow. We used a condom and it was a safe time of the month, but I skip hop with relief at the arrival of my next period.

CHAPTER 13

'June is early in the year to teach you the T bud process of propagation,' Mr Blake says to Damian and me, 'but I'll start you off now and you can work at it during the summer.'

It's a complicated process and I watch closely. When he gives us each a rooted stem and a bud and tells us to have a go, I lay them carefully on the bench, arrange the tools so that they're to hand in the order in which I'll need them and then make the incision. I gently lever back the outer layer of the stem until I can insert the bud and bind the finished scion, as Mr Blake calls it. I attach the label with the name of the rose.

Mr Blake doesn't say anything. He pushes a second root and bud in my direction. I arrange my tools again and repeat the process. I'm utterly absorbed in the work and when I finish and look up I see a bemused expression on his face.

He inspects Damian's and says, 'Not bad.' To me he says, 'Wear a shirt that's less revealing tomorrow.'

I flush with embarrassment and realise that as I've been leaning forward, he's been looking down my scooped neck Tee shirt.

The following morning the foreman directs me to a potting shed. On the bench there are twenty roots and buds and I'm to graft them all. He leaves me to get on. I assume this means that Mr Blake approved my efforts even if he can't bring himself to say so. I lay them out along the bench, get a carry-all for my tools, and move my stool from plant to plant. The finished results lie in a neat row.

Mr Blake comes in toward lunchtime when I'm just shaking my hands to relax them after holding the tools all morning. I'm wearing a button up blouse.

'I've two more to finish,' I say and get on.

He picks up one after the other to inspect the grafts.

'You can pot them up after lunch,' he says. 'Graham will give you the size of pot and one of the lads will bring the compost. Don't forget to water them.'

It's a strange way of knowing that my work is satisfactory. Why can't he praise me?

I hope my outward behaviour hasn't altered while I'm having an affair with the elder son of the family. I don't see much of Nick, he doesn't work with me and he takes off about nine o'clock most nights in his BMW. I sometimes hear him come back in the early hours. He and Gareth both live in the family home.

The suggestion that I could have a baby has been food for thought ever since Gareth mentioned it. Hoping for permanent love between a baby and me would be a naive reason for bringing a child into the world. The love between my parents and me wasn't permanent. It ground to a halt after twenty-one years.

Having a baby would be a way to assert my womanhood but I hadn't thought about exercising that particular function. I'm disconcerted by a rush of feeling that brings tears to my eyes. I would love to have a baby of my own in my arms, grow a baby instead of plants! What would it mean with regard to my career? I'd have to down-size my ideas. I couldn't stay at Blake's and I wouldn't be able to work full-time. If Mr Harrison could re-employ me part-time at Kerryhall Nursery I could live at home, as long as I had enough money to pay the mortgage and keep the baby and me comfortably. Would I be able to run my car? I start to look at babies in prams and pushchairs and try to imagine myself in a mother role.

If I had a baby, my parents needn't know. They'd have a rare old time determining which sin was the greatest of the three I'd committed. Otherwise, I haven't a multitude of friends who would find it necessary to disassociate themselves from me.

I imagine Mrs Harrison and Edith might enjoy contact with a baby. I do feel lonely and I must not use that as an excuse to have a child. On the other hand, I do have a lot to offer. I'm loving and very capable. I would see that a child had a good education and a comfy home. The idea of having a baby is certainly less alien to me. I'm a little afraid that I might will pregnancy to happen. The reality might not be so easy to live with.

I've been driving to meet Gareth miles away and we're both fed up with making love in a vehicle. I have a key cut for him but the nights are light and he daren't let himself into my chalet until late, and then he has to walk up the road and drive back. We only chance this arrangement twice. The walls are not very soundproof and we have to whisper and stifle giggles. Gareth is not amenable to a quiet orgasm and I dread that his grunts of pleasure are heard through the open windows.

We go to a midsummer folk dance that's held in a barn. When the band has a break, a DJ plays pop music. It's a fun night.

In the summer time when the weather is high, Mungo Jerry sings at the beginning of my thirtieth summer.

Gareth is friendly with the farmer's family. He must have sworn his friends to secrecy because no word gets back to his father when we're out together. We sit on straw bales to eat our pie and pea supper and drink beer.

I'm the driver on this occasion and I stop half way home.

'You see that mound with the Scots Pine trees Gareth? That's a fairy knoll. Have a look and see if the field is clear of cows.'

He can't see any livestock.

'It's a lovely night. I don't think the fairies will mind if we trespass on their ground for one night of love-making. I'll get my blanket.'

Lying in the balmy air is lovely and we don't feel pressured to have sex and hurry away. This certainty that I'm wanted is the most glorious feeling I've known because I'm entirely happy in Gareth's company. Does the fact that it has to be kept secret make it more exciting? We don't discuss the future.

'We're nicely hidden from the road here and not too far up the hill to upset the fairies,' I say.

'You don't really believe there are fairies do you?'

'Who knows? There's no harm in thinking there might be. Tonight feels magic.'

'Now that endears me to my fanciful girlfriend, come here.'

Conversation is out of the question until we've made love. We stretch our damp bodies out in the night air, enjoying our nakedness.

'Oh no!' Gareth says with alarm, 'the condom, it broke!'

We look at each other in dismay.

'Where are you in your monthly cycle?'

'Bang on ovulation time I reckon.' I lie back and look at the stars. What happens now? Reasoning about having a baby is quite different from knowing that we may have made one.

'Would it be so very dreadful if we had a baby?' Gareth says shyly and leans over me. 'I'd be a good dad and you and the baby wouldn't want for anything. Have you given some thought to being a mother?'

'As it happens, yes I have. I like the idea ... but finances, living arrangements? We don't want to be married do we? If you were to fall in love with a man you'd break off with me and if I fell in love with a woman, the same would happen. I'll return to my home in Hylton if I'm pregnant. I don't quite know how I'd manage financially.'

'Look, I've said you wouldn't want for anything. I can support you and the baby without any difficulty and would want to, so don't worry on that score. There needn't be a drastic break from each other anyway. We'll always love each other's company, there's no reason for that to change.'

'You're making it sound too easy. Would you be satisfied with seeing the baby occasionally? A father-child relationship couldn't develop until the child was old enough to visit and stay with you. That's the arrangement my erstwhile friend Dee has with the father of her girls. I'm sure thousands of children are brought up in single parent situations. But oh Gareth, look after me.' I shiver and bury myself in his arms for reassurance.'

'I will Helen. Don't worry. I could cope with being an "at-a-distance dad" to start with.' He helps me into my jacket and lies close to keep me warm. 'However, I'm a determined "father-to-be" Helen, my love. There's nothing half-hearted about my intention. And I consider that a broken condom is too doubtful and unsatisfactory a way of making a child. We must ensure propagation.'

'I can't imagine that I will ever again experience such deep purposeful loving,' I whisper, when we've done our best to make a child. 'What will your mother say?'

'She'll be astonished, speechless. She knows about my predilection for men and assumes Nick will be the one to produce a grandchild, not that she's said so.'

'What about your father?'

'I can't say. He made two children himself didn't he?'

'I'm afraid the baby will be a little short on grandparents.'

'Why is that, Helen? I notice you don't talk about your parents.'

'My father's very religious and he and mum have disowned me.' I can tell him half the truth. 'They object to homosexuality.'

'Cripes! Not that I've been open with Mum or Dad. As long as I keep the firm in my sights I don't think Dad cares what I do in my spare time. Mum makes a point of not mentioning girlfriends. But she approves of me seeing you, I can tell.'

'I've a few friends that will be happy for me.'

'Of course you have, and I promise I will look after you.'

'We're talking as though I'm pregnant already.' I raise myself on my elbow and look at him. 'Gareth Blake, it could be that I'm going to have your child.'

He holds me close. We're so at one with each other – but as usual, we have to separate and make our own way home.

I reckon I know the next day that I'm pregnant. I feel strange as though I'm insubstantial, perhaps the result of conceiving a child on a fairy knoll! I walk on air for the next few days. My feelings seem to have a heightened sensibility. I want to laugh and cry. Gareth is away for a fortnight in America. I miss his reassurance and could have done with seeing him. A letter arrives, written at the airport while he was waiting for his delayed plane.

Darling Helen
*I hate this separation from you, particularly now ... I hope **we** are well ... This hole in a corner friendship has to stop. I've given in to dad's wishes for too long. We'll talk about it when I get home.*

Blake's Nursery has a successful summer. The assistants work hard at the propagation of next year's plants. Mr Blake has increased the sale of annuals and plants imported from other sources. I'm on duty in the shop on alternate Saturdays. I'm exhausted after standing all day and spend the evening lying on my settee in front of the telly.

In the last week of July I suddenly have to dash to the toilet to be sick, when I'm preparing my tea. I hadn't counted on this aspect of pregnancy. I'm relieved to have evening sickness. It means that I can keep my condition a secret from the workforce but it is not pleasant! I make an appointment with the doctor. He confirms the pregnancy and makes an appointment for a blood test at the local maternity hospital.

Gareth and I decide to go along with the present situation until it's obvious that I'm pregnant, because he's working on some plans for the future which he says will include me. We feel different now when we're together. We're gently loving and full of amazement at the fact that we're growing a baby and going to be parents.

I tell him that I won't make any preparations until the first three months are safely past but I look in shop windows in town and drift round the Mothercare shop calculating how many of the articles on display will be necessary for our baby. I buy knitting needles, a pattern and white baby wool. Now I wish I'd taken more notice in handicraft lessons, I drop stitches and have difficulty with the pattern.

I daren't think about my mother. I need her. I need the advice of experience and someone to share my news. I make up my mind that I have to tell someone. I can't go through with this alone. I ring Mrs Harrison and ask if I can pop over on my day off, in the morning.

'Oh Helen!' she says but then she smiles. 'I like babies. Is this to be a secret?'

'Please, for the time being. I might as well keep my job for as long as possible. I'd be sacked on the spot if Gareth's dad knew. Can you and Mr Harrison keep an eye on what's happening with my house, please? I'll need to move back there before Christmas, and can you please help me with this knitting?'

She laughs, unravels my attempt and starts me off by knitting the welt of the little baby cardigan.

'I'll be back when and if I get to the armholes,' I say, 'because I've no idea how to cast off.'

I feel much happier about everything. I have my blood test but don't agree to register my name for a bed for the birth.

'I won't be living in this district,' I tell the hospital receptionist. 'My baby's not due till next March.' I know exactly when.

I'm unhappily throwing up one Wednesday evening and it's nearly the end of August. This can't go on forever! I hear someone call, flush the loo, and hold a face flannel to my mouth. My eyes widen with alarm when I see Mrs Blake.

'I'm sorry to barge in like this, I couldn't make you hear. Are you all right, Helen?'

I rush off to the bathroom. This is all I need! She's still there, when I've retched my heart out, standing by the window with her back to me.

'That hopefully is the last of that,' I say with a weak stab at amusement, 'must have eaten something that doesn't agree with me.'

'Is it Gareth's?' she asks and turns round. She's holding my knitting and the pattern.

'Yes.'

'How far on are you?'

She's not going to suggest that I have an abortion is she?

'Nine weeks and five days.'

She dabs her eyes with her hanky. She's crying!

'Well, so much for rejoicing that your son is bringing a child into the world,' I say bitterly.

I've had enough of fucked up parents! I throw myself down on my settee. What is she doing here anyway, unannounced? She sits down at the other end of the settee and hands me a package.

'It wouldn't go through your letter box.'

I might as well open the package while she pulls herself together. I take out the dearest little blue embroidered jump suit for the baby, made in Germany. Gareth's note says, '*not that I'm hoping for a boy!*' I smile. I don't think I want a boy.

'Is Gareth pleased?' my visitor wants to know, 'he's been very cheerful lately.'

'We're both delighted, despite the necessity for keeping the baby a secret. Don't worry it's all planned. I won't be giving you any trouble. I have a house and I'll give in my notice as soon as I can't hide the pregnancy any longer. Gareth has promised to help financially and I'm hoping to be taken back as a part-time employee at Kerryhall Nursery.'

'I thought Gareth was gay,' she says quietly. 'I never expected to have a grandchild by him. I'm sorry I reacted as I did, the news was overwhelming.'

'Didn't you know he's always wanted to be a father?' She shakes her head. 'Yes, his sexual preference is for men. It's just that he and I really suit each other. It isn't a grand love affair, we're very happy together and we don't expect that to change. We won't be getting married. The baby will be my responsibility to start with until its old enough to have a relationship with him.'

'And with me.'

I look at her in surprise.

'Helen, I'm delighted. I've longed to have a grandchild.'

'I wonder if our child will have your hair,' I say and she smiles.

'Will you promise to bring the baby to visit me?'

'Would I be welcome in your home with a baby?'

She doesn't answer and fidgets with her handkerchief. There's the same disturbed look on her face that I saw when she made her inspection call, as though her mind is full of something uncertain.

'I can only say ... at this stage ... that your visits will give me great joy and I hope you'll keep me in touch with baby's development.'

That's an odd thing to say. What are these plans that Gareth spoke of and when will I be told about them?

The sickness stops and I begin to feel great. My breasts are less sensitive after being tender for weeks. When I measure them they've grown larger and my waist is thicker. But otherwise, it doesn't show that I'm pregnant. Bib and braces overalls have a lot of room in them.

It helps to know that I've got two kindly women friends looking out for me.

I don't tell Liam. He mentioned in his July letter that his sister miscarried at eleven weeks and is very upset. He asks about Gareth. What will he think of me when he knows about the baby and that Gareth's the father? I was supposed to be pointing Gareth in Liam's direction and instead I've attracted him to mine. Will our friendship stand the emotional entanglement? I'm sure that if I add the news of a child born out of wedlock to the story of my prison sentence, the Spencers will think less kindly of me. Perhaps when there's better news of his sister they'll feel able to welcome my baby.

CHAPTER 14

Gareth has been preoccupied these last two months, here one day gone another, all very mysterious but that has suited me. Coping with the nausea has used up my spare energy.

By the seventeenth week of my pregnancy, we're in October and the main work of dead heading and attending to the roses is nearly over. The cycle of plant production never stops and the standing hurts my back. I hope the lads don't notice that I work more often sitting on a stool.

Mr Blake seems tetchier than ever and I keep out of his way as much as possible. Unfortunately he's nearby when I pick up a potted Camellia and let it slip. The accident shakes the root out of the soil and I apologise.

'Get it seen to,' he says angrily and I see the cause of the furrows on his forehead. I wouldn't like to be around if he flipped.

I'm quite giddy when I feel the first flutter of my baby and can't wait to let Gareth feel his child. We sit in the back of his car in the darkness, his warm hand resting lightly on my abdomen. He feels the movement that thrills us both. We've been sexually abstinent for weeks. His wandering fingers rekindle the passion that we hope the third presence appreciates.

'I shall hate going back to the use of a condom after this bliss,' Gareth complains.

'We've got plenty of time,' I say.

He's quiet for a few minutes.

'Helen, do you remember my mention of possible changes in the future?'

'Of course I remember.' I wonder what's coming.

'I've been away a lot because I'm working part-time for another firm, in Shropshire.'

Near Liam ... I think.

'I've only hinted that Mum and Dad have problems because I could see that you felt it was none of your business. Mum decided back in April that she's had enough of the life dad makes her lead. He doesn't like her to go far afield, keeps a jealous eye on her social activities and her friends are not welcome in the home. There are lots of other reasons why they don't get on. He objects to her financial independence and tries to bring her under his control. It's embarrassing to tell you this, for both their sakes, particularly as one of the ways in which he dominates Mum is by making love to her. You must admit that she's a lovely looking woman. He doesn't realise that he's just made her desperate and she wants to get away from him.

'I've seen to the purchase of a house for her, near my work. It has four bedrooms, three bathrooms and a beautiful garden. There'll be room for you and the baby, either to live there, or to stay over when you visit. I'll move in with Mum until she's settled. It'll be a relief I can tell you, not to hear my mother being subjected to Dad's desire and feeling powerless to intervene.

'The thing is, Dad knows about my job. He's training Nick up to take over my work, but he doesn't know about Mum's decision. She daren't tell him and you know he has a bad temper. I feel rotten in that I have to deceive him, in more ways than one. We're moving out on Friday the twenty-ninth. We'll tell dad before he goes to his conference at Blackpool on the twenty-seventh. When he gets back on the Friday night it will all be over, he won't have to witness the move. Promise that you won't mention this to a soul.'

'I promise I won't tell.' I haven't the heart to say that my birthday is on the twenty-ninth.

'Helen, I think it's time I told him about the baby. You'll have to give him notice in November if you're to finish work at Christmas.'

'Will I see you?'

'Good Lord yes! Mum's expecting you to come for your days off. You haven't had a holiday this year. You could spend Christmas with us.'

That cheers me up but I feel a sense of approaching dread for Nick and his father. Gareth and his mother can't be very happy either at having to steal off in Mr Blake's absence.

I dearly wish I hadn't to work on Saturday the thirtieth. I'd like to take off on the Friday after work and stay overnight with the Harrisons. I'd prefer to be well away from the nursery when Mr Blake gets back from his conference and I'm not sure that he should be told about the baby. Part of me wants him to know that I'm pregnant and be pleased for Gareth and me. He might look forward to having a grandchild. Our news will hopefully pale in comparison with the disappearance of his wife from the scene. I don't want to be around when he feels the full force of that separation. The prospect frightens me for the whole family.

I feel as though I'm creeping round at work on the Friday and it's my birthday. Edith hasn't remembered, neither have the Harrisons and Madge promised a cake with three candles. There's a card from my parents as usual. Liam and I didn't do birthdays.

The furniture van arrives at eight-thirty and not long afterward I watch Gareth and his mother leave in their own vehicles. I feel desolate, even though I'll be seeing them soon.

Nick finds me in the potting shed.

'What are we going to do without lover boy?' he says jeeringly. 'Think I didn't know? You should keep your windows shut if you don't want anyone to know you're having sex or hear you throwing up every night for weeks. When's the baby due?'

I'm shocked to hear that Nick knows about Gareth and me, and about the baby, yet he didn't betray our secret.

'Nick, I'd no idea you knew. You're a pal. That was really decent of you not to split on us. I owe you one.'

'You could start any time with what you and Gareth do in the back of his car.'

'Nick!' I can see that he's miserable. 'That's not worthy of you, Nick. I'm sure you don't go short on girlfriends. Do you want your niece or nephew to know you offered to have sex with their mother because you were unhappy?'

He turns away and I see his shoulders shake.

'I'm sorry Helen. I'm an idiot. I'm not thinking straight because I'm scared ... of what it'll be like with dad when he gets back,' he chokingly admits. 'I don't think he'll take it out on me but he might smash things up. I could go over and help Mum and Gareth to settle in but I don't want to leave dad alone.'

'You'll be able to visit them soon. You see, you're a nice considerate guy. Tough and nasty doesn't suit you. I'll be around. Come and have a coffee with me, when your dad's not looking of course.' I give him a hug.

I'm not sure whether I don't concentrate on what I'm doing. Half my attention is on the removal and my thoughts are full of fear for Friday evening and Saturday morning. I work in the greenhouses all morning, which is routine. The radio plays but my mind keeps wandering.

After my sandwich lunch, I drive the tractor down to the far field, where I began weeding and loosening the soil yesterday. I switch off the engine but, in jumping off the tractor, I somehow miss my footing and land smack on my bottom where the ground is rough and stony. I scream with pain and keel over in a faint. When I come to I'm lying on the ground. The pain is less severe but I don't feel I can move. My baby ... will I have damaged my baby? Perhaps if I lie quite still the baby will recover from the shock. Hot tears fill my eyes and I lie and weep. I've done so well with everything, but now I'm hurt and alone.

Sometime later, I'm relieved and embarrassed when I hear the noise of a car engine and see Nick hurrying over to me. I can't stop crying. He helps me to get up and holds me tightly.

'What did you do?'

'I missed my footing when I jumped off the tractor and landed on my bottom on that pile of stones there. What if I've damaged the baby, Nick?'

He wipes my face with his hanky and makes shushing noises. 'Don't think like that. Let's get you up, and back to your chalet.'

Once in the chalet, he makes me lie on the settee, covers me with a rug and brews a pot of tea. He suggests that a couple of Paracetemol tablets wouldn't harm the baby.

'You've got your colour back,' he says with relief. 'You were as white as a sheet. I was scared. If you think you'll be okay. I'll go and get on. Don't worry about the tractor, I'll send one of the lads down to the far field to bring it up to the garage. When I knock off work, I'll make us an omelette for tea and you can stay put.'

'Will you just wait until I've been to the loo please Nick? I feel a bit unsteady.'

I dread taking off my pants in case I'm bleeding. It's a relief to see there's no sign of blood but I'm very bruised and sore and glad to lie down again. I manage to doze fitfully during the afternoon.

Nick is true to his word and sits beside me as we eat bread and butter and cheese omelette with another cup of tea.

'You'll make someone a good husband,' I say gently. 'I'm grateful to you Nick. I lay on the ground thinking that I hadn't a friend in the world to help.'

'Well, I suppose I'm a sort of brother-in-law and the baby's uncle, aren't I? If it's a boy you can give it one of my names, Benjamin Nicholas.'

He looks out of the window and his eyes widen with alarm.

'Dad's back. I'd better go.'

'Yes, thanks Nick. I hope everything will be all right. I'll see you tomorrow morning.'

I put on my nighty and dressing gown when he's gone and find I'm more comfortable lying in bed. I've nearly finished reading *Watership Down*. If anyone had said I'd enjoy a book about rabbits I'd have laughed, but the story's kept me enthralled. I picked up another second hand paper back in the bric-a-brac shop in the village. It's very well thumbed so a lot of people must have found it worth reading – about two ladies that lived together in Llangollen. The front cover shows an old picture of two oddly dressed women, clothed entirely in black and wearing top hats. I'll read it next. At ten o'clock I'm ready to switch my bedside light off and go to sleep. I look across at the house and see that all the lights are on.

I wake terrified. My back door bangs, hitting against the fridge. Shivers of fear run down my back. I jump off the bed, grab my dressing gown and wrap it round me. The bedroom light flashes on and I see Mr Blake. He lurches forward and stands holding on to the wardrobe. He's drunk. The smell of whisky wafts round the room. I cower back when he comes toward me. He grasps the fronts of my dressing gown and pulls me strongly until I'm pressed up against him. I get the full blast of his intoxicated breath. Just as suddenly, he pushes me away and opens my dressing gown. I'm aware of my full breasts and rounded abdomen. I pray that he's in no condition to want to substitute me for his absent wife.

'I can see now,' he says thickly. 'I can see you're carrying my son's bastard. You've been hiding it inside those baggy overalls, carrying on with my son against my wishes. I'll never forgive Harrison for sending me a whore to mess up my family.'

He feels his way to the dressing table and slams an envelope down on it.

'There's your pay. In the morning you get off my premises.'

I find my voice but it's difficult to stop it from trembling. I speak to his retreating back.

'Thank you for my pay and everything you've taught me Mr Blake. I shall not tell our child that you called it a bastard and me a whore. I'll say that its grandfather wants nothing to do with it. If you really want to mess up your family ... tell Gareth that the mother of his child served a prison sentence for manslaughter.'

I see him hesitate briefly before going out of the door.

I don't know why I added the prison information. Yes I do! I'm mad! I'm blazing! I'm sick and fed up. What does one have to do to be appreciated and treated with respect? What right have miserable parents to be so hatefully judgemental? That's three grandparents off the scene! Secrets are useless. Doing your best is useless. Let the whole fucking world know everything about me.

CHAPTER 15

I close the door and lean against it, tears pouring down my face for the second time today. I must get away from here. I'll have to go to the Harrison's. I can sit in the car until it's time for them to get up. I dress quickly and take down my suitcase and rucksack. I open and empty drawers and the wardrobe, fill carrier bags and shopping bags, open the boot of the car and stuff my possessions into every available corner. Bathroom, kitchen, living room – cushions, Gareth's rug, postcards, my growing collection of baby clothes, shoes, wellies, overalls, I don't stop till the place is bare. I leave the key on the kitchen counter, pull the front door to and heave the last bag on to the back seat. As I lift, a dragging pain tears at my abdomen and I stifle a shriek. Wet warmth spreads between my legs. My baby! It's dark. I can't see if it's blood. I can't take any chances with my baby. The pain rips again. I head for the maternity hospital. Three miles ... clear roads at this time of night ... groaning with pain, can't be quiet, mustn't think.

I park at the entrance and lean on the buzzer until a porter opens the door. I stagger to the receptionist's desk.

'My name's Helen Burns, please save my baby,' I say. I offer my car keys to the porter and crumple on to the floor.

The clock in the room says eight when I wake. I'm lying flat. I remember the emergency measures taken last night to save my baby and the relief when the pain eased. The doctor advised that sleep would be the best thing to help us both. I'm in a side ward by myself. I lift my head off the pillow and see a lady doctor and a nurse.

'Good morning, Helen,' the doctor says. 'I'd like to check that everything's okay down below. We've managed to save your baby, thanks to your prompt action in getting here quickly but I want you to lie flat and very still for the next few days.'

I don't listen to any more; I'm crying with relief.

'Is there anyone we can contact?'

I shake my head. I don't want to bother any of my friends until I'm able to manage by myself.

'Not at the moment,' I say. 'Will someone see that my car is safely parked please? All my worldly possessions are in it. I was sacked last night and had to clear everything out of my accommodation.

'I'll get the message to security,' she says and doesn't press me for more information.

There's only me and my baby now. Perhaps I shouldn't have tried to save the baby. Does it want me for a mother? Work is the only area in which I succeed and I've been sacked. I'm a nuisance to the Harrisons who care for me. I don't command respect from friends once they know the truth about me. Gareth and his mum won't want to know an ex-prisoner. How will I manage financially without Gareth's support? He might still honour his promise as it's his child. He might insist on his family having custody. I'm at an all time low and relieved that I have nothing to do except lie and cry.

The doctor returns in the late afternoon. She closes the door behind her and stands over me.

'I won't beat about the bush,' she says. 'Are you the Mary Helen Burns who served a sentence for manslaughter at Stonebridge Women's prison?'

I nod.

'I thought so. I had to check with a friend of mine before I asked you. Do you remember Doctor Tupman at Stonebridge?'

I nod again.

'She was upset about your case and shared her concern with me. She said you should never have been imprisoned for what was blatantly an accident. Anyway, rest now and I'll see you tomorrow.'

I sleep a lot. Now that I've stopped being in control, the effort that I've made to keep going catches up with me. I feel some reassuring flutters from my baby and weep and sleep some more.

On Sunday morning, I'm allowed a second pillow and take more notice from the raised elevation. I hear the visitors arrive in the afternoon but before I can bemoan my isolation I see Margaret Pennyfields come into the room, closely followed by Frances.

'There you are,' Margaret says and draws up two chairs for herself and Frances. 'Are you surprised to see us?'

I smile, of course I'm surprised!

'Dot Tupman rang Frances and asked if she remembered you. That's how we found out where you were. Is the father Gareth Blake?' She's busy emptying the contents of her bag on to the bed and into my locker, fruit, her famous shortbread biscuits, toiletries and magazines. The unexpected kindness brings more tears to my eyes.

'Here you are, tissues to mop up those tears, but it's time for you to stop crying. Your baby doesn't want a sad mother. You haven't answered my question.'

'You haven't given her chance, Margaret,' Frances laughs.

'Well, someone's got to see that she's doing the right thing and I did have three babies.'

She makes me smile again and I confess that Gareth is the father of my baby.

'You see Frances, I was right. We wondered Helen ... the possible connection of nurseries, you and roses. Guess where Gareth goes to have his ginger curls kept in control? Yes, to Barry's salon. Barry and Gareth are old buddies. We knew that Gareth was excited about his girlfriend Helen having a baby but he hasn't been back since for Barry to ask him if the Helen was Helen Burns. We didn't know it was definitely you until Dot Tupman rang. It's a small world.'

'I think it will be all over between Gareth and me,' I say wearily. 'I was so upset when Mr Blake got drunk on Friday night, and called me a whore and my baby a bastard, that I threw my prison sentence at him. He'll tell Gareth. Somehow it didn't seem important that Gareth should know when we were having fun. I've worked hard at Blake's and I know Mr Blake was satisfied, though it didn't occur to him that I might like a word of praise. When he sacked me, out of hand, it was like my prison sentence all over again – being punished undeservedly. I wanted to wipe out my connection with the family.'

'Like you've wiped out your connection with mine?' Margaret puts in quickly. 'Is that what you do when you're hurt?'

'Ever since my prison sentence, yes it is.' I bridle. 'If I feel I'm unfairly blamed I cut the people out of my life.'

'And were you blamed last Boxing Day morning?'

'I was.'

'I see ... but now's not the time to sort things out. Perhaps matters can be remedied in the future. I know Dee's missed you. She's been cross with herself ever since that morning, particularly as you went out of your way to be helpful to her. Annabel wasn't very pleased either.'

'Is there anything we can do for you, Helen?' Frances wants to know.

'I'm worried about my car. I had to pack all my possessions in it, in the middle of the night and then drive here. I left my keys with reception. Could you phone the Harrisons at Kerryhall, please, and tell them what's happened. I'd like to get back into my own home as soon as possible. My lodger will have to find other digs.'

'I'll do that. You're going to be here for a few days. Do you want anyone else to visit you?'

'No thanks. I'll be fine as I am. I've a lot of thinking to do. It's been lovely to see you and thanks for everything.'

'I'm glad we've met up again Helen,' Margaret says convincingly. 'I hope we'll keep in touch this time. Be good and listen to the doctor.'

So Dee has missed me. I'm pleased to hear that. Perhaps it was shirty of me to cut her off completely. I must examine the chip on my shoulder. And Annabel ... when she knows I'm pregnant she'll rejoice that she ran off in the night before she got further involved with a reprobate.

I'm dozing off on Monday evening when I recognise a voice.

'Well, I don't know, Helen Burns! You can't keep out of trouble for five minutes. You'd better come back to our neck of the woods so we can keep an eye on you.' Mr Harrison plonks a posy of carnations on the bed.

'Sh ... Roger, let the girl be. How are you, Helen?'

'I'm feeling much better, thank you. I think I was ready for a rest but it was a painful way to get one. Those flowers smell beautiful, Mr Harrison.'

'Is baby all right?'

'From her vigorous activity I'd say she's fine. I think she likes me to lie here and do nothing.'

'That's wonderful. I'd say this baby has no intention of parting from her mother. We keep saying "her" and "she" don't we? We'll get a shock if it's a "him". Now look, I've made these for you.' She unwraps three beautiful nighties in a soft cloth, with pin tucked yokes and little embroidered rosebuds. 'Babies are not for show in my opinion, not while they're very new but you do want them to look nice. I'm knitting a lacy bed jacket for you to wear in hospital but that won't be ready till near the end of your term. How's that cardigan coming on?'

I pull a woebegone face.

'I see. Well, we'd like you to stay with us when you leave hospital. No, don't look like that ... you're not a nuisance and you won't be any trouble until your house is ready. Roger says it will be vacated by the middle of November. It's only what I would do if I had a daughter, besides I want to keep an eye on you and your bump – and make sure you get one cardigan finished.'

'John's on his way home in your car at this moment,' Mr Harrison says. 'We'll put your things in the spare bedroom. I'll drive over to get you when the hospital says you can come out. Any news of Gareth?'

I shake my head. 'I don't think I'll be hearing from him. He knows now that I was in prison.'

The bell rings to end visiting and my good friends leave. A nurse puts my flowers in a vase on the windowsill, where I can see them.

I'm comforted. I let myself lie back against the pillows. Things are not all bad. The Harrisons are kind. I'll have to allow myself to be looked after for a few days because I don't feel as though I could manage by myself at the moment. I feel strange and fragile. One minute I'm a healthy outdoor girl and the next I'm incapacitated, needing to be looked after. I don't feel quite such an emotional mess – but I mustn't be a nuisance to anyone. I must get better soon.

I am surprised to see Edith walk in on Tuesday evening, accompanied by Grace. I'm thrilled with the little pink flower arrangement she brings. It's quite something to have a Horsfall creation as a gift. The Harrisons have let them know I'm in hospital.

'Of course, we both hope you're having a girl. I've bought a white pram outfit until baby is born and we know which colour to buy.'

'I don't think for one moment that Helen is into sexual stereotyping, Edith,' Grace butts in, 'we talked about this! You fancy rainbow striped dungarees, boy or girl don't you, Helen?'

I love to hear them go at each other. They don't need an answer from me.

'You'll have to come over to the bungalow, won't she, Grace? There's a nice spare room for you and baby and a conservatory. We've had your room decorated in pale lemon and I think you'll like the Sanderson print curtains. We'll look out for a pram for you to use when you visit us. There's room in our shed to store it. '

'You fare better than me,' Grace says grudgingly. 'I have to sleep in a room that's mainly white and elegant. It's your fault – I believe you said something complimentary about Edith's taste and now I have to suffer.'

Edith seems delighted with the criticism. 'You've got your grumpy old study emblazoned with colour so don't complain, woman. Honestly Helen, she's got an oriental rug on the floor, Indian throws over the chairs, white walls with Mexican hangings and goodness knows what about the room.'

'Sounds interesting,' I say in defence of Grace's taste.

'The two of you are hopeless,' Edith tosses her head at us but we're smiling. 'Mrs Harrison said the baby's due in March, Helen, is that right?'

I nod.

'We'll see you before then I hope. We won't stay longer now because the nurse said we haven't to tire you. Keep in touch.'

I get hugs and kisses and off they go.

Edith's transformation is much more successful than mine. She just had to open out and become more confident in herself. I started off confident and was happy when Gareth and I were together. Now that he's gone I feel vulnerable, not very sure of where I'm at. Edith's older than me. I'll persevere. Her flower arrangement is on my trolley table and looks so pretty. I can smell the carnations on the window sill, warmed by the sun.

On Wednesday morning I'm allowed to walk to the bathroom.

'If you promise to rest, Helen,' the doctor says, 'you can go home tomorrow. I hear that you're going to stay with a friend and I have her assurance that she'll keep a close eye on you. You've been very brave,' she says gently. 'Your baby can be proud of her mum.'

Is it true? I wish I could believe what she says. How does a baby be proud of a mother like me?

CHAPTER 16

Mr Harrison has me back at Kerryhall Nursery before lunch on Thursday. I agree to Mrs Harrison's suggestion that I go upstairs and rest. It's comforting to see that my possessions have been neatly stacked in the room. There's a coal fire burning in the little fireplace and an armchair has been placed where I can watch the flames and see out of the window into the yard. I sit back and relax, touched by the careful thought that has gone into making me feel at home. I hear footsteps on the stairs.

'Here we are. It's a new mushroom soup recipe from a vegetarian cookery book that John gave me for my birthday. Some recipes in the book use *tofu* which I don't fancy, and there are stodgy lentil dishes, but the soups seem all right. See what you think. John's got a girl friend that's vegetarian so I have to be prepared for when she comes for a meal. Hope you like my rice pudding. Eat up. Roger'll come up for your tray.'

She expects no effort from me and leaves me alone. Her kindness affects me. It makes me grieve because my mother doesn't want to know me ... and I didn't even celebrate my birthday. I cry in between mouthfuls of soup.

Mr Harrison brings a cup of coffee.

'You've made a good job of clearing that. Madge'll soon have you right. 'Bye for now.'

I see him and the lads in the yard. A week ago I was busy working. I sit and watch the flames. I don't want to do anything. I'm tired. I get on the bed and sleep.

I'm not asked if I would like to go downstairs. I could manage it physically but I don't want to make the effort. I stand by the window on Friday morning and watch the van being loaded for tomorrow's market. Mr Harrison waves. I sit in the armchair with my hands lightly clasped over my baby. I want her to believe that everything's going to be all right. I sleep and eat. Mrs Harrison is quite sure the rest and quietness are doing us good.

My knitting is hanging in a pocket from the arm of my chair. On Saturday morning I get it out and work the rows up to the armholes. Mrs Harrison sits with me and shows me how to cast off. I'm pleased to have her company. The cardigan back grows faster with fewer stitches but I tire and have a rest before lunch.

Mr Harrison brings up afternoon tea.

'There weren't too many people about so we knocked off early. I told young Myra that you're back in town. Her lad's coming on fine. She was interested to hear that you're going to have a baby. She's got another on the way by the look of her. You'll be able to compare notes. I'll go down for my tea now and check that the lads have left everything straight.'

He pauses at the doorway.

'Oh, and Miss Priestley asked after you. She knows what's happened evidently. I said you were doing as well as could be expected in the circumstances; told her you were staying with us until your house is empty. Nice woman that.'

So Annabel Priestley knows that Mary Helen Burns is pregnant and has been sacked. And she was worried about my reputation a year ago! She made her escape. Her censure is likely to be multi-fold. How will she rate me as a second Christmas approaches?

Why am I thinking like this? I must keep my thoughts away from imagining that other people have negative opinions about me. For my baby's sake, I have to concentrate on the resolution I made last New Year to value the person I am. I must add a new assertion, that I'm fit to be a mother, but I'm not sure I believe it. I'm disempowered, leaning on the Harrisons' care. How do I believe in me again?

'Would you like to come down and watch *The Muppet Show?*' Mrs Harrison calls upstairs. She settles me on the settee. '*Miss Piggy* makes Roger laugh, he'll be in soon.'

Miss Piggy makes me smile and I stay up to watch James Stewart and John Wayne in *Who Shot Liberty Valance?*

'I don't think this is very suitable film for Helen to watch, starting with a funeral!' Mrs Harrison objects.

'Wait till it gets further in, it's a good story,' Mr Harrison insists and I'm glad in the end. I do like stories where the hero triumphs over violence and a whole town benefits from his influence. I find myself saying, 'Yes! Yes!' vehemently when justice is done.

'Thank you for a nice evening,' I say before I go back upstairs.

My life takes on the aspect of a diary. On Sunday I go downstairs for my meals and help with the dishes. I still don't feel chatty and that's understood. Mrs Harrison enjoys telling me stories while she's working.

'And for heaven's sake, call me Madge,' she says at the end of one of them. 'I suppose you'll have to keep calling Roger, Mr Harrison, because of working for him.'

On Monday I go for a walk round the nursery. I come to a bed of roses that haven't been dead headed and automatically work my way along the row with secateurs. I hear a vehicle and Dee's Land Rover parks in the yard. She goes over to the house and I see her and Madge in conversation. Madge shakes her head. Before she drives away, Dee looks in my direction and waves. I acknowledge her wave but I don't make an effort to go over to her.

'More flowers for you in the living room, and a parcel,' Madge says. 'It seems the Hattersley folk are glad to be back in touch with you. Your young friend is genuinely concerned.'

I open the parcel and find a brightly coloured size 9-12 months Parka for the baby.

'Now isn't that grand?' Madge says, 'just right for next winter. You'll have to drop them a line, writing paper's in the bureau.

'Dear Dee, Thank you for the jolly little jacket. I find it hard to believe there will be a child wearing it this time next year. Sincerely Helen'

'Madge, do you think that baby will have been harmed by what happened?'

'Good gracious me no! With a healthy young mother like you and a great lad like Gareth! You feel your baby don't you?'

I nod.

'Well that's proof enough. They'll have gone into all that at the hospital.'

I work in the greenhouses each morning, deciding for myself what needs doing. The lads give me the thumbs up – less for them to do and they leave me to get on. By Thursday I want to hear some music and switch on the radio. I cope with the memory of Gareth and me dancing.

You to me are everything, the sweetest song that I can sing, Oh baby ...

We were so happy.

I'm not prepared for the song that comes next. When I hear Diana Ross sing, I bury my head in my hands and sob wildly.

Do you know where you're going to
Do you like the things that life is showing you
Where are you going to
Do you know?
Do you get what you're hoping for
When you look behind you there's no open doors
What are you hoping for
Do you know?

The radio is switched off abruptly.

'That'll do, young lady. Off you go back up to the house, Madge's got your drink ready.'

'A letter's on the table for you,' Madge says, 'care of our address. I don't recognise the handwriting.'

Dear Mary Helen,

Who is writing to me as Mary Helen? I look down quickly to the bottom of the page – Elizabeth Blake!

I'm hoping that this letter reaches you and we can arrange for you to come over for a visit. I've been anxious about you. We heard of your accident and dismissal from Nick and then we had to wait for Gareth to return from China, before I had the Kerryhall contact address. You must tell me the whole story. I don't imagine Ernest was gentle with you.

Gareth was surprised to hear about the prison sentence from his father. I didn't think it was necessary for him to know, so I never mentioned it. He doesn't feel that your past has anything to do with the three of you. Oh yes, Mary Helen, I knew who you were as soon as I put your face and your name together. I don't think I missed reading one newspaper article about you. You poor long suffering girl.

I hope Mr and Mrs Harrison won't mind giving me a phone number where I can contact you. Please let me know where you are and how you are. Will it be convenient for Gareth and me to take you out to lunch? Gareth shares my anxiety.
Yours with fondest love, Elizabeth Blake

I let Madge read the letter. 'That's nice,' she says.

'What could I wear?' I say. 'I'm growing out of my clothes.' I show her the safety-pin holding up my jeans.

'We'll go shopping into town tomorrow. You're at that in-between stage but we'll see what we can find.'

'I'll drive,' I say. 'It'll feel as though I'm functioning.'

The shopping trip on Friday is successful and I return with maternity trousers and a slightly flared jumper top that suits me. I have a fight with Madge over my keep. I want to pay something towards my food and she won't let me. In the end I get her to budge when I mention a Kenwood mixer, I know she's been hankering for one. I leave her studying the operating instructions when she sends me upstairs for a rest. At teatime there's a lovely surprise.

'Ta dah!' Mr Harrison says and in comes Madge with a birthday cake.

'The news of the Blake split-up and then your accident put your birthday out of our minds, I'm afraid. We've been waiting for a convenient day to celebrate with your three candles. Make a wish.'

I could wish for so many things ... but I blow out the candles knowing that the main wish must be that my baby is healthy and we get to full term with no more mishaps.

'Happy Birthday to you,' Madge and Mr Harrison sing, 'and here's to my Kenwood mixer,' Madge says. We raise our tea cups. The sponge is light and delicious.

We arrange for Mrs Blake and Gareth to come on Sunday. I'm hugged lovingly by both of them. They take me to a hotel for lunch and in between the courses quiz me about my accident and departure from Blake's Nursery. For their sakes, I don't make much of Mr Blake's bad behaviour. They're pleased that I'm looking well. They both appear to be much less strained. I won't agree to any plans for the immediate future about where to live. I'm rather looking forward to time in my own home.

'Here's your November cheque,' Gareth says and gives me a copy of the papers he's drawn up with a solicitor, re my allowance. He asks permission to have my bank details so that he can transfer the money into my account. I look with surprise at the monthly sum I'm to receive. It's as much as my former wage.

'It'll be my pleasure to look after you both,' he says.

I assure Gareth and his mum that I look forward to accepting her invitation to visit their new house and I'm hugged again when it's time for them to leave.

'Toward the end of November will be early enough for you to be on your own,' Madge says.

'What about having a week to recover, and set your home in order, then you can come back to work in the first week of December,' Mr Harrison suggests. 'I'm a hand short now your lodger has gone and you'll need some wages.'

CHAPTER 17

I close the front door of 12 Willoughby Street with a great sense of relief. The house has been left in good condition but it needs loving back into being my home. My morning is spent with the vacuum cleaner, dusting and adding my treasures; Gareth's rug on the settee, the little Valentine's card on the mantelpiece and the postcards from abroad pinned to my kitchen notice board. I drive to the supermarket and stock up with food.

'There we are,' I say to my baby when the shopping is neatly stowed and I'm sitting with my feet up and a mug of tea, 'this is where we belong, doesn't it look nice? Now let's see what we have here.'

My lodger has left a stack of adverts and my unopened mail on the kitchen counter. There's a very out of date New Year card from Edith and Grace which hadn't arrived before I left for Blake's Nursery. I open a letter from Dee dated December 27th 1975.

Helen, I'm sorry, sorry, sorry! It was awful of me to speak to you as I did yesterday. I don't know what Annabel was playing at. I shouldn't have assumed that you had upset her. You haven't answered my phone calls so you must be mad at me. I do hope we can kiss and make up before New Year. Love Dee

I'm pleased that Dee wants to be friends. We'll get together again, sometime.

The stamp on the pink envelope is French and the letter arrived by airmail. I open it cautiously.

Paris 27 decembre 1975 – so Annabel wrote the day after she got to her mother's.
Ma chere Helen
I don't know what to say … probably that I'm a coward and/or that I don't trust myself. My head was so out of sync after our embrace that I don't know how I got here. I never went to bed and left just after half past one. I should have written you a note. My mother keeps pumping me to find out what's the matter. How can I tell her? I don't know myself! Am I in love with you? I hope you enjoy New Year with your friends and please meet up with me when I get back.
Amitiés – Annabel

A huge wave of regret sweeps over me. I hide my face in my hands. It was love. It was nothing like the playful affection that Gareth and I feel for each other. I loved her and wanted her. As soon as I admitted it to myself, she'd gone. I've coped with the disappointment by stamping on the emotion, disliking her, running away and pretending the love never existed. Too late, we missed the boat Annabel. I'm not in a state where you'd be interested in me now. I assume that 'amitiés' means loving thoughts or something of the kind, I remember *j'aime* which means 'I love'.

I leaf desultorily through the receipts left by my lodger and pick up a piece of notepaper that was trapped in between the envelopes. It's in my mother's handwriting!

Your father and I were visiting nearby and waited in the car for you to come in from work. A young woman let herself into your house and we felt we couldn't cope with the situation. We hope you are well. Mum and Dad.

They saw my lodger! I wonder what she thought of the note. Once my parents received the change of address that I posted from Blake's, they would know that I wasn't in residence at Willoughby Street when they called.

I'm ready for work by Monday 29th November. It feels like old times and my spirits lift. Mr Harrison has allotted half of one of the long greenhouses specifically for my work, when I've got time. The first week I don't do the markets. I buy an evening paper and see that a touring ballet company is on at the theatre. I haven't been in touch with Mrs Hurst since we exchanged Christmas cards last year. I decide to phone.

'Mrs Hurst, its Helen, Helen Burns.'

'Helen!' It's Helen, I hear her call to Mr Hurst. 'I didn't know you were back in the district.'

'I came back in October. I'm working at Kerryhall again.'

'You didn't like the other place?'

'There were complications – some of them nice. I'm ringing because I wonder if you've booked for any of the ballets.'

'I'm going to *The Nutcracker* on Friday. Do you want me to get you a ticket? It wasn't sold out. We won't be able to sit together but we can meet in the foyer at six forty-five and have a chat before the performance. We'll order a glass of wine for the interval. Shall I get you a ticket?'

'Yes please!'

'Can you get here okay?'

'I have a car, so yes, transport is no problem. Mrs Hurst, don't get a shock when you see me. I'm six months' pregnant.'

'Good gracious! We will have a lot to talk about. I can't wait till Friday.'

Mrs Hurst welcomes me like a long lost friend and we talk until the bell rings for the performance to start.

I find my seat in a very happy frame of mind and let myself relax into the colourful ballet and lovely music. I'm sure my baby is listening and sharing my enjoyment. Mrs Hurst is waiting with the drinks at the interval and we mingle with the crowd until we move into a space where we can lean against the wall. I'm jolted by the sight of Margaret, Frances, Jane, Dee, Annabel and a woman I recognise from Annabel's party. They're talking animatedly and don't see me.

After the ballet, I run Mrs Hurst home from the theatre and pop in for a cup of tea and some garden talk with Mr Hurst.

'I'll drop a line to your former employer in Spain,' Mrs Hurst says. 'She'll be interested to hear your news.'

'How is Mrs Watkiss?'

'Fine, she's still enjoying the sunshine.'

I'm heartened by my friendship with the Hursts, despite their knowledge of my prison sentence and my return to their acquaintance as a mother-to-be. It must mean that they like me? We've promised to book seats the next time the ballet comes to town.

The following week, I feel I can cope with the market and on Wednesday and Saturday we take a chair so that I can sit down when we're not busy.

Myra stops by on the Wednesday without Nathan, he's at toddlers' play school. We go for coffee and fit as much chat about pregnancy and babies as we can into half an hour.

'Helen, we never talked about that night … '

'That's okay, it was pretty dreadful.'

'I recovered from the fright after a day or two but I had to do some thinking about the lesbian name calling. Do you mind if we get something straight? Are you a lesbian and did you ask me to your house to get me into bed?'

'It seems I'm more lesbian that not and no I didn't invite you to my house to get you into bed, not that the idea hadn't occurred to me.' I grin. 'At that time I really wanted a friend. I was crazy with disappointment.'

'I'm sorry I was so distant with you afterward, I didn't know how to behave. My new partner is more open about sexuality and he told me not to be so silly – said I would hurt your feelings if I ignored you because you like women. Anyway, it seems you like men too!'

'I met one nice guy and we're happy about the baby but we won't be living together. I still like women but you don't have to be scared.'

'I'm glad we're back to being friends. I have to pick up Nathan now but I'll see you soon.'

I'm given the next Saturday off to visit Elizabeth.

'I thought Granny and child had better get acquainted,' I say as she hugs me.

She and I have a lovely time. I don't want to meet anyone else so we go for a little walk, do a tour of the garden and eat nice meals. She's working a cross-stitch sampler for the baby. GARETH AND HELEN 1977 is all she can definitely sew as yet, but the border patterns are delightful.

Gareth comes for Sunday lunch, looking very well and cheerful.

'I'm so glad you're okay,' he says to me while his mum is in the kitchen.

'And you? Have you bumped into Liam?'

'I didn't just bump into him. I sought him out after he was highly recommended by a beloved friend of mine.' He hugs me and dances me round. 'We get on.'

'So I'm jilted good and proper?'

'I shall love you and our baby to the ends of the earth but I fancy my new friend.'

We laugh. Granny Elizabeth is coming to my house to have lunch next Sunday.

'Miss Priestley was at the market on Saturday, Mr Harrison says on Monday morning. She was asking where you were, says she saw you at the ballet. She didn't come over and speak because she could see that you and your friend were deep in conversation and she wasn't sure it was polite to leave the company she was with. She's a nice woman.'

'I've heard you say that before.'

'I'm not sure you're listening.'

'I know what you're trying to do.'

'Well, you could do worse.'

Oh yes, I'm listening. I don't tell him about the spasm in my gut when I saw Annabel or when I hear her name mentioned. I hope my baby enjoys the excitement. So Annabel saw me at the ballet. I wonder if she and the woman I recognised are an 'affair'. Why can't I convince myself that she and I are a 'no go' area? Is there any chance that she still feels affection for me, despite my pregnancy?

Frances comes over to me at the Wednesday market and asks if I'm well. I assure her that I am.

'I notice you haven't ordered a Christmas tree from us this year, Miss Pointon.' Mr Harrison says.

'No, we won't be at home this Christmas. Dee's children will be with their daddy, Jane and Dee are going to take off abroad and Margaret and I are spending Christmas with a friend on the north coast of Scotland.'

'It'll be chilly up there. I hope you have a nice time if I don't see you again.'

'Goodbye Helen,' she calls. I'm busy with a customer.

I shop after work on Friday so that I have the ingredients ready to make a meal for Elizabeth's visit. I'm always in bed by ten o'clock.

A customer brushes against me on Saturday and I nearly wobble over when I'm lifting a crate of potted hyacinths from the ground to the counter. A firm hand steadies me.

'Helen, is that you?'

I face Annabel for the first time in eleven months. She's wearing a colourful mohair hat and scarf, a green duffle coat and warm boots. The wind blows her blonde hair across her face and I feel a thrill of pleasure but I say coolly, 'Yep, it's me, my balance is a little out of kilter these days. Thank you for the support *mon amie*.'

'How are you?'

'As you see from my shape, twice as disreputable.' I'm making it easy for her but she frowns.

'That attitude's not called for.'

'Isn't it? You don't want to be in a position of having to escape a second time – Miss Runaway in the Night.'

She turns her back on me and disappears between the stalls. I didn't mean to be bitchy, my Scorpio sting, but I don't feel like letting her off lightly. I'm in a 'don't care, my life is in a messed up with regard to her' mood. She can't know that I daren't open myself up to her. I'm clinging on to the security of my home and my few safe friends.

Uncertainty makes me wild; it brings up the despair of my hopes having been kicked out for under my feet in the first instance by circumstance, in the second by Annabel and in the third by Mr Blake. How do I learn how to forgive her for putting a stop to our friendship in that abrupt way? Do I even want her to come back and talk to me?

I see Mr Harrison watching me and deliberately serve a customer. Annabel reappears and she's wiping her eyes. I experience a stab of guilt. What do I know about Annabel's feelings, why she ran away last Christmas and how the year has gone for her? She hovers nearby until I've finished with the customer and then comes over to me.

'Do you think we could start again? How are you, Helen?'

'I'm very fit as you see, thank you. All efforts to crush my spirit have failed and I'm well on the way to reproducing – there will be two of me.'

She smiles and says shyly, 'I was looking forward to seeing you. Can we meet?'

'Not tomorrow, I'm afraid. I'm involved with extended family.'

'Oh dear, and there are no more Sundays before Christmas. My mother's coming for Christmas.'

'It will have to be after Christmas then,' I say to show her that I'm not in a hurry to get into her favour. Her next question comes as a surprise.

'Would you by any chance be interested in going to a Candlelit Carol Service on the twenty-second, that's Wednesday next week? Mum likes these events and you could meet her?' I point to my bulge and raise 'you can't be serious' eyes to her expectant face. 'So, you're pregnant, it doesn't mean you can't meet my mother. I told you she was a midwife, well, Sister-in-charge by the time she retired.'

'I'd forgotten. She'll have seen enough pregnant women to last the rest of her life-time. Besides, mother figures I'm doing very well for thank you. I've two on the lookout for me already. My own won't receive the news till next week. It'll probably spoil her Christmas.'

'Helen, stop it! It doesn't suit you to be bitter.'

I can't help it. Tears pour down my face. She's punctured my defence. When I can get the words out I say, 'I broke my heart when I wrote the Christmas card to my parents last night.'

'It's okay, Helen,' she says gently, 'I have some idea how you must feel, you know. I couldn't bear for my mother not to share what was happening if I was pregnant. My mother would make three mothers for you. It seems to me that your guardian angel knows you have need of more than one! Your hanky's a bit damp, let me.'

I stand miserably with my hands in my pockets and she wipes my wet face.

'I'd better get back to work,' I say.

'Yes, but can I tell my mother that you'll come to the service?'

I rally. I don't want her to think I'm miserable on any account, and particularly not because of her.

'If I'm spared my propensity for trouble, I'll accept your invitation to the carol service, thank you. Oh ... and by the way, I got your letter three weeks ago. It was waiting when I returned to my house. Better late than never ... thank you for that too.'

She flushes with embarrassment.

'It's okay. I won't refer to anything it said. The content made me sad, in the circumstances.' We both stand uncertainly.

'The circumstances have certainly changed but there's no need to be sad,' she says perkily. 'I'd better go, you've got customers waiting. I'll pick you up on Wednesday at six-thirty.'

'I could make my own way, I've got a car.'

'Did you hear me say I'll pick you up?'

'Yes, ma'am.'

'Until Wednesday.'

I confess to confused thoughts as I go over and over the reasons why I should not take up Annabel Priestley's offer of friendship and yet the fact that I want her to like me, to want me, defies all reason. I'm back to Mr Prison Shrink and his 'attachments cause pain.' I suppose this is the way of all tentative relationships. At the outset one is vulnerable and with Annabel and me, it's for the third time. Could I bear another rebuff? But according to Dee, and Annabel's letter, she didn't mean to rebuff me. She just didn't know how to handle her emotions and ran away. I'm making excuses for her, being ruled by what I want rather than my common sense. Can I settle for friendship and not hope for a more intimate relationship? A church service and Annabel's mother surely won't add up to a recipe for disaster.

My self confidence is wobbly and that's a bad starting point. Yet, if I hadn't travelled along the prison route I wouldn't have met Annabel. Was it fate?

Annabel arrives on Wednesday evening with plenty of time to spare before we need to leave for the Carol Service. She hands me a large carrier bag with a French name printed on the side.

'What's this? Where's your mum?'

'It's an early Christmas present. Mum's waiting in the car.'

I stand and look at her, a number of thoughts going through my mind. I haven't prepared for Christmas and presents on this scale. Apart from writing cards and buying presents for the Nursery folk, I haven't given Christmas much thought. I planned to buy a chicken and small Christmas pudding for myself,

'Come on! Get it opened or we'll be late.'

'Am I not to leave it till Christmas Day?'

'The whole idea is that you wear it tonight to make yourself presentable enough to accompany my mother and me.'

She's smiling so there's no reprimand intended and she's right. I haven't bothered about my appearance lately.

'Take off your coat, slowcoach. Now, try this on.'

She takes out of the bag, a soft off-white duffle coat with toggle fastening, a hood and deep welt pockets. I'm so astonished that I let her dress me like a tailor's dummy.

'You do well to be impressed. Latest Parisian style, now available off the peg in clothing stores, thanks to Mum. I told her I had a badly dressed friend and she did the rest.'

She's fastening up the top toggles and her face is very near mine. There's that unsure but hopeful expression on her face that I witnessed a year ago when we were dancing at Hattersley.

'For a second there I wondered whether you were going to kiss me,' I say.

'For a second, I wondered whether I was going to kiss you. However, the second passed.'

'Having a baby hasn't de-sexed me.'

'I'm glad to hear it. You look great, now can we go?'

I'm seized by a wave of gratitude for her caring, undemanding gesture. I take hold of her fur collar and draw her closer.

'Thank you,' I whisper and kiss her very gently on the forehead.

'I meet you at last, Helen,' Mrs Priestley says from the front passenger seat of Annabel's car. 'The coat ... I make a good choice, no? I give you the kisses when we get out of the car.'

'It's a fabulous coat, thank you very much.'

'And now you and Annabel go to help me sing carols in English.'

I'm greeted with three kisses, French style when we arrive at the church.

The church is beautifully festive with fairy lights and an angel on the Christmas tree. Holly and ivy entwine on pew ends and above picture frames. Christmas Roses have been added to the clusters of greenery that decorate the sills of the stained glass windows. The Crib is at the front below the altar and near a pot of Poinsettia flowers. The woman vicar relates a colourful story about a poor girl in Mexico. She had only a bundle of sticks to take to church as an offering to God. Miraculously, the sticks changed into a Poinsettia – the message being that God values heartfelt gifts.

Annabel sits between her mother and me and we each hold a white card circle with a candle through the middle. The candles are lit while we sing *Hark the Herald Angels sing* and then the electric lights are switched off.

I reach for Annabel's hand as we sit listening to the reading of the Christmas story. I need her to keep hold of me. The softly lit darkness and solemnity move me to tears. Years since I was in church with my parents at Christmas and so much has happened that has separated me from them. I read the words of the carols but I can't trust my voice to sing. Perhaps my tears can wash away some of the sadness and I can enjoy a fresh start along with my unborn child.

We drive to Annabel's home first, as it's nearer to the church. The huge building was not very warm and her mum is chilled. After a glass of ginger wine, shortbread and mince pies, we're all feeling warmer.

'You will join us for the Christmas Dinner?' Mariette asks.

'That's very kind of you. I haven't thought that far ahead. I was planning to spend Christmas by myself at home. I've only bought presents for the few people with whom I've been in touch.'

'*Eh bien*! We are not thinking of presents! You and baby, it is not good to spend Christmas without friends. You come and relax with us and I prepare for you the Christmas meal. If Helen is contented, it will make Annabel and her *maman* very happy, *oui* Annabel?' Her daughter nods.

'Anyway, I haven't bought presents for you, only for your baby,' Annabel says which makes me smile. 'Did you realise in church that this time next year, if all goes well, you'll have a child on your knee, unless of course it wants to sit with its Aunty Annabel.'

'You're more bothered about this child than you are about me,' I say with mock peevishness.

'Of course I am! You're far too difficult a case. I've given up on you. Your baby will be quite a different matter. The poor child will need good friends and relations. Come on, I'll take you home. What time shall I tell Helen to come on Saturday, Mum?'

'Eleven o'clock for coffee,' Mariette smiles.

I'm tired. The market was busy today – everyone buying Christmas Wreaths, Poinsettias and potted hyacinths. I'm very grateful that the Priestley mother and daughter want to keep me from being lonely on Christmas Day. I don't talk on the way back to my house until the car stops by my gate.

'Thank you for driving me there tonight, Annabel. It was nice to be transported for a change. You and your mum have made it a very special evening and this superb garment hasn't just made me look good, it's made me feel cared for.'

'We'll see if we can make Christmas Day as special – with perhaps a better ending than last year.'

I twist sideways in my seat to look at her. 'Annabel, I retain the distinct impression that last year ended with the most beautiful kiss I've ever experienced.'

I let that statement hang in the air. It was her behaviour on Boxing Day morning that ruined the excitement and hopes I had for both of us. This year could have been so different. She doesn't reply.

'Good night Annabel.'

CHAPTER 18

On Thursday we prepare for tomorrow's Christmas Eve market. I dash to the shops to look for presents for Mariette and Annabel.

I feel well but I'm ready to sit down and eat my tea in front of the telly when I get home. At a quarter past seven, the phone rings.

'Helen it is Mariette. I would like to talk to you while Annabel is at her little party. I am welcome?'

I scoot round tidying and straightening everything, once I've assured her that it will be all right to call. My house is small and plain compared with Annabel's home but with Gareth's colourful throw on the settee, decorative objects on the bookcase and hearth and my Christmas cards, it's quite attractive – and it's warm. I change out of my overalls into my one outfit. Mariette takes in the room with an admiring glance, doesn't want a drink and makes it quite obvious that the talk is to be serious.

'Helen, last night, my Annabel is upset after she take you home. It is one year since she came to me in Paris and was also troubled about you. You tell me why.'

'She hasn't said anything about me?'

'At her college you were a clever student and she likes you. You help her once when she forgets to eat her snack.'

'I met Annabel in the summer of 1970 when I was in prison and began to study horticulture. I needed reference books. The prison governor asked Annabel to supply the books from Deanswood College. I only saw her once. I let her know which books I needed by sending notes.'

'The prison governor she is Jane?' and when I nod, 'Jane I like very much and Deanna and her two girls, also Margaret and

Frances and their beautiful Hattersley House. You were in prison why?'

I tell her the story and she purses her lips.

'This punishment, it is not very fair?'

'It didn't feel very fair. When I was released from prison I worked for a year in a shop and studied for exams at Deanswood College. Annabel and I sometimes talked after class and she invited me to a Christmas party at her house. I didn't see her for the two years I was at horticultural college.

'You have unfortunate liaison with college tutor, Annabel tells me.'

'Does she indeed! Her own liaison with porcupine head Deirdre wasn't very fortunate.'

'What you call Deirdre ... porcupine head?'

'It's an animal with prickles over its back.'

'Ah ... *porcépic oui,* I like it. *C'est* Deirdre,' and she laughs.

'The college tutor was good to me and we're friends now.'

'Your parents?'

'They don't want to know me. The prison sentence and homosexuality are more than they can cope with.'

'But they will be the grandparents to your baby!'

I shrug. I don't like to think of my child not knowing its grandparents.

'The baby's father?'

I smile. 'He's called Gareth Blake.'

'This Gareth, he wants the baby?'

'Yes, he's looking forward to being a father and he's arranged a generous allowance with his bank for baby and me.'

'That is good. You will marry?'

'No, we'll be loving friends. He's gay.'

'And you, you like men?'

I smile again. 'I like women.'

'You like my Annabel.'

'I like your Annabel. We've had some good times and some disagreements. There hasn't been much opportunity for me to get to know her. Last Christmas she left for her visit to you without saying a word, after we'd had a lovely evening together. I was hurt and decided I didn't want to see her ever again. She looked me up at the market last week and I'm puzzled as to why she's being kind to me. You can tell her that there's no need for her to feel guilty about what happened. It's probably unfortunate that she had to meet me. I'm someone whose life isn't very straightforward.'

'I thank you, Helen, for telling me the story.

'That's okay. I'm a bit despairing about me most days, but I'm looking forward to having a baby and I hope I'll be a good mother. I like my little home. My employer is happy to keep me on the Kerryhall Nursery staff and Gareth will see that I'm comfortable financially.'

She stands up and I expect her to go.

'I have to tell you, Helen ... you make the joke with Annabel about the baby. Annabel loves babies. I hear her cry only because she will not be a mother. I was midwife for many years and Annabel begs me always to tell stories about babies. Her dolls she treat like babies. I say "Annabel, adopt a baby", but it is a process complicated and she answer "no". I say to her, "have the insemination artificial" but she answer, "no" and she will not go with a man. It is that she is very interested in your baby, Helen. I hope you will let her be a good friend to you and the baby.'

'That's fine by me. I hope she'll bring along some of your knowledge and experience because I'm a total beginner.'

'I think you are a good girl, Helen. I like you. Now I will go. Annabel is not to be knowing that I visit you. How you say ... a secret?'

'A secret.' I walk out with her to her smart Renault Coupé. She has friends in England and likes to drive everywhere. Her plan is to spend New Year with her husband's family in Sussex.

CHAPTER 19

The festive season starts once the Friday market is over. This year again, the staff's invited to the Harrisons for a Christmas drink of sherry, savouries and mince pies.

'Only one drink at a time, young lady,' your baby won't appreciate alcohol,' Mrs Harrison warns.

I've bought Mr Harrison a new clock for his office wall, a tray of non-stick patty tins for Mrs Harrison and a gift box of three Yardley's Lavender tablets of soap, her favourite. I put them under their little Christmas tree.

The staff has clubbed together for my present. They give me a receipt to say that when my baby is born I can collect a baby bath and stand from Mothercare. It's a lovely idea but it makes my tum turn over with excitement to think of the inevitability of the birth and having a baby.

I've been listening to their enthusiasms and spent a long time in Our Price choosing their favourite music on forty-fives. I add a tub of hand cream to each package to make odd shapes so the presents are not too obviously records. Many jobs in the greenhouses require delicate handling. We can't wear gloves and take care of our hands as we ought. Painful cracks open on our fingers.

'And this is for you, not for your baby,' Madge says. I squeeze the soft parcel.

'Is it what you mentioned at the hospital, finished already?'

She nods. I give her a big hug.

When I get home, I look again at the present I've bought for Annabel. It's useless really, but a beautifully made cuddly toy, a teddy bear dressed up like a schoolmistress. Annabel's home is tastefully furnished and decorated. Her clothes are expensive. She always smells fragrant. I wouldn't know where to start choosing jewellery, toiletries or cosmetics for her. I wrap up the teddy. Then I wrap the Spode *1976 Christmas Plate,* with the decoration of Good King Wenceslas that I've bought for Mariette. I'm taking a box of Bendicks chocolate mint crisps.

I'm in bed once again by ten o'clock.

On Christmas morning we open our presents at coffee time and I'm pleased to see that the teddy and the plate delight Annabel and her mother. As Annabel forecast, my presents are for the baby except for a pretty nighty to wear in hospital and a book about having a baby. I'm going to be a well informed mother-to-be. I open Mrs Harrison's parcel and the lacy bed jacket is greatly admired. More twinges of excitement as I imagine where I'll be, and what will have happened when I'm wearing the nighty and bed jacket.

'That is good,' Mariette says. 'The new mother must feel pretty.' She has given me slippers. 'These you slip in your feet when you hear baby cry.'

I pull a face at the prospect and the three of us laugh.

I save my one drink on Christmas Day, for a glass of wine with our Christmas Dinner and relish the meal with a French flavour, cooked by Mariette. We have a lovely relaxed day.

Sunday, Boxing Day, I spend quietly reading about what to expect of my body in the next few months and watching films on telly.

On Monday I spend an hour in my garden as the sun shines. The ground's very hard and I can't see green tips yet. I watch more telly.

Tuesday I'm back at work preparing for Wednesday's market. I begin clearing and cleaning the half greenhouse that I've been promised, where I can develop some new roses from budding.

I bring in the New Year quietly by myself on Friday. I've kept a bottle of beer for the occasion and sit mulling over the last year. I know it's only dates and calendars that change, but somehow New Year's Eve feels serious. 1977 will be very different for me. I switch the telly on before midnight, to join in the festive mood, and toast my baby and me. I can lie in on Saturday morning and I have lunch at the Spencers' to look forward to. There's no Saturday market on New Year's Day.

Mr Spencer phones on Saturday morning.

'Helen, I'm sorry we've left it a bit late but we were wondering if you've a friend you'd like to bring to lunch?'

'There's one person who might be free, I'll ask her and ring back.'

I know Mariette has set off for Sussex and Annabel's friends are away. I take a chance that she hasn't been invited out and ask her if she would like to accompany me. It would be an opportunity for me to return some of the kindness she and her mum lavished on me at Christmas. I phone her.

'Good morning Annabel, Happy New Year! Does the prospect of a drive to Shropshire for lunch with my friends appeal to you?'

It does. She's pleased to accept the invitation but insists on driving us there.

'It's great that Helen's got a partner to take care of her,' Mr Spencer says to Annabel while we sit having coffee.

'The inference being that I won't manage to successfully reproduce, and look after a baby, unless Annabel supervises me?' I say with mock resentment.

'You know we think you're very capable, Helen,' Liam puts in. 'It's nice to think you won't be on your own.'

'I've no doubt that Annabel will organise me very well because she's into seeing that this baby has an aunty Annabel. She's a good friend,' I add deliberately and smile at her – let them not get the wrong idea about our relationship. 'She gave up on me many moons ago.' I know it's stupid of me to say that when I'm hoping it's not true.

The lunch party is seven in number. Liam, his now pregnant sister and husband, Mrs Blake and Gareth, Annabel and I, join the Spencers at the table.

I'm delighted to see Gareth and after lunch we sit on a window seat together to check in depth how we feel about the changes in our lives. Liam takes Annabel on a conducted tour of the Spencer Nursery hot houses.

'Is everything still well with you and the baby?' Gareth asks anxiously. 'By the way, you won't need to acknowledge receipt of the allowance every month. I know it goes into your bank on the first of the month.'

'Thank you, Gareth. It's great that I can count on receiving the money regularly. It means we'll be okay when my maternity leave starts. We're both fine. Our child must have been determined to defy all mishaps.'

'What's with you and Annabel?' he says suddenly. 'It doesn't look as though she's given up on you.'

'She made overtures a year ago and backed off which makes me wary. I like her ... a lot. Lucky for me she's crazy about babies. Her mother was a midwife so I'll stick with her for the help ... if nothing else.'

'I wouldn't be surprised if she isn't sticking to you, you very attractive creature. Pregnancy suits you.'

'I'm glad you still find me attractive, O faithless one.' He hugs me. 'How did your mother cope with Christmas?'

'She loved it! She insisted on celebrating alone so that Nick and I could keep Dad company. She says it's the most peaceful Christmas she's had. Now she's busy with her embroidery.'

'The sampler's going to be a beautiful piece of work for our baby to treasure. I think your mum's house is super and she looks happier.' I'm not going to enquire about Mr Blake though I'm curious about his situation.

'Dad and Mum have to talk sometimes, about the business,' Gareth offers. 'He's not as aggressive since the shock of the separation, less overbearing. It's obvious that he adores Mum and he's lost without her. He might be prepared to change if it means he can keep in touch with her. She won't have him back but they might be friends ... you'd think it was possible after forty years of marriage wouldn't you? He knows he won't find another woman like Mum.'

'What has he said about you and me and the baby?'

'I've told him I'm gay, which he said he'd already suspected. He wanted to know why I was messing about with you; that was how he put it. I said we have a wonderful friendship and that we both want to be parents. He just said, 'Hmph,' and would the child be called Blake. I said we'd discussed Burns-Blake, and he said, 'Blake should be sufficient, it's the father's name.' He hasn't used the word bastard again. I think he's ashamed of that night. I get the impression that he won't turn me away when I arrive with his grandchild.'

'And how are you?' There is that in my question that is more than 'how is work' and he knows it.

'I like my new friend,' he says shyly.

'Does he like you?'

'If I tell you that we're going down to the orchid exhibition at Kew in February and have booked into a double room at a hotel, will that answer your question?'

I just grin at him, so pleased for the two guys I like best in the world.

'You've got some nice friends,' Annabel says on the drive home. 'Gareth will be a good father when baby is old enough to spend time with him. He and Liam, are they a couple?'

'It seems they are, so baby Burns-Blake will have two father figures looking out for it.'

'Don't say "it".'

'What shall I say, him/her?'

'Just say "baby". How much French did you do at school?'

'I took it for three years, dropped it when my science courses started. I swotted up the grammar you accidentally sent to the prison or did you sneak it in deliberately?'

She laughs. 'I sneaked it in deliberately. What about coming to the Holiday French class I'm running in the spring term? It starts next Thursday at seven o'clock for two hours. You were the one that pointed out that women need to be fulfilled by diversity in their lives.'

'What have I let myself in for? The French teacher said I had a good accent and it was a pity I couldn't include the subject with my options.'

'Good. Baby will appreciate a more cultured mother and my mother will be impressed if you study her language.'

'Well, I know I'll never be right in your opinion but I think it will be worth cultivating your mother. She might invite me over to see the rose gardens in Paris and I'll leave him/her with you. I should have finished breast feeding by June/July.'

'Don't be so sure. Six months would be better or even longer.'

'Oh heck! I won't be able to go anywhere. No, it's bottle as soon as possible and then you or anyone can feed him/her.'

'Don't be aggravating!'

'It's called self preservation, return to normality, having a life, not being devoured by child. I'm your original selfish mother – in the best sense of the word selfish.'

'I hope you're joking. There is no best sense of selfish.'

'Oh yes there is. In my book it means that which is good for oneself. And here I am home! Goodbye Annabel and thank you my friend, for driving today. In case I decide to attend your French class, do you think you could drop a follow-up French grammar book through the letter box before Thursday? Or I could pop round and collect one. I need to refresh my mind.'

There's a French book on the doormat when I get in from work on Monday. Annabel isn't in so I leave a message on her phone

'*Merci professeur*, so begins the umpteenth stage of my cultural development.'

I stretch out on my sofa and am pleased to find that I'm familiar with, *un, une, le, la, les* attached to their respective objects. My vocabulary is way beyond, *la plume, le miroir, les enfants*, etc., which is encouraging.

On Tuesday evening I remind myself of the conjugation of verbs, *je, tu, il/elle, nous, vous, ils/elles*, etc. I think I'm going to be okay with this.

After market on Wednesday I nip into Waverley's bookshop and buy a small English/French dictionary. I lie on my settee reading exercises from Annabel's book aloud, to practise my pronunciation.

On Thursday evening I'm nervous as I drive up to the college. I've scrubbed up and my hair's looking good but I'm not happy in my clothes. My trouser fastening is on the last notch and I'm wearing a baggy sweater over my bulge, because the air's cold. I'll have to go shopping on Saturday. I park my car and notice a beautiful maroon Jag in the next bay but one. Is it Jane Pennyfields' car?

The classes are listed on the notice board and I arrive in the upstairs classroom at seven o'clock. The door is at the back of the classroom and I look at Mademoiselle Priestley after I find a space at a table. I can't read from her expression whether she's pleased that I've made it to class or not. The Jag is Jane's and she and Dee are sitting at the front of the class. I have mixed feelings about meeting them.

Evidently we're not to sit at our tables and work from books. We have to get up and walk round introducing ourselves – not like the lessons I was used to, where we had to open the book at page so and so and read the passage.

And would you believe it? The first person I have to shake hands with and say, '*Bonjour, mon nom est Helen. Enchanté,*' is Dee. I'm not altogether enchanted to find her there and she knows damn well what my name is. I don't have any problem with pretending that it's the first time I've met her but she's equal to the occasion. She doesn't let go of my hand and makes me look at her face.

'*Bonsoir mon amie,*' she says.' I am very happy to see you again. You look well.'

I'm pleased.

'French please,' Mademoiselle Priestley insists, 'no relapsing into English.' Dee grimaces and moves on.

The next person is Mademoiselle herself, '*Bonsoir Mademoiselle, je m'appelle* Helen. How do I say I'm not enchanted,' I mutter in her ear.

With Jane Pennyfields I'm suitably distant and deliberately miss out the enchanted bit. '*Je m'appelle* Helen but you know that,' I say with a smile that doesn't reach my eyes, and prepare to move away. My hand is held tight for the second time this evening.

'*Je m'appelle* Jane and you know that too. I can tell you're not *enchanté* but I have to say that I'm glad to see you. Could you forgive and forget?'

This time my smile is my mischievous usual one. '*Oui, c'est possible* but you'll have the teacher on to you if you don't speak French.'

I'm pleased again. I feel as though the chip on my shoulder is reduced in size. Mr Harrison will be happy.

Annabel is your lively, lovely teacher, in her element being charming with her students. She pushes her hair back off her face when she's answering questions and perches on the edge of the desk while we write an exercise. She walks round looking at exercise books. I cover mine with my arm but she moves it to one side and with her red pen rings an ending that shouldn't be there. Perhaps being corrected counts as special attention, she doesn't do it to anyone else.

It's a relief to go down to the cafeteria at break with the rather nice woman who's sitting next to me.

We work at the French alphabet after the break and have to spell in French individually. It's light-hearted because it's a leisure activity, non-examination course, and it doesn't matter if you don't get the answers right. At the end of class, I collect my homework study sheets and walk out with the same woman, after we've said our collective, '*Au revoir mademoiselle.*' Dee and Jane, stay behind to speak to her. I remember that they're just back from Christmas abroad.

CHAPTER 20

'Is it really necessary to buy maternity garments,' I ask Mrs Harrison 'can't I put more elastic in the trousers I've got?'

'Oh my goodness no! You'll get very big in the next three months.'

I shop for enveloping maternity clothes on Saturday. I buy a sleeveless top so that I can wear shirts, blouses and jumpers underneath it and hideous trousers that allow for my bulge.

Mr Harrison gives me two pairs of large size of overalls which are fine for the waist but I have to shorten the legs. As soon as I've had my tea and done the dishes each evening, I change into my nighty and dressing gown. That way I should be able to manage with just the one outfit to go out in. I don't work full time at the Nursery but I like to pop in for a chat with Mrs Harrison and Mr Harrison includes me in discussions on all matters concerning the business.

Not very cultured, Annabel, but good at my job …

I rest more in the evenings with my feet up and study hard at the French homework. I was riled by Annabel's suggestion that I need to be more cultured and am determined to keep up with the other students. From what I can gather, they want to understand the basics for travel abroad. We learn about eating out, finding directions, booking a hotel room and finding a camp site – none of which I will be doing.

I do look forward to seeing Annabel each week but I don't presume to make contact with her, in or out of class – I'm not sure if she counts me as one of her friends. I don't know what our relationship is. If she wants to be involved with him/her, it's up to Aunty Annabel to make the move.

I don't give Dee or Jane the opportunity to talk to me. I'm pleasant enough when we have to work in a group in class but that's all. It's not that I haven't forgiven them – it's that I must hold on to a good opinion of myself and I'm not sure that they can be trusted to respect me.

Annabel rings me up six weeks before him/her is due, to remind me that I must enrol for ante-natal classes.

'I enrolled last week.'

'Would you like me to come with you to the classes?'

Let me think ... do I want her to go with me? It might be nice to have someone with me who's in touch with what's happening – promise to Mariette and all that. Lots of the mothers-to-be were accompanied by partners or friends at the enrolment. It's a bit tough to go it alone and I would see her twice a week.

'Yes okay,' I say but without too much enthusiasm.

My suitcase is ready packed for hospital, strictly according to what the book says I'll need.

The Harrisons acquired a second-hand cot for me with a firm mattress and I've stitched remnants of flannelette into little sheets. I've bought a pretty cot-sized eiderdown. There's a corner in my bedroom where the baby will be out of draughts. I can't imagine what it will be like to have another presence in the room with me – until him/her is okay to sleep alone. Terry-towelling nappies, Annabel's baby clothes and gifts from Mrs Harrison and the Spencers are neatly stacked on shelves in the airing cupboard. Elizabeth has promised a pram for her first grandchild. I've followed the book's instructions about bath-time and having everything to hand.

Not very cultured, Annabel, but very practical ...

Why do I feel annoyed with her? We feel like mates at the ante-natal classes and then say 'bye' and drive off in our cars. Where did the beautiful closeness of the Carol Service go, or the fun of Christmas Day? Is it me that's too cagey? Aunty Annabel sounded nice and possible at Christmas, but now I feel that it was a pipe dream on my part.

The last Thursday class before Easter is pleasant, with talk of French customs and holidays. We take food and have a little party. Dee brings her accordion and plays from a music book of French songs. We sing *Frère Jacques, Allouette* and *Savez vous plantez les choux*. Some class members have already departed for France.

I have problems getting comfortable. My bulge won't fit under the table and I wriggle about on my chair. The slice of quiche, piece of brioche and glass of white wine has made me feel slightly sick. I'm relieved when the bell rings at nine o'clock. As we stand to say our, '*Au revoir*' to Mademoiselle, a sharp pain shoots across my lower abdomen. The scraping of the chairs hides my gasp. Dee and Jane go up to Annabel after the class as usual. This time I don't leave the classroom and she notices I'm waiting to speak to her. She excuses herself and comes over to me.

'*Eh bien,* Mademoiselle Burns,' she says but I'm not into pleasantries at the moment.

'Have you finished for the evening?' I say.

She looks affronted, as though I've no business to be asking about her plans for evening.

'I take it you've a reason for wanting to know?'

'Do you think I'd be asking, interrupting your *tête a tête* with your friends, if there wasn't a reason?' I whisper fiercely, annoyed again. 'Forget it,' I say savagely and make as dignified an exit from the room as I can. I was going to ask her to drive me from my house to the hospital but I've got the taxi number at home. By all accounts a first baby takes its time to appear.

I don't reach the bottom of the stairs before another pain and dampness between my legs remind me that him/her is on the way. Please God don't let my waters break here! I've heard enough frightful stories of the sort.

I feel safe in the car, as though sitting on a seat will prevent the baby from coming out. Two more pains in the ten minutes it takes to get home and park in my drive. I leave the front door open, ready to jump into a taxi. One more pain in the bathroom; I pad myself up in case of leaks and collect my suitcase. I disconnect plugs and head for the telephone. The next pain makes me double up and I groan. I hear a shout.

'Helen, where are you?'

'Here ... just a minute,' I pant.

'Give me your suitcase and key.' She locks the door and steers me to her car.

We don't speak again until I'm de-clothed and on a hard bed in a small room, being felt and measured, listened to and injected with something that makes me woozy when I stagger to the toilet. I'm surprised Annabel's still there. I thank her for providing the taxi service.

'I realised after you left what might be the matter. I came as quickly as I could,' she says. 'You weren't exactly clear as to what was happening, you know.'

'It was no use telling you I needed a lift to the hospital if you were tied up for the evening.'

'I couldn't of course have cancelled a former arrangement because you needed a lift? Words like "My labour's started" "Annabel I must get to the hospital" would have put me in the picture. "Have you finished for the evening?" made me wonder if you wanted to go out for a drink.'

'You know I wouldn't presume to ask you out for a drink!'

The nurse wades in. 'Not a time for in-fighting you two, shush your arguments until after baby's born.'

Annabel whispers, 'It was Dee who said "Isn't Helen's baby due about now? She doesn't look as well tonight." I'm sorry I was slow on the uptake.'

'Dee's been through this twice with Thea and Maddy, she probably recognised the signs,' I whisper back. 'Don't worry, you did the necessary. Thank you.' I reach for her hand and give it a squeeze – which probably bruises her slender fingers as it coincides with the next contraction. I groan.

'Breathe properly,' she prompts and stands over me.

'This promises to be a big baby,' the Irish Sister says, 'we must do everything we can to ease its passage. I'll be giving you an enema.'

'I should make your getaway on that note,' I say to Annabel and close my eyes for a rest between contractions.

Half an hour later she's back but I haven't the energy to query why she's spending the early hours of Friday morning at my sweaty bedside.

'I'm going to be sick,' I call out to anyone who's listening and someone holds a bowl while I retch, again and again, just to make sure there's no relief in the intervals between the pains. A clean bowl is there every time I need it.

'Oh ... I didn't know I had to be sick as well,' I moan.

'Mum told me she was sick when she was in labour,' Annabel's voice says calmly. She's still there, it's her fingers I see holding the bowl.

'I'm afraid the delivery theatres are occupied,' we hear the Sister say to a nurse. 'She'll have to have her baby in this anteroom.'

I see a little cot. It's strange to realise that my baby will be a separate entity and lying in that cot in a very short while.

I don't quite understand what I'm supposed to do with the gas and air supply and Annabel holds the nozzle to my face when I need it. I hear her explain to the nurses that her mother was a midwife for years and she's grown up with births. They seem content to let her help. Perhaps they think she's my partner. They're very busy. Lots of babies must have been conceived last midsummer.

'I think we're nearly ready, let's have you over on your back now, young lady,' the Sister says and I heave my bulk over as instructed.

'You don't want to see the blood and everything,' I gasp to Annabel 'why don't you go? I know you think I can't manage to do this without you ... ohh ... '

'Time to push down, that's it, now breathe,' the nurse says.

'Panting breaths,' Annabel leans over me and imitates what I must do.

'Drink please,' and she holds a cup of water for me.

'Bear down lovey, now breathe. We're tight here nurse, episiotomy, little snip.'

'Ouch! Drink. Let me push in my own time,' I say and with the next pain I push with all my strength.

'That's it! You've moved your baby,' the Sister's praise helps.

Another drink, another two mighty pushes and I feel my baby slither out warm and wet between my legs.

'It's a girl!'

Annabel gives me another drink.

'We wanted a girl didn't we?' I whisper.

'We did, and you were wonderful.'

My abdomen is rubbed firmly by the Sister. 'Can we have another little push then?'

I oblige and out slides the after-birth. I don't want to see it. I'm squeamish about blood and body parts but the Sister gives me no option. 'Look!' she says holding it up by the umbilical cord and I marvel at the structure that has supported life for my baby for nine months.

A stabbing injection and, a few minutes later a doctor is stitching up the cut down below. I'm padded up and my baby is presented to me, wrapped in a white cloth blanket.

'Give her to Aunty Annabel,' I say and watch Annabel's awed face as she takes the eight pounds thirteen ounce bundle of newborn child. I have tears in my eyes because I know how much she wanted giving birth to be her experience. It's the nearest she can get to it – and she's shared it with me.

CHAPTER 21

Annabel has been busy. News of the birth travels fast.

Gareth and Mrs Blake arrive for visiting that afternoon with a bunch of cheerful daffodils. They bring a catalogue photo of the superb *Silver Cross* pram that is to be mine/ours, white with a navy hood and streamlined patterns on the coachwork.

The babies are beside our beds in this ward, so that we learn to look after them from the word go. Gareth holds his daughter shyly and hasn't far to look for family resemblance – the baby's hair is ginger. His mother is delighted when he hands over her granddaughter.

'What are you going to call her?' Elizabeth wants to know. She looks so content with a baby in her arms.

'How were the orchids at *Kew*?' I ask quietly while Elizabeth's occupied.

'Magnificent! We had a lovely weekend. I'm sorry, Helen, it made me realise that I never gave you any fun like that. I should have made an effort to whisk you away from our "hole-in-the-corner" affair. I was so taken up with everybody's concerns that you lost out. Perhaps Liam, Mum and I can take you and the baby away in the not too distant future, cottage by the sea?'

'Oh yes, that would be nice.'

'Come on now, name? We can't say baby forever.'

'I haven't made up my mind about a name.'

'Why not Elizabeth after Mum? Baby could be Betty, Beth, Babs, Liz, Liza.'

'Babs! I like the idea of Babs, I think that's what she'll get for now.'

'I'd better put Elizabeth on the sampler hadn't I?' Elizabeth joins in the conversation. 'She'll be registered as Elizabeth, won't she?

'Oh yes, Gareth! Will you leave soon and go to the Registry Office before it closes please? I'd like you to register our baby as Annabel Elizabeth Burns-Blake.

Annabel is there for evening visiting and sits with Babs in her arms the whole time. She doesn't think much of Burns-Blake or the name Babs – tough. It's my baby and now I won't tell her that I've added Annabel.

She makes me feel like a delivery girl, but the Harrisons don't, when they visit on Saturday afternoon. They make me feel like a clever girl and a proud mum. Mrs Harrison has stitched a pretty patchwork coverlet for the pram and Mr Harrison presents me with a red rose. I'm weepy and Mrs Harrison hugs me.

'You'll be emotional for a while, be gentle with yourself.'

I'm told that I can go home on Monday as Babs is feeding well and I've no other problems. I ask Annabel on Sunday evening if she'll arrange transport to my home for me, as she'll be at college in the daytime. She doesn't answer straight away.

'Do you think it's a good idea for you to be alone with the baby so soon after the birth? Usually two people manage the adjustment to a new baby in the home.'

I was half expecting her to cook up an excuse to get Babs to her house. 'I've got everything organised. I should manage all right,' I say.

'Yes I know but, Helen, would you consider living at Leahurst for the first six weeks until you've had your check up and your body's back to normal? I could help when you're tired and Babs would get to know me. You can choose either of the two spare bedrooms and we can get the cot and baby clothes over from your place.'

I agree to her suggestion. Why? I'm nervous of being in sole charge of another human being, a helpless one at that. Whatever will it feel like to arrive home with my baby? What does one do first? Most people have their mother to stay ... In six weeks a routine will be established and I'll be more confident on my own.

At the moment I'm not quite sure when to feed Babs or whether I've got her wind up properly. It's easy here in the maternity hospital where my meals are provided, but how will I fit in the housework and my meals at home? Annabel's house is nicer and warmer than my house and she's got a washing machine. I would have someone to talk to and it's only what friends are supposed to do – help each other out.

I choose the bedroom that's across the landing from Annabel, we can see each other's light. The baby gear is in my bedroom. Annabel likes to bath and dress Babs and I'm amenable to having a clean child placed in my arms ready for her feed.

More presents arrive, this time the promised carry-cot with love from the Hattersley crowd. I write a thank you note.

Mariette sends two pairs of stylish colourful dungarees and tops for Babs – and a smart tie-belt stone coloured jacket for me!

I think you will want to feel attractive again, her note says, *and thank you for being a good friend to Annabel. I hear that in the delivery room you were an excellent patient!*

I write a warm, friendly note of thanks.

Edith posts the white matinee set. I phone my thanks and am glad to have a chat with her. We plan to meet when I'm out and about.

The Spencers send a rosebush, 'Queen Elizabeth' for my garden. I thank them over the phone. The Spencer grandchild is due in May.

I wait until Annabel is out before I dare to communicate the news to my parents. I don't want her to see me cry. I use a card that announces the birth of a new baby.

Annabel Elizabeth Burns-Blake, weighing eight pounds thirteen ounces, was born on Friday 11th March 1977 at 4 a.m. She will be called Babs.

On the back I write the information that I know will be of concern to them.

I shall be living in my own house and working part-time at Kerryhall Nursery. With a generous allowance from the father, Gareth Blake, Babs and I will be financially comfortable.

She and I are both well, as I hope you are. Love Helen

I take Babs for a little walk, as far as the post box further along the street. I'm shy pushing the smart pram. One neighbour, out for a walk with her dog, wants to look at the baby and ask questions about age, weight and name. That makes me feel accepted as a mother.

I tell Annabel that I've let my parents know and show her the reply when it arrives ten days later. There's a greeting card for a new baby girl and a letter.

Dear Helen

Thank you for your note. We are pleased to hear that you and the baby are well and provided for.

Your father has put £10,000 in trust for her to have when she reaches the age of twenty-one. I enclose the documents relating to this transaction.

We wish you well.

Love Mum

This time Annabel sees me cry. 'If it was for me, I'd refuse the money,' I sob, 'but for Babs it will be proof that she has grandparents who care for her in the only way they know how. I'll send photos every now and then.' I write a thank you note and walk along to post it ... alone.

Easter Holidays and Annabel and I rub along together comfortably, I would even say we're happy. If I'm up in the night, Annabel takes over in the morning. I hear her singing snatches of songs in the kitchen and she serves me breakfast in bed. I like watching her dance with Babs in her arms – Mariette was right, she's a natural with babies. I'm learning. I'll dance with Babs when I get back to my home. Annabel can have her turn now.

I rest in the afternoons and Annabel takes Babs to show her off to the Hattersley crowd. When she visits other friends with Babs I wonder what she says to them. 'My friend's just had a baby and she's staying with me for a few weeks'? Do they ask where the father is and why I'm not in my own home – how she got to know me – why she's doing this for me? I'm prickly.

Annabel is a different woman when she's tending Babs. She's so gentle and loving – her face is alight with tenderness and her halo of blond hair makes her look beatific. I love watching her hands. She has long slim fingers, quite unlike mine which are square and practical. I don't feel envious of the time she spends with Babs because Babs and I belong together, but I can understand that a husband might feel his nose put out of joint when he sees his wife so bound up with a new baby.

Once or twice Annabel has raised her head from adoring Babs and transferred the affectionate gaze to me. She quickly realises it's me she's looking at and not Babs and her expression shuts down. It makes me long to be loved and looked at adoringly for real, instead of by mistake. Gareth and I loved playfully – it was a blithe relationship that we knew wasn't going to be permanent – we couldn't show affection unless we were miles away from Blake's Nursery. If Annabel was to catch me out when I think she's not watching, she would see that I love her. When we do speak, I'm pleasant and courteous, the perfect house-guest.

I'm not allowed to relax my French studies. Sometimes Annabel insists on speaking French while we're doing chores or playing with Babs. My little dictionary is very well thumbed.

College resumes; Annabel is at work and I have the days to myself.

'Oh, it's nice to come home to you women,' Annabel says to Babs on more than one occasion.

I'm very glad to share the pacing about with Annabel when Babs has a period of evening colic. It would have worried me silly to nurse my tiny baby with her legs drawn up in pain, when nothing seemed to soothe her. Annabel rings her mother for advice. She sometimes gets up in the night when she knows I'm breast-feeding Babs and brings me a mug of tea.

I keep an awareness of four o'clock in the afternoon and Annabel's diabetes. She doesn't make any mention of her condition but I have the kettle on, ready for afternoon tea, and if she's late home I feel a knot of worry in my stomach. Usually she tells me if she'll be late and I remind her about eating something. She tells me not to fuss. She's very private about her injections and her medical equipment is kept high up, out of a child's reach, in her bedroom.

We share the cooking of the evening meals and each week we go over to my house to collect my mail and see that everything's in order. She's very thoughtful about things like that, but I am too. We have the same caring attitude to Babs and each other and the same attention to detail. It makes being in someone else's house fairly easy.

I feel much freer when I'm ready to drive and take my car over to Leahurst.

Annabel sends photos of Babs to Mariette. She has duplicates printed; one or two for my parents, the rest for the large scrap book I'm making into an album. I sit in the evening with scissors and glue, sticking in cards and photos and recording dates.

I visit the Harrisons regularly. They're always pleased to see Babs and me. Babs gets taken off my hands for an hour or two and I spend time in the greenhouses. I need this connection with my former life.

I tidy up the garden at Leahurst after the winter, while Babs sleeps in blissful comfort in her luxurious pram. I drive us over to my house and she sleeps in the carry-cot while I tidy up the garden at 12 Willoughby Road. I must prepare for my return.

Annabel makes no mention of the fact that the six weeks are up.

I park Babs with Madge while I go for my check-up. I'm pronounced fit and rejoice that I no longer need to wear pads. I begin to feel like my sexy self in my jeans and re-double the effort I put into the exercises that are to get my tum back into shape. Now I just need this breast-feeding to come to an end so that I don't feel like an ever obliging tap.

Return to normality brings problems. It felt part of the routine to see Annabel bring a drink into my bedroom, wearing her pink angora dressing gown, with her long wavy hair tumbling on her shoulders. Now I notice that she doesn't tie the belt and I'm tempted by her lacy nighty and soft inviting breasts. She skips about in her petticoat or in her bra and briefs, to and from the bathroom, when she's getting ready for work. It's time I left. I'm back to finding Annabel a very desirable woman.

During the following week I spring clean the bedroom I've been using and relay belongings to 12 Willoughby Road. I shop, stock up my cupboards and order milk to be delivered for next Monday. I walk the three miles with Babs in the pram, leave it at Willoughby Street and catch the bus back. Annabel doesn't notice that the pram has gone out of the garage because the weather is fine and we leave our cars in the drive. I wait until Sunday.

'Annabel,' I say at lunchtime, 'I'm going home tomorrow. I'll be gone when you get in from college.' I wait for a response in vain. She collects our empty plates and serves the dessert.

'I hope you know that I'm very grateful for the help and comfort you've provided in these first few weeks with Babs,' I say when she sits down. 'I would have found it difficult to manage on my own. Don't be surprised if I'm on the phone to you every five minutes. You'll keep up your contact with her now that the two of you have bonded, won't you? When this breast-feeding stops she can come and stay with you.'

Babs cries and Annabel picks her up. I mix the little portion of baby rice that Babs can eat before her milk feed. I'm disappointed that Annabel doesn't comment on our forthcoming departure. I suppose it was too much to hope that she might say she would miss me. I know she'll miss Babs. On the other hand, she may have been hoping I would make the move so that she can return to her friends and social life.

CHAPTER 22

Babs makes the transition to 12 Willoughby Road okay. Her little tum is appreciating the introduction of solid food and she sleeps soundly. I lie awake into the small hours and then it's time to feed her again. She lies between my breasts and I feel tremendous love for this little scrap of daughter. I mustn't fall asleep. I change her nappy and put her down. This was Annabel's job. She's probably glad to be relieved of it.

I'm so mixed up about everything. It doesn't seem fair that Annabel ran away from me and yet I've provided her with the access to a child that she wants most in the whole world. I can't fault her care of me. She probably knows that her rejection contributed to my eagerness to leave the area, move to Blake's, and she's spent the last three months trying to make it up to me. She's fulfilled her obligations. She can go on her way rejoicing.

Will my job and the affection of the Harrisons and Edith be enough to get me through as a single mother? There's Myra and Mr and Mrs Hurst and I might make more friends as the months go by. I could join a mother and baby class.

Or would it be better for Babs if she was adopted by Annabel and I clear off to distant parts and make a new start with my life? The idea cuts me to the quick. I can't bear to entertain the idea seriously but it has crossed my mind – it's a possible solution to my messed up reputation.

Annabel might have been positive and active in her effort to settle Babs into the world, but my personal relationship with her ends in frustration for the second time. It's only what I should have expected. I'm annoyed with myself. I hoped for love and now I'll have to content myself with loving Babs unless I find love elsewhere. Am I loveable?

Next week I'm due to start work part-time and my mind will be more occupied but if I admit it, I'm bitterly disappointed.

Tuesday morning is clear and bright. I put Babs out in her pram for her morning nap and do some washing. I'm pegging out nappies when I hear the click of the back gate and stand astonished to see Frances and Margaret. This is the second time they've turned up unexpectedly. They must make a habit of it. Once again, news has travelled fast! I'm not altogether pleased to see them and leap to defensive mode.

'Have you been sent to check up on Babs' welfare? She's quite unharmed after one night alone with me I can assure you.'

'Helen!' Margaret says gently but reproachfully.

My eyes fill and I stammer, 'Would you like coffee? I have instant and a percolator but I only have mugs to drink out of.'

'Mugs will be fine,' Frances says firmly, 'I'll come and help.'

'May I spend a few minutes with Babs?' Margaret asks and I nod.

'I reach in the cupboard but I'm shaking with sobs. 'They're very pretty mugs,' I try to say.

Frances takes them out of my hands and puts them on the counter.

'They're very pretty mugs, Helen, now sit down and I'll boil the kettle.'

But she doesn't boil the kettle. She sits on a chair opposite me.

'Boxing Day morning 1975 Helen,' I look at her with surprise. 'We haven't got to the bottom of what happened at Hattersley that made you break contact with us. Margaret and I would like to know the story behind that morning, if you wouldn't mind sharing.'

I can't see any harm in telling them what happened, might be a relief after months of feeling resentful.

'I was really happy that morning and looking forward to seeing Annabel and all of you. She and I had a long talk in my bedroom and discussed starting a relationship. We were going to make breakfast together if you remember, and when she wasn't in the kitchen I was going to tease her because I'd beaten her downstairs.

'Dee said, "Annabel's gone, did you do something to upset her last night, Helen?" Her question and Annabel's absence came like a blast of cold water. She could have said, "Any idea why Annabel's gone early, Helen?" or "You're on your own for breakfast duty as Annabel's gone early" but no! "Did you, Helen, do something to make Annabel leave?"

'I didn't dare speak; I'd have howled with disappointment, I just asked Jane to take me home. I haven't felt able to trust either of them since. I decided that I would be better away from close contact with people who can't forget that I was a prisoner or who know that I've had affairs. Dee wrote me a letter of apology and Annabel posted a note of explanation from Paris but I didn't get their mail until I returned home in November. The disappointment plus my parents' rejection felt like a deal of hurt to suffer. Now there are only a few people I'm at ease with.'

'What's this about a relationship – you and Annabel?'

'Annabel asked me to dance on Christmas Day evening. She was really seductive. She came into my bedroom, sat on my bed and said she'd always liked me but in the early days of knowing me she was put off by my past. I didn't want her to assume that it was okay to play with me because of my lesbian reputation and make a fool of me in front of all of you. She said she'd like to try going about with me. Before she left my room, she wanted to be kissed. I don't honestly know what happened next. I've heard it said that lovers can't tell where they end and the partner begins, and the kiss was like that. She gasped and buried her face in my breasts.'

'Thank you, Helen that makes the whole situation clearer.'

'I lay awake for hours last night wondering what to do,' I say dolefully.

'About what?'

'The future, I'm never going to escape my past, am I? Would it be better to let Annabel adopt Babs? I could sell up and move right away where my reputation can't follow me.'

'Didn't a certain Miss Horsfall get to know about your prison experience from as far away as London?' Frances says with a teasing smile. 'How far you would have to go, Australia?'

I manage a faint smile but I feel very miserable.

'I think you might be suffering from a bout of post-natal depression, young woman. Now, let's have a mug of coffee.'

Margaret comes in and sits down at the table.

'Babs looks so cosy and healthy, Helen. You must be producing good quality milk. She's grown a lot in the weeks since Annabel brought her to visit us. I've been sitting on the seat out there and listening – hope you don't mind. I think the young women at my house know very well that they weren't helpful to you. Jane and Dee both admire you and Dee was enjoying your friendship. I'm told that Gareth Blake is a very pleasant young man and promises to be a responsible father. I imagine that making a baby with him wasn't all bad!'

'We did have some lovely carefree fun, despite having to hide our relationship from Gareth's father. Babs is a Midsummer's Eve baby.'

'You, Dee and me, we're alike,' Margaret says 'we're open to loving a man or a woman. Frances only likes women, so does Annabel. Jane and Dee think you've coped wonderfully.'

'I'm tough in some ways and Annabel has helped a lot.'

'And so she should, by the sound of it! It's extraordinary really. She ditches you and then gets the chance to make it up to you – meanwhile you provide her with a much wanted baby to care for.

'Jane and Dee said they were going to come across to see you tonight, Helen, if that's okay? Would you and Babs like to come to Hattersley tomorrow morning to stay until Sunday? Barry and Jim are anxious to see Babs and the nurse in me is concerned about your depressed frame of mind.'

'I was going to start work part-time next Monday.'

'And so you probably will; we'll see about that when it gets to the weekend. Now, are you okay to pack up what you need for tomorrow? And you can find your way? We'll expect you for coffee at eleven. Now – ah, thank you, Frances, I'm ready for this and,' she rummages in her bag. 'Here we have some of my very own shortbread biscuits ... and if I'm not mistaken, I hear that a very young lady nearby wants Margaret to nurse her.'

I get up to go out to the pram but Frances catches my hand and Margaret goes for Babs.

'What about Annabel?' she says.

'What about Annabel?' I repeat and sit down again.

'Well?'

'It will be difficult with Annabel now. She wants to be involved in the baby's upbringing. Once I stop breast-feeding Babs, Annabel can have her at Leahurst to stay, perhaps at weekends and in the holidays. She'll be visiting Gareth and his mum too. I'll have a lot of time to myself!'

'You're not answering my question, Helen. What about you and Annabel?'

'Oh, I don't know. What can I say? She's always turned me on, ever since we first met. For seven weeks I've been her lodger, a wet nurse, a nanny, cook and gardener and there's been no intimacy between us. We've both been intent on seeing that Babs is okay. There was just one lovely evening before Christmas, when Mariette was here, and we went to the Carol Service together. Annabel and I held hands. There's been no touch since then. I think she only wanted me at Leahurst because Babs couldn't do without the milk supply.

'I did hope that Annabel would get to know and like me and that we might develop into a long term love relationship. And then lately she got careless about me seeing her undressed, which was not considerate. She and I had no physical contact and yet she was flitting about in front of me half naked. You know Frances – I'm still the same sexy woman I was before I got pregnant. I've kept my love for Annabel in wraps for years and there she was coming into my bedroom, bending over me to scoop up Babs with her dressing gown unfastened and her breasts within reach of my face and hands! I had to pretend I hadn't noticed! That was when I knew I must leave.'

Frances laughs. 'That was exactly the situation with Margaret and me a few years ago. I was on the verge of leaving Hattersley because I was in love with her and couldn't bear her physical closeness. It wasn't Margaret's fault, she wasn't being deliberately provocative. She didn't know I was in love with her. Annabel however ... hmm ... I don't know about Annabel, she has experience of women lovers, I'm not sure she's so innocent. You didn't say anything to her, about your feelings for her?'

'No. You know, I've never needed to ask someone to go out with me. Women fancied me and made the moves. Annabel gave me no indication that she wants to be intimate. She's been pretty critical of me in the past and I wouldn't chance being rejected by her. She said I wasn't cultured enough and suggested I go to her French classes. You know I was riled enough to take her up on it.'

Frances laughs. 'You don't think she wanted to make sure that she would see you one night a week?'

'That hadn't occurred to me! I know I was glad to see her once a week.'

'Whoever is to be Annabel's partner will need to speak French because of going to Paris and staying with her mother?'

'That hadn't occurred to me either.'

'And how is your French progressing?'

'I'm doing okay. Annabel brought home an easy reader play last week and we had some fun reading the parts. She's very patient with me.'

'I'm sure she's pleased to have an able student. I've heard Jane and Dee trying to keep up a conversation in French but they're short on vocabulary and they're not as fortunate as you in having a tutor on hand.'

Margaret brings Babs in and it's evident that the squirmy, smelly bundle is ready for a change of nappy and another feed.

'This is where I have pleasure in handing her back to you,' Margaret says, 'and we must make our way. We'll look forward to seeing you tomorrow, Helen.'

Frances and Margaret have further reduced the chip on my shoulder. I feel much easier in my mind until Babs is asleep in her cot, and then I get anxious about the arrival of Jane and Dee. How will we greet each other? I tidy away the baby bits and pieces and make my living room look as welcoming as possible.

I needn't have worried.

'Helen!' Dee says and folds me in her arms. 'Forgive me?' and she looks in my face for my answer.

'I've missed you,' I say accusingly 'I could have done with you around.'

'Oh I know, I feel dreadful! I didn't know how to get back in your good books. How are you?'

'I'm okay.' I hold out my hand, 'Jane?'

'I'm sorry, Helen, really sorry,' Jane says sincerely. 'We weren't there for you. We can't undo what's happened but perhaps we can make amends. Can we have a peep at Babs?'

They've brought a bottle of wine and a Guinness for me – Margaret's orders. We sit chatting. They want to know details and I relate the good and the bad of the past sixteen months. It feels comfortable. We talk and listen as if we're long term friends. I hear about their holidays, Jane's decision to retire soon, Dee's accordion playing and Thea and Maddy.

'I'm not sure whether the girls' enthusiasm at tea-time was for you or Babs.' Dee says. You might get a look in. They haven't forgotten the fun you had with the board games. You'll get roped in, I'm afraid.'

We don't mention Annabel.

I have a glorious time at Hattersley. With three willing nursemaids I'm only required to breast-feed Babs.

Dee encourages me to renew my acquaintance with a recorder. Thea has been playing the piano and recorder for five years. When she comes in from school, we sit in the music room and she plays for me.

'I hope Babs learns to play the piano and is as good as you by the time she's thirteen, Thea.'

'Listen to me,' Maddy says and pipes easy tunes on her recorder.

The three of us manage to play a tune in simple harmony, with much laughing in between attempts. I haven't felt this happy since ... ever felt this happy? I realise with astonishment that there aren't any clouds on my horizon!

In the daytime, I spend ages in the grounds examining and appreciating the plants. Mr Green, the gardener, is only too pleased when I ask for a kneeler and trowel to titivate the soil in the rose beds. The enjoyment of working alone, at a job that I enjoy, returns

My Friday afternoon rest is on one of the benches in sight of an archway overgrown by a tangle of Clematis stems and seed heads. I determine to tackle it when I wake. I get the secateurs and string that I carry whenever I'm in a garden and start to work.

I'm underneath the trellis with a fistful of ties and branches when I hear Annabel.

'So that's where you are!' She lies down on the bench and watches until I've finished. 'I'm very impressed with your skill, rustic maiden. Now can you come and sit with me? She picks leaves out of my hair then turns my face toward her – and kisses me!

'What's that for?' I ask, perplexed.

'It's Friday afternoon and on Friday afternoons a rustic maiden with an adorable baby has to be kissed by a female lover, I'm sure I read it somewhere.'

I have to laugh. I love it when she's funny and she's in a very good mood. Her shirt is tantalisingly buttoned so that I see too much of her breasts. She's a confident madam.

'So what sort of time have you been having? Are you all friends now?'

'I'm having a wonderful time,' I say without looking at her.

'I've been sent to get you. Babs will be ready for her drink soon. I'll let you go if you kiss me.' I give her a peck on the cheek. 'Babs doesn't want her drink that quickly!'

There she is, back to being a seductive woman, just like she was on Christmas Day, months ago. Do I fall for it a second time? I know the answer. This time I rise to the bait and make the move. I've longed to kiss this woman. Babs has to wait for some time before the two of us get back to the house.

'We'd better discuss sleeping arrangements,' Dee says aside to me during the evening. 'Do we carry on as we have done since you came?'

'Yes, leave the arrangements as they are. Annabel hasn't broached the subject, though I suspect that I may get a visitor after lights out.' We both grin.

I am rather interested in what will happen at bedtime. I wash and get into bed as usual and the door opens to admit Annabel in her dressing gown. She sits on the bed.

'I thought I'd leave my dressing gown unfastened so that you can see my breasts,' she whispers.

'You monkey! So it was deliberate.'

'Of course it was. I had to see whether you were stimulateable after having a baby, I didn't expect you to up and leave however. I've been frantic, scared in case I'd put paid to my plans. I had to rope Margaret and Frances in to help.'

'What plans?'

'Oh haven't I mentioned them?'

'You know damn well that you haven't mentioned any plans to me.'

'I've got another job.'

That ... I hadn't expected. I hold my breath and wait for more information.

'Yes, it's at a college in Paris. I'm to teach English as a foreign language.'

My head spins with shock, and fear of losing her, until she turns and snuggles up to me.

'I wondered if you and Babs would like to come with me.'

'As?'

'Well, there are a few choices really. My lodger, my wet nurse, nanny, cook, gardener ... '

I push her away from me. 'You've been talking to Frances!'

'Of course I have. I told you I had to use my friends as spies. You never gave me any clues as to whether you loved me. I used to look at your face and you were always correct and pleasant. I couldn't see that there was any affection for me.'

'You should have seen my face when you weren't looking. I watched you with Babs and was hoping that one day we'd adore each other.'

'You see if I'd known that I wouldn't have had to pry information out of Frances.'

We need a few minutes to begin the process of adoration.

'By the way, there are other options for a relationship in France,' Annabel says. 'I believe the terms these days are lover or partner.'

I'm so delighted I'm speechless.

'Helen?'

I can't think what to say so I kiss her instead.

'Is it done to make love in the same room as one's child,' she whispers urgently.

'This mother is also Annabel Priestley's lover, try to stop her,' I say as my hands find the soft places I so much want to caress and arouse.

Babs wakes us at six with her happy crowing and gurgling. Annabel brews a pot of tea. I watch her lovely body as she moves about. I'm elated that she's learnt to trust me enough to respond to my love making. We sit with Babs between us. We have much to discuss and I start with us.

'I'd like an explanation please as to what's been going on since I returned to the area. How did you make the transition from disinterested friend to being in bed with me?'

'Was I disinterested? I think I was very interested. I wangled things didn't I, with one excuse or another? I introduced you to my mother, invited you to my French class, went to ante-natal classes with you and got you into my home. I had to know if we'd get on together. Babs gave me the opportunity.'

'I thought you just wanted Babs.'

'That was part of my deviousness.'

Babs is in danger of being squashed as we need to make up for months of no physical contact.

'What will we do about our properties?' I want to know.

'One option is that I let Leahurst and you could let 12 Willoughby Street. We'll come over for visits and can check that the houses are being kept in good order. I'm not keen on agents but we may have to employ one. Option two is to sell. We can buy one house for our family when we return.'

'Where will we live in France?'

'Mum's spotted a house that she thinks will be suitable. I'll fly over next weekend and look at it. I'll take photos to show you. It would be too much of an upheaval for you and Babs for a weekend.'

'Gosh! It's so exciting! I'll be sad to leave my friends though. They'll miss us and Gareth won't see much of Babs. I'll have to give notice to Mr Harrison.'

'We'll keep in touch with our friends and Gareth travels a lot so he'll be over frequently. Are you okay about your parents?'

'I'll never stop missing Mum, Annabel. My joy would be complete if I was to see her walk through the door. But I've accepted that Mum and Dad don't want to be part of my life. It won't be too hard to leave the country.'

'I doubt we'll spend the rest of our days in France but it will give you the complete break from your past that you need just now.'

I look at her gratefully. She's been thinking and preparing for the best for both of us, without saying a word to me. I put a contented Babs back into her cot.

'Oh dear,' I moan as I slip under the bed covers.

'What? What's the matter?'

'I'm having an attack.'

'What sort of attack?'

'Being in love is the term for this type of attack these days.'

'Okay, I deserved that. I shall not attempt to cure you. I may even succumb to the same malady.'

We're late for breakfast which seems to cause no surprise.

Annabel delivers our news when we're all there at coffee time. It makes for a very excited Saturday morning.

'So, Elizabeth Burns will grow up to be bi-lingual,' Margaret says.

'Annabel Elizabeth Burns-Blake will grow up to be bi-lingual like her second mother,' I add and look fondly at the delighted face of the person concerned.

'Did you notice that I pretended I couldn't find the birth certificate?' I say to Annabel. 'You were so critical of my daughter's name that I wasn't going to tell you I'd added Annabel, until Babs started school. But a change has come over my heart. I might drop the Blake if Gareth doesn't mind. He can be satisfied that his name is on the birth certificate. Burns-Blake is an unwieldy surname. Annabel Elizabeth Burns, that's better.'

I see Annabel's mind working nineteen to the dozen. She opens her mouth to speak and I think I know what she's going to say.

'No,' I stop her. 'I won't call her Anna or Bel. Babs it is.'

AFTERWORDS

My name is Katherine Burns. My husband and I can't figure in this story as it is written by our daughter Helen, after a nine year separation from her former life, which was with us, her family.

Our two daughters, Mary and June, were the joy of our lives. I would have defied anyone to claim that their home life was happier. Wesley, my husband, has a good position in banking and I haven't needed to go out to work.

Mary never gave us a moment's trouble and her academic progress delighted us both. June has said since that she felt shadowed by her clever sister and that's why she was so defiant in her teenage years. It took considerable tact on my part to help prevent June from ruining her young life by getting pregnant. I pointed out the life she would miss if she encumbered herself with a child. She's twenty-eight now and she did have fun. She loved going to the cinema, dancing and she belonged to a tennis club. She's married to one of the assistants at Wesley's branch of the bank and they live nearby. I have a grandson William who is four years old and a granddaughter Jessica who's just had her first birthday.

Mary didn't show much interest in boys. She was into netball and swimming and one or other of the sports kept her busy on Saturdays. She said once, 'I ought to be dressing up to go out tonight instead of coming home tired out and needing a bath.' She used to confide in me about the dates she had with boys at university and refused to let anything interfere with her studies.

Wesley and I ran her back to the university that autumn term. I particularly wanted to see what the accommodation was like where she was going to live. We unloaded her belongings into the bedroom that was to be hers. Her roommate hadn't arrived so we went out for a meal before leaving for the drive home. That was our last happy time together.

I can't adequately describe the feelings that accompany opening one's front door and seeing a male and female police officer standing on the doorstep.

'Mrs Burns?' The male officer said.

'Yes, is something the matter?' I was certain from their demeanour that they were bringing bad news.

'May we come in?'

'Is someone dead?' I asked fearfully.

'Not anyone from your family. We've sent a police officer to bring your husband home as we need to talk to you together.'

'Would you like a coffee?' I asked when we were standing in the hall.

'That might be a good idea, Mrs Burns,' the lady officer said and we all went into the kitchen. Making the coffee gave me something to do while we waited.

The policeman had noticed the silver cups in the hall, that my husband had won at flower shows, and wanted to talk about his chrysanthemums but I could hardly concentrate. When the three of us were seated with our mugs of coffee, we heard the door open and there was Wesley.

'What's this about?' he said. 'I'm dragged out of work without a word of explanation!'

'It's about your daughter Mary. There's been an accident at her lodgings. The young woman who was sharing accommodation with her is dead.'

'Enid?' I gasped.

'Yes, her name's Enid. I'd like you to get ready to accompany me to the police station where your daughter is being held.'

'Being held? Mary is being held, what for?' Wesley was incredulous.

'I can't say any more Sir. Shall we make our way?'

A white faced Mary looked at us bleakly from the far side of a table in an examination room at the police station. We none of us spoke. The usual greetings seemed out of place. Anxious eyes said it all.

The detective began once we were seated.

'It appears that your daughter pushed her roommate, the young woman called Enid Thompson. As a result, Enid fell backwards, tripped over a stool that was behind her and hit her head against the corner of the tiled mantelpiece. The blow killed her.'

Again we didn't speak. What was there to be said? What were the implications of Mary's actions? Why had she pushed Enid?

'In answer to the question we put to your daughter, as to why she reacted as she did, she replied that Enid's approach was ... shall we say amorous and unwelcome. The whole thing is very unfortunate and it's a pity Mary employed that method of repulsing her friend.'

'But it was an accident!' Wesley said as though the whole world would realise that.

'Mary will be held in custody overnight and there will be a hearing in the morning.'

We were allowed a few minutes with Mary. A female police officer stayed in the room.

'What happened?' I said immediately.

'Enid decided this afternoon to tell me that she's ... was gay. She said she wanted us to room together because of her feelings for me. I said I wasn't ready for a relationship. She seemed to think that telling me she was gay gave her permission to try an embrace. She came at me with her arms open wide and I said, 'No Enid, don't!' I wanted to stop her. I've said all this in my statement.'

'What do you mean, 'You're not ready for a relationship'?' Wesley said coldly. 'Were you thinking that you would eventually have a relationship with Enid?'

'Wesley!' I said.

'No, Katherine, Let's be clear on this. You agree to room with a lesbian and say you're not ready yet? What are we to think? It seems peculiar to me. There doesn't seem to be anything else we can do tonight. We'll book into a hotel and see you in the morning.'

We were introduced to Enid's parents the next morning as we waited in an ante room. They were terribly sad but gentle toward us.

'It's nice to meet Mary's parents,' Enid's father said. 'We've heard nothing but Mary and how lovely Mary is all summer! Enid was thrilled that she and Mary were going to room together. This is a dreadful end to her dreams of a life together.'

Wesley stiffened perceptibly but commiserated with the stricken parents as best he could. As he said afterward, he couldn't feel too much sympathy because his own daughter was in serious trouble because of this dead young woman.

I needn't write about the outcome of the hearing because Mary has told the story.

Wesley's main concern was the newspaper report and how it would reflect on our family if the lesbian aspect was emphasised. The word lesbian was not mentioned in the papers, which rather implied that it was a vicious action on Mary's part to push a woman hard enough to kill her.

As a family, I would say we've never been happy since the day the police officers knocked on our door.

Stonebridge Women's Prison is up in the Midlands. Wesley's faith in Mary was shaken to a point where he didn't want to see her. I didn't want to go against him. I felt it was my job to support him through the disappointment. After hours of discussion, we decided that it was Mary's life. We'd given her a good start and now it was up to her.

Mary wrote letters in defence of lesbianism which further upset Wesley. I argued that it didn't mean that Mary was a lesbian but I couldn't persuade him to think otherwise. Communication between us and the prison stopped.

We also had to consider what was best for June. Homosexuality, to this day, is frowned upon in our social circles.

'I couldn't tell Peter if it turns out that Mary is a lesbian!' June screamed. 'You should hear him and the guys at the pub going on about queers.'

She cut Mary out of her life. She said she wouldn't have to cope with questions from her friends if her sister was never mentioned.

I was sad. When Mary and I went to the opera, *La Traviata,* I remember how she scorned the plot. She couldn't believe that the father would ask the lovers to part and claim that *Violetta's* reputation would damage his daughter's chances of a good betrothal. Something similar has happened in our family. We protected June, we rejected Mary.

Our relations enquired politely as to Mary's well being, at first, and we replied that as far as we knew she was well. My younger brother was disgusted with us. He said he would visit Mary in prison but we needn't expect to see him again. He's my favourite brother and I miss him.

We didn't let her down financially, I'm sure she's told you. We knew her life would be hard enough without being short of money. We felt we'd helped to pave the way to her college course, by providing money for her fees.

Once we heard that Mary had passed out of Neston College with honours, we could say that she was doing well in her line of work. I wanted to go to the Graduation Day but Wesley wouldn't entertain the idea. He said we wouldn't be able to keep up the connection afterward and that it would cause a storm of curiosity in the neighbourhood if Mary was to come home. He was adamant that should Mary be a lesbian, he wouldn't have two women sleeping together in his house. In his opinion, there was no point in renewing the acquaintance – that it wouldn't be fair to June or Mary. I wanted to say that June had been well favoured by both of us and that Mary, lesbian or not, had suffered nine years of our unfair behaviour, but I didn't. I could follow his reasoning.

I've saved all her cards. I can't get used to calling her Helen – my beautiful daughter. I show the cards to Wesley and then put them in my dressing table drawer. I take them out, look at her familiar handwriting and hug and kiss them. I'm proud of her success. If it's true, that to surround a loved one with the light of God affords help and protection, Mary will have been cared for. She's my first and last thought every day.

It's easier for Wesley because he has his work, his club and church meetings. Sometimes when the door closes after he leaves in the morning I feel desolate but I can't cry. Even if I cried, the pain would still be there when I'd wet half a dozen handkerchiefs. I'm involved with the church, of course, but I'm aware that most of the women there are quietly sorry for me. The stigma, of having a daughter who's been in prison, does not go away.

I have a woman doctor in whom I can confide. She advised me to make more of a life for myself, not long after Mary was lost to me. I said I enjoyed my garden but she said I must get out of the home. I'm pleased that Mary has taken after Wesley and me with regard to horticulture.

I joined the Women's Institute. I enter the monthly competitions and go on outings. I sing in a women's choir and am a member of a women's reading group. We each choose a novel, read it and discuss. At the moment we're reading Marilyn French's *The Women's Room* and it's a breath of disturbing air! It's making me see a woman's life from umpteen different perspectives. I'm looking forward to the discussion next week.

Recently, I've dared to try my hand at water colour painting. I'm afraid it's rather a heavy hand. I can't get the delicate touch. There's a nice woman tutor Kit Merrol, who encourages me.

'I'm a Katherine too,' she said 'but I preferred to shorten it to Kit.'

She's a confident woman. Her grey hair is cut really short and it suits her. She wears jeans or trousers with colourful patterns and interesting tops. I feel boring in my same skirts and blouses.

She and I were the only ones at class today. The other students said they would be away on holiday. The two of us did more talking than painting. She's retired early from teaching.

'I've got a dodgy back,' she said and laughed, 'just bad enough to get me out of the classroom before I went crazy.'

'Surely it wasn't as bad as that,' I said, surprised.

'One's nerves get a bit frayed after thirty-four years as a teacher. I'm really enjoying the freedom to do my own thing.'

'Have you any children?' I asked and then regretted the question. I was laying myself open.

'No such luck, I've had to make do with hundreds of other people's. Have you?'

'I've two grown up daughters. Can you help me with this shading please, I'm making a mess.'

We concentrated on our work and packed up at noon. We walked together to the bus stop.

'I suppose I'd better head for home,' Kit said. 'My better half has a day off. With a bit of luck, lunch might be ready for me.'

'How nice, my husband has never made my lunch.'

'Ann's a good cook but she works long hours so I'm chief cook and bottle washer most of the time.'

'What's her work,' I heard myself ask but my head was spinning with the news that Kit's partner is a woman.

'She's a doctor, moved out from London to the local hospital. Her remit is to develop a department of education re infectious diseases, particularly sexually transmitted ones. I say, are you all right?'

No, I wasn't all right. Kit's words had broken the carefully constructed dam to my emotions. I was a mess of hysterical weeping and terribly embarrassed because I was drawing attention to myself. I couldn't stop.

'Into my car,' Kit said. She took my arm firmly and I was across the road and into her car in a jiffy. 'Anyone in at your house?' I shook my head. 'Right, we'd better get you to mine.'

She helped me out of the car and the front door was opened for us.

'Damsel in distress, Ann ... brandy and strong coffee?'

'Coming up.' Ann disappeared into the kitchen.

I was made to sit on the settee with my feet up and covered with a rug. They both stood over me to see that I drank the brandy. Then the three of us sat with coffees and I told them everything. They were silent throughout the story. I lay back exhausted, feeling giddy with relief.

'I think lunch for three,' Ann said and laid another place at the table 'and a goodly glass of vino for one and all.'

I stayed until four o'clock and cup of tea time. I apologised to Ann for spoiling her day off.

'We feel privileged that you've felt able to share with us, Katherine. You've been tremendously brave. In my job, the attitude of parents is often the worst problem for my patients. I think Helen will believe that you never stopped loving her even though you felt you couldn't keep in touch.'

'But I'm ashamed. I'm reading Marilyn French, about women who learn to stand up for themselves. I've just gone along with my husband and society's views on homosexuality. I abandoned my own daughter when she most needed me.'

'French is fiction. No two people's circumstances are the same. If you'd disobeyed your husband, what sort of atmosphere would it have created in your home? It may have meant divorce. I would say that you behaved according to the light that was given you ... until today. How do you feel now?'

'I feel as though I want to go home, get my car out of the garage and drive up to see Mary.'

'For a start, you'd better call her Helen if that's her choice of name,' Kit said. 'And you need to explain to your husband that you want to resume contact with Helen before you dash off.'

'You're right. I'm so excited I'm not thinking straight. If I'm going to change from traditional housewife to liberated woman, I'll have to break it to Wesley gently. But my main concern must be Mary, I mean Helen. Everyone else in my family has had my best attention for the last nine years. They can adjust to my wishes now.'

'You're on the right lines, stand up for what you believe in,' Kit backed up my intention, 'but what will you do if Helen's not pleased to see you?'

'I'll write first. I'll be waiting with baited breath for her reply. Thank you for making me see sense and for your wonderful friendly help.'

'That's okay. We're glad to make a new friend in this town. We must do some things together and for heaven's sake keep us in touch with what happens! Take our phone number. I'll see you at art class next week.'

I begin my letter with, *Dear Helen and Babs,* but all I can think of to write is, *Can you please forgive me and may I come and see you? Love Mum*

I stand behind an elderly person in the post office when I queue for stamps. She and a young man talk seriously and the woman says, 'Your mother will see you right, mothers always do.'

I hope for this mother that it's not too late.